JESSE –
FOR JUSTICE!

THRUSTS OF JUSTICE

MATT YOUNGMARK

THRUSTS OF JUSTICE

*WITH ILLUSTRATIONS
BY THE AUTHOR*

CHOOSEOMATIC BOOKS, SEATTLE

An imprint of Atherton Haight

THRUSTS OF JUSTICE. Copyright © 2012 by Matt Youngmark.
All rights reserved. Printed in the United States of America.
No part of this book may be used or reproduced in any manner
whatsoever without written permission except in the case of brief
quotations embodied in critical articles and reviews.

First edition, 2012

atherton
HAIGHT

Chooseomatic Books and the Chooseomatic Books and
Atherton Haight logos are registered trademarks of Atherton Haight.

www.chooseomatic.com

Illustrations by Matt Youngmark

Library of Congress Cataloging-In-Publication Data
is available upon request.

ISBN 13: 978-0-9840678-1-7
ISBN 10: 0-9840678-0-9

Dedicated to two
grandmasters of cartooning,

Sergio Aragonés *and* **Phil Foglio**

Because discovering GROO THE WANDERER
and MYTH ADVENTURES *in the mid-'80s*
made me fall in love with comics
in the first place, all those years ago.

The truth is, you never really wanted to be a reporter, anyway. Sure, you've been single-mindedly working toward a job in journalism since junior high, but it wasn't out of a true passion for the news or anything. It was because reporters get to hang out with superheroes, and you realized at the age of 12 that, short of tragically-murdered billionaire parents or a freak accident involving radioactive waste, "superhero" probably wasn't a viable career path.

"Man, screw the *Cleveland Tribune*," Dale says. "After we make a billion dollars with ClevelandNewsExplosion.com, we'll buy the damned *Cleveland Tribune*. And fire all those guys."

"Have another drink, Dale." That's Melah. She's just as inebriated, judging from the number of empty whiskey glasses in front of her, but carries it better. The three of you are having

(continue to the next page)

what's essentially the same argument, at the same bar, for the eleventh consecutive day since being laid off by your common employer. Theoretically, you're exploring the idea of launching a website, but deep down you all know it's empty talk. Drunken rambling about the internet is just what unemployed journalists do.

Today, however, will offer a break in your routine debauchery. Before you can flag down the bartender for another round, the room is flooded with an intense white light, followed by a strange sense of weightlessness that makes the hair on the back of your neck stand on end. Whoa. How drunk *are* you? A deep, soft voice calls out from what feels like the inside of your head, rattling your fillings.

"They're coming."

What? Who's coming? *"Heed my words,"* the voice continues. *"They're coming, and you alone can stop them. The way forward is twisted and there is very little time, so do not hesitate. Choose your actions carefully. The fate of this world is in your hands."*

The light subsides and the voice fades away with it. You silently meet your friends' eyes and find that they're as shaken up as you are. Whatever that was, it knocked the drunk right out of you. "Heed my words?" Dale mutters. "Who talks like that?"

In case an ominous psychic warning isn't enough, suddenly the entire bar shakes from a concussive blast. Gainful employment or not, your reporter's instincts kick in and you leap from your bar stool to investigate. Outside you see pedestrians fleeing in all directions from a smoking crater in the middle of the street, and three unmistakable figures dotting the landscape. The first is an enormous man in a horned helmet who you rec-

(continue to the next page)

ognize as the Ox, a famous New York supervillain. He's carrying several large, unmarked bags, and you realize that much of the rubble comes from the busted-through wall of a bank building directly behind him.

The second is a cloaked figure with glowing eyes—Nightwatchman, the most mysterious of the whole crop of costumed heroes. His modus operandi is to hide in darkness and strike terror in the hearts of criminals. He's old school, and seriously badass.

And inside the crater itself is a figure in some sort of high-tech battle armor. Could that be the Cosmic Guardian? He's a legendary hero who disappeared some time in the mid-'90s. From the looks of things, he appears to have just saved downtown Cleveland from a stray meteor.

Superheroes! And villains! Right in front of your favorite bar! The three of them exchange glances, and you're pretty sure you're about to witness a superpowered smackdown. But then the Guardian launches into the air, sputtering off on a wild trajectory (and, from the sound of things, crashing back to earth a few blocks over). Nightwatchman disappears into an alley, leaving the Ox alone amid the chaos. What the hell is going on here? Could a simultaneous meteor strike and bank robbery be pure coincidence? And if he's not here to battle the Ox, what could Nightwatchman possibly be doing in Cleveland?

Melah is the first to say what you're all thinking. "If you two still want to start that website, I think we've got our first story."

"We should split up," Dale says. Sirens are approaching, which means the Ox is about to go toe-to-toe with Cleveland's finest. That's front-page news for sure—cell-phone video

(continue to the next page)

of the Ox in action would generate the kind of page views a typical start-up news site could only dream of. Then again, the darkness-lurking, fear-inspiring reason you always wanted to be a superhero just fled down that alley. And a long-missing champion may have saved the city from a meteor. That's some big-time, interplanetary space hero stuff right there. Which lead should you follow?

▶ *If you stay put and report on the Ox situation,*
   turn to page 6.

▶ *If you chase after the Nightwatchman,*
   turn to page 8.

▶ *If you track down the Cosmic Guardian instead,*
   turn to page 11.

The real Nightwatchman is still out there somewhere, and if you wreck his jet, you're pretty sure he's going to kick your ass. Human Torpedo grabs Ocean Boy by the waist and flings himself out the open hatch. Man, those guys get to have *all* the fun.

You start scanning the cityscape for a suitable landing pad. Wait a minute—shouldn't a jet this awesome have some kind of autopilot? Before you can start digging through the manual, though, an alarm goes off in the cockpit. You ask for a report, but the display doesn't respond to your mental command. Uh-oh. You quickly discover that you've lost all telepathic control—you grab the flight stick and pull up, but the plane ignores your panicked attempts at steering and falls into a tailspin, plunging to the city streets below.

What the hell? Is someone shutting down the jet's systems remotely? Did its owner finally realize that you stole his plane? You were totally going to bring it back! You start to realize that this whole villain-bashing joyride was doomed from the start. Plummeting to your doom, you try to figure out where you went wrong. Was it not sticking with Magnifica back at her Florida rest home? Thinking you could fill Nightwatchman's boots in the first place? Deciding to even get out of bed this morning?

These are your thoughts as you crash into downtown Washington, D.C. The exploding aircraft also takes out three or four truly horrible supervillains along with it, though. Feel free to think of that as a silver lining if you'd like.

THE END

If you're serious about launching a local news site, the Ox duking it out with the Cleveland police department is a no-brainer. By the time the local press arrives it'll be long over, and after one late night with too much coffee and a free Wordpress template, ClevelandNewsExplosion.com (the name might still need a little work) can debut with an eyewitness scoop.

Your friends bolt in opposite directions. Are they chasing down other leads or just plain fleeing? Either way, your whole career has been leading up to this moment. You don't have your notebook on hand, but you're a trained observer. Taking a mental snapshot of the scene, you commit everything to memory down to the finest detail, and creep into the street for a better view.

At which point you stumble directly into the giant crater, hit your head on a chunk of meteor, and immediately black out.

* * * * *

You regain consciousness in what looks like a cheap motel room, tied to a chair. Judging from the numbness, you've been there for some time. Looming above you, hunched over a little to fit inside the room, is the Ox—even without his horned helmet, there's no mistaking him.

He grunts. "So, you got superpowers now?"

Superpowers? "What? Uh, no."

"Meteors give a lot of people superpowers," he says. "You know that Verminator guy? Leather suit? Talks to rats and stuff?" He seems to expect a reply, so you nod.

"Meteor," he finishes.

(continue to the next page)

"I don't have superpowers!" You're pretty groggy, and although you still want to get this story, you'd also really like to live through it. Are you a hostage here? If you can convince him that you're not any kind of threat, will he let you go?

"Plus, you kinda melted into a puddle of purple goo for a couple minutes outside the bank," the Ox says. "That sounds like superpowers to me."

"I promise you that I don't have—wait, what?" *You melted into a puddle of purple goo?* Holy crap, maybe you *do* have superpowers. You feel sort of weird, now that he mentions it. Testing the ropes, you find that they have a surprising amount of give. Either your captor isn't great at tying knots, or you're about to rip right through your restraints. Your mind is racing—if that meteor gave you superpowers, they could be anything. Super strength? Super speed? Laser beam eyes? You stare at the Ox as hard as you can, but he just looks back at you like you're stupid and fails to burst into flames. Probably not laser beam eyes, then.

He leans toward you. Unless you have some kind of super bone density, you're fairly sure he can squeeze you into pulp with one hand. You strain against the ropes with all your might and feel them tear away. Um, did you just free yourself with newfound powers far beyond those of mortal men? Is there any chance you could actually take this guy?

▶ *If you punch the Ox right in the face with everything you've got,* **turn to page 14.**

▶ *If you run like hell instead,* **turn to page 27.**

A supervillain shootout may be the local Cleveland angle here, but you know what? Screw Cleveland. The Nightwatchman just fell into your lap, and your inner twelve-year-old superfan won't let you pass up this opportunity.

You've got a mysterious vigilante to track.

You hit the alley just in time to see a dark cloak at the top of a rusty metal ladder on the building in front of you. He's getting away! You throw yourself onto the ladder, but the life of a journalist is a mostly sedentary affair, and by the time you've reached the rooftop, you're desperately out of breath and the Nightwatchman is already several buildings over and quickly disappearing into the skyline.

(continue to the next page)

It turns out that rooftop scrambling is an awkward, grimy business, and although there's no gap between buildings, the various architects involved clearly didn't put much thought into the needs of anyone trying to participate in an action sequence on top of them. By the time you reach the end of the block, your quarry is nowhere to be seen. Catching your breath, you scan the area for any clue to where he went. The next building is at least 30 feet away—way too far to jump. You also notice that the alley directly below you is blocked on one side by a brick wall and on the other by an ancient-looking dumpster and pile of debris. There's a fire escape leading down into it, but other than from the rooftop you're currently standing on, there's really no way in or out.

Curious. You climb down, and the area appears altogether abandoned. The only marginally interesting feature is the metal dumpster, which looks like it's been rusted shut for decades. You give it a shove, but it doesn't budge.

Suddenly a blast of steam hits you in the face from underneath the dumpster. There's a loud click, and the entire thing shifts about four feet to the side, knocking you to the pavement in the process. It's on rails! The moving dumpster reveals a circular hole in the asphalt and a ladder leading down into the darkness.

You've just discovered a secret passage—could the Nightwatchman have some kind of safehouse here? In *Cleveland*? Or maybe it's a villain's hideout—this could be a *lair,* for all you know. After a bit of hemming and hawing, curiosity finally wins out over good sense and you hesitantly climb down into the hole. As soon as your head is clear, the dumpster slides

(continue to the next page)

closed above you, shutting you in the darkness with a clang. You frantically grasp around for some kind of control mechanism, but feel only cold, rough stone.

Crap. Well, it looks like you're committed now. You find the floor about ten feet down, and the wall here feels like smooth tile. You stumble upon a switch, which bathes the underground chamber in light—it's a tiny room with a ledge built into one wall that houses a computer terminal, a nondescript office chair, and that's about it. There's a door on the opposite wall, but you discover that it's locked tight. Thrown over the chair is a big, dark blanket, a pair of funky gloves, some goggles and . . .

Holy crap—that's not a blanket. It's a cloak. *This is Nightwatchman's stuff.*

Your heart skips a beat. You're definitely alone here—the room just isn't big enough to be hiding another person. Also, you're pretty much trapped in it. You test the computer, but it just gives you a blank screen with a command prompt. So you examine the gauntlets, and notice a small touchscreen built into one of them. There's a message on the display.

"System reboot completed. Set controls for new host?" A little green button onscreen is labeled "Set host controls," and a red one reads "Shut system down."

Is that glove asking you what you think it's asking?

▶ *Yes. Yes. A thousand times yes. If you don the Nightwatchman's costume and set the host controls to YOU,* **turn to page 16.**

▶ *Whoa, there! You don't know where the real Nightwatchman is, but if he finds you messing with his stuff, you could be in serious trouble. If you play it safe and shut the glove down,* **turn to page 21.**

Melah and Dale can stick around and report on the local angle if they want. As far as you're concerned, superheroes from outer space trump anything that's happened in the entire state of Ohio, ever. You hazard a guess at where the Cosmic Guardian —if that *was* the Cosmic Guardian—might have landed based on the erratic flight path and miscellaneous crashing noises. It's not an exact science, but after canvassing a few blocks you spot a thin column of smoke wafting out of a broken window on the fifth floor of an apartment building. That's a pretty good bet.

Some teenaged stoner is standing in the front entryway as you approach it, so you scoot past him and head up the stairs. The building isn't in great shape, and is apparently the kind of place where you can crash through a plate glass window without making a stir, because when you arrive on the fifth floor (panting and sweating, thank you very much), you don't see a single concerned tenant milling about in the hallway.

Okay, the smoke was coming from the third window, so . . . apartment 503 or 505? You take your best guess and knock gently on a paint-cracked door. "Uh, hello? Is everything all right in there?" The door shudders violently, as if someone on the inside had smacked it with a baseball bat. Or . . . unlocked it with an energy beam? You gingerly test the knob and find that it's open.

Lying by the window is an armored figure with one arm stretched toward you, still smoldering. The battle suit is bulkier than you remember from the posters in your childhood bedroom, but from the gleaming blue metallic polymer and pattern of circuits on the arms and chest, there's no question: this is the Cosmic Guardian. His helmet is open, revealing a pale, emaciated face crisscrossed with blue veins.

(continue to the next page)

"Keep it . . . *secret*," he says in a whisper. There's a flash of light, and the man inside the suit literally dissolves into smoke before your eyes.

His empty armor remains frozen in position. Then its arm suddenly stretches toward you. You try to leap out of the way, but it strikes you in the chest, knocking you to the floor. Struggling to get up, you feel the suit envelop your entire body. For a moment, everything goes black. Then the room in front of you crackles into view, tinted green and overlaid with a horizon line and various digital prompts and readouts.

Before you can get your bearings, the suit launches you off the floor and out the broken window. You're flying! And utterly out of control! You don't feel any sense of motion inside the armor, but the city quickly disappears beneath you. A voice pops into your head—it seems to be bypassing your ears and streaming directly into your mind, and yet somehow has the feeling of an educational film from the 1950s.

"*In respect 197, rather you can get selection sector galaxy 'delicious,' and this is called brown*," it says.

What? It's gibberish. And it's not audio, exactly, but nevertheless you can almost hear the announcer's booming, cheesy tenor, and the crackling of an old projector. You half expect it give you a stern warning about auto safety, or syphilis.

"*Not easy task*," the message continues. "*And if you do there is only a great life you congratulations, you and the mercy of the universe.*"

Whatever translation software this thing uses clearly needs a lot of work. You continue to rocket skyward, breaking through the Earth's atmosphere, traveling onward until the entire globe

(continue to the next page)

is within your field of vision, crisp blue oceans and the contours of continents visible through a swirl of clouds.

Holy crap. It's *magnificent*. And you're not at all sure what the suit is trying to tell you, but if it's asking if you want to be the new Cosmic Guardian, the answer is *yes*.

With that thought, you feel something click. You wiggle your arms, and discover that you can move them effortlessly, as if . . . well, as if floating in space. You concentrate on changing course, and slowly the Earth starts getting larger on your helmet's viewscreen.

You're pretty sure you just became a superhero.

What now? You happen to know that a villain just held up a bank somewhere down there in Cleveland. Stopping that sort of thing is what superheroes are supposed to do. But you consider the dying words of the suit's previous owner. Keep *what* secret? Your civilian identity? The entire existence of the Guardian armor? Should you try to keep things on the downlow, and stay out of the public eye until you have a better handle on what's going on?

▶ *Onward to battle! If you charge ahead and stop the Ox before he gets away with his nefarious scheme,* **turn to page 18.**

▶ *That would be impulsive and irresponsible! If you retreat to safety and use your skills as a journalist to dig up some information on the Cosmic Guardian before doing anything rash,* **turn to page 46.**

You throw all your weight behind your fist, driving it straight into his massive jaw. You've never felt this kind of strength before, and you somehow manage to execute the maneuver with the grace of an acrobat. Fist hits face with a loud crack and an explosion of pain. Son of a *bitch*! It's like punching a steel plate!

The Ox doesn't budge a centimeter, but his face breaks into a wide grin. "I felt that," he says. "You *do* have superpowers."

Powers or no, you're way out of your league here. And your hand feels like it's broken in about six places. This is the end of the road, you think. The Ox stares at you for a moment, and you just stare back, dumbstruck.

"So, you wanna team up?" he asks.

"Excuse me?"

"You know, team up. I used to roll with Megawatt before he switched sides and joined the stupid Justice Squadron. You and me could hang out, do crimes and stuff. We could get you a costume. I got a guy."

Until now you've never given much thought to villainy as a vocation. It occurs to you that if that meteor really has given you great power, then you've got a choice to make. A real hero would find a way to defeat the Ox and bring him to justice. Then again, your hand hurts something awful from your first attempt at that whole justice business. Perhaps you'd be better off taking his offer and seeing how things play out.

▶ *If you tell the Ox you'll never join with the likes of him,* **turn to page 48.**

▶ *If joining with the likes of him actually sounds like a pretty good idea,* **turn to page 31.**

You wake up many hours later with a blistering headache and a stomach raw from what can only be the long, sustained expulsion of eighteenth-century pirate rum. Your drinking partners—not to mention your superpowered battlesuit—are nowhere to be found.

You eventually recover enough strength to explore the cavern, and find a large, blue, metallic pod that bears the markings of the Cosmic Guard. It's covered in moss and barnacles as if it's been here a very long time, and although you try every conceivable method of interacting with it, it remains inert.

What you don't find is any kind of food or drink other than the second vat of rum, and just the thought of that makes your stomach turn. As time wears on with no sign of your companions, you start getting really worried. Without fresh water you can't possibly survive more than a couple of days down here, and no suit means no way back to the ocean's surface. Seriously, could the Human Torpedo and Ocean Boy have just abandoned you? Short of a global catastrophe, what could possibly be keeping them?

You never find out.

THE END

You put on Nightwatchman's gauntlets and boots (which are way too big for you), followed by the utility belt, goggles, and cloak. You're still wearing your jeans and an ironic 1970s beer t-shirt underneath, but the cape covers all that if you drape it right. You push the green button on the touchscreen and are treated to a high-pitched squeal. The gloves and boots start to compress, forming themselves to your extremities until the fit is quite comfortable. What just happened?

"Control reset complete," the screen reads, as if responding to your thoughts. Wait a second—your thoughts? *Situation report*, you think, and text immediately starts spitting out onto the screen. You're controlling it with your mind! You scan the information and discover that Nightwatchman had been investigating the murder of Brain Stem, a member of the Justice Squadron.

Whoa. This is big. If Brain Stem really is dead, somebody has taken pains to cover it up—that's the sort of thing that would normally inspire round-the-clock cable news coverage and special commemorative editions of terrible magazines. Your notes also reveal a list of superhumans that are somehow tied to Crexidyne Megacorp, the theoretically legitimate business run by notorious criminal mastermind Reginald Thorpe. Brain Stem is second on this list, and the Ox is first. Is that what Nightwatchman was doing in Cleveland? Following up on a lead?

Well, you always wanted to be a superhero. Maybe you'll just pick up where he left off.

The world's foremost authority on Crexidyne and its misdeeds would be Nancy North, the legendary reporter who's been

(continue to the next page)

hounding Thorpe since the 1970s. She's famous for her dealings with the hero crowd, too—she'd be a good place to start if you intend to continue Nightwatchman's investigation. Or are you jumping the gun here? Maybe you should devote your resources to finding out what happened to the *real* Nightwatchman. And, you know, making sure he doesn't beat your ass for taking his stuff.

▶ *If you contact Nancy for help with the Crexidyne connection,* **turn to page 42.**

▶ *If you concentrate your efforts on tracking down the Nightwatchman,* **turn to page 80.**

Two words: superpowered battlesuit. Technically, that may be anywhere between two and four words, but grammar is the type of thing you started caring about *after* you gave up your dream of fighting for truth and justice at the tender age of twelve.

Now that the dream lives again, the last thing you intend to do is *research*.

You will yourself back toward the planet, pushing through the atmosphere within moments. After a few navigation-related errors—honestly, Lake Ontario looks about the same as Lake Erie from this altitude—you find Cleveland and swoop down in front of the bank. It looks like someone swallowed a city block and barfed it back up. Flattened police cars litter the street and there's some kind of gooey, purple splat at the bottom of the meteor's impact crater. Perhaps you should contact Hazardous Waste Disposal about that? You rush to a fallen officer to see if he needs help, and although his face is a mess of bruises and abrasions, he flashes you an incompletely-toothed grin and gestures with his thumb down the street. "White van," he wheezes.

That's all you need to know. You launch back into the sky and scan traffic for a vehicle matching that description. He headed away from the freeway, so he doesn't seem to be . . . wait a second. Bingo. You spot the van pulling into a motel a couple of miles away from the bank, and see the Ox climb out of it as you zoom to intercept.

It's business time. "Stop where you are," you say as you make your landing just behind him. Your voice comes booming out of your suit through some kind of loudspeaker, giving it a deep resonance that you don't normally possess. It's kind of awesome.

(continue to the next page)

"Huh?" The Ox turns and looks you over. "What the hell are *you* supposed to be?"

"I am the Cosmic Guardian." You use your most authoritarian tone. "Surrender and you will not be harmed."

"Wait, I've hearda you." He looks unimpressed. "You're the dead one, right?"

"Missing," you say. "In space. I'm back now." Man, your superhero banter is just *awful*. "Lay down your weapons!"

"What, these weapons?" He balls up his hands up into two enormous fists. "Okay."

The Ox lunges, but you leap into the air and hover just out of his reach. If you recall correctly, the Cosmic Guardian's force beams should be strong enough to stop a tank. You concentrate, and a ball of blue light forms in the palm of your hand. Tingly! With an outstretched arm, you fire a blast of energy that shakes your entire body.

When it subsides, the Ox is standing there unfazed. "My turn," he says. With a truly impressive vertical leap, he grabs one of your legs and pulls you to the earth, which you hit like a steel-plated sack of meat. Your suit absorbs the impact, but he pins you the ground and follows with a punch to the chest you can feel even through your armor. Uh-oh. The blows start coming in rhythm, and with each one your chest plate creaks and moans. Maybe if you work up a force blast strong enough to—BAM! Or if you can just get yourself airborne, then he'll—BAM! That last punch shorted out your visual display for a moment, making you—BAM! Okay. You're not sure how much more of this you can—

BAM.

(continue to the next page)

When you regain consciousness, you find yourself face down in a field, half covered with rocks and dirt. You feel like you've been run over by a train. As your systems slowly come back online, you realize you can't even see the motel from here. Did he *throw* you? You also note that there's a black helicopter on the ground 20 yards away, its rotors still spinning. A small man in a tweed jacket runs toward you, shouting over the chopper's noise.

"I'm so glad you're here!" He pulls out a fancy little tablet computer and makes a note on it. "We didn't know if the emergency signal would reach you!" The helicopter starts powering down, allowing the man to lower his voice. "I'm Agent Moretti. And you're Mr. Janssen? Or has the suit . . . um . . . changed possession?"

Sten Janssen! Ha! Back in journalism school you did an exhaustive paper speculating on the secret identities of the Justice Squadron. Janssen was a Swedish athlete who went missing about the same time the Guardian disappeared. You *knew* it! However, you're still pretty confused from your beating. Are you *supposed* to be Sten Janssen? Was that the secret you were trying to keep? Inside that giant armored battlesuit, you really could be anybody, and the speaker makes you sound like James Earl freaking Jones.

▶ *If you tell Moretti that you're Janssen,*
   turn to page 181.

▶ *If you come clean and say Janssen passed the suit on to you,* **turn to page 64.**

You're reading a choose-your-own-ending book about superheroes, and immediately decide *not* to become one? Okay. No, it makes sense. If Nightwatchman comes back, he could be really mad. We're with you. You just caught us a little off guard is all.

As you shut down the suit, the door in the back wall opens with a hum of machinery. You think about calling Melah and Dale to tell them what you've found, but can't get a signal. You also consider taking some of the gear with you, but decide that it probably wouldn't be wise. The door shuts behind you and after briefly navigating the city sewers, a ladder and manhole cover bring you back up to the street, somewhat stinkier but otherwise none the worse for wear.

You backtrack to the bar, only to find a smattering of trashed police cars and some paramedics tending wounded officers. The Ox appears to have made a clean getaway, and your friends are nowhere to be found. Neither of them answers their cell phone, so, for lack of a better plan, you head into the bar to wait for them. One beer follows another without any sign of your compatriots and eventually you start to get hungry. The nachos here are decent, and of course hot wings are usually a safe bet. There's also that weird side dish on the menu, which you've often considered trying but never actually committed to.

▶ *If you order nachos,* **turn to page 30.**

▶ *If you go with the buffalo wings,* **turn to page 30.**

▶ *If you throw caution to the wind and get the deep-fried ravioli blasters,* **turn to page 248.**

Relax and act cool. You need to handle this just right to avoid coming across like a complete doofus.

"Magnifico! Um, hey. I can't believe I'm actually talking to you!" Ouch. So much for acting cool. But you're blathering now, and it's too late to do anything about it. "You must be here to capture Lightning Queen! I was going to help out with that —you know, because I'm a superhero? But then somebody stole a bike, and I thought it was more important to stick up for the little guy. I mean, not that what you do isn't important."

He just stares at you.

"I think you're *very* important," you finish lamely.

"I applaud your sense of civic duty," Magnifico says in an even tone. "But when you see a crime being committed, even one as heinous as property theft, it's vital that you contact the police and let them do their job."

"No, it's not like that!" Aw, crap. You've blown it. Perhaps this calls for a demonstration instead. "Here, look!" You throw your stretchy arm across the street and stick it to a telephone pole. Then you retract it, accidentally tearing off several fliers for local bands and adult chat lines in the process.

"Great Scott," Magnifico says, finally looking impressed. "You really do have superpowers, don't you?"

You're unable to contain your excitement. "This isn't even a costume! It's some kind of organic goo that I secrete from my skin!"

He pauses, deep in thought. "You know, the Squadron could really use someone of your talents. Just the other day we needed to squeeze into a tight space, and I had to tear apart half a city block because we couldn't get in. Are you good at squeezing?"

(continue to the next page)

"Maybe? I'm not a hundred percent sure, because it's my first day!"

"I like your moxie, kid. How would you like to come back to Squadron HQ with me and meet the rest of the gang? Do you see that Justice Squadron transport parked just around the corner?" You turn to look where he's pointing, but don't see anything that looks like a supervehicle. Could it have a cloaking device or—

SMACK.

Something hits you hard in the back of the head, and for the second time in less than 12 hours you black out.

* * * * *

When you regain consciousness, you find yourself in a big glass vat in the middle of a poorly lit room. You can make out a Justice Squadron insignia inlaid into the intricate tile work on the floor, but very little else, since the air outside your container is thick with a putrid-looking brown smoke. Wait a minute. Something's moving out there—huge, asymmetrical figures shift around in the darkness. They're coming toward you. Then a vent opens and gas starts seeping in.

It's the last thing you ever see.

THE END

North may be a famous newscaster and your own personal journalism idol, but with the sneaking into your apartment and all, you worry that she's just freaking nuts. Her contact turns out to be Girl Friday, the long-retired sidekick of Professor Medium Maximus, the Gentleman Mentalist. Your impression was that Friday (it turns out her real name is Octavia) had no superpowers of her own, but Nancy insists this is not the case.

You track down Octavia in Santa Fe, working in her backyard garden. She's in her late sixties, with a deep tan and a gentle smile. "Um, hi," you say, trying to avoid landing on her asparagus. "I'm, uh . . . I'm the Cosmic Guardian."

Octavia laughs. "Nancy phoned ahead," she says. "Let's have a look at you, then. I never met the first Cosmic Guardian, you know. He was after my time."

You stand awkwardly for a moment as she circles, peering intently at you from every angle. "Mmmm, there's definitely something else in there with you," she says. "It's very closed off, though. I'm not sure if it's blocking my mind or if it's just so alien that I can't find my way in." Octavia proceeds to lead you in a variety of what she calls "transgenic exercises," most of which involve stretching, deep breathing, and helping her tend the garden. You suspect she may be pulling your leg. By nightfall you've made very little progress with the suit, but quite a bit on the fall harvest. That was a waste of time. You're exhausted, so you agree to spend the night.

Her spare bedroom is cozy, and for once the armor responds to your commands immediately, shuffling off and settling into a heap in the corner. You catch a whiff of yourself. Wow, it gets pretty sweaty in there. You briefly consider a shower, but as soon

(continue to the next page)

as your head hits the pillow, you're out like a light.

In your dreams, you've just won a shiny new toaster. It's terribly exciting. It can toast an entire loaf of bread at once! You carefully fill its slots and push down the lever, but no heat comes on. You're starting to worry. You need toast! All the people are coming! You can feel that the toaster wants to make toast for you—making toast is the toaster's whole purpose. But it just can't bring itself to do it. What's the point of making toast? What's the point when everything you'll ever care about dies?

The sun is bright when you awaken, and Octavia is sitting in a chair next to your bed, watching you. That's creepy. You hear the quirky monotone of NPR wafting in from the other room.

You grunt. "What time is it?"

"Ten o'clock," Octavia says. You decide not to tell her that since joining the ranks of the unemployed, ten is actually an early start for you. Sitting up, you notice that your battlesuit has moved to the foot of the bed, and a large appendage is curled around your feet like a labrador retriever.

"The alien armor isn't designed to communicate with its wearer through verbal commands," Octavia says. Has she been poking around in your brain while you slept? "It's meant to join with the wearer as one—to bond with you, so the two of you think with a single mind."

"That sounds great," you say, yawning. "Can we make that happen?"

Octavia's voice is soft. "You must understand—this isn't something you can undo. The armor's life cycle involves finding a host and grafting to it, forming what is almost a single entity.

(continue to the next page)

You must be absolutely certain that this is what you want."

That's a lot to take in first thing in the morning. "And then there's the matter of what *it* wants," Octavia continues. "Normally, the armor itself would initiate the bond. But I sense a hesitancy. Remember, it was with the previous Guardian for decades. It's mourning. Also, your subconscious apparently thinks of it as a toaster."

You hear the radio announcer raise his voice slightly in the other room (this is public radio—*any* vocal inflection is enough of a surprise to grab your attention). He says that a trio of supervillains has just descended on the nation's capitol, and the Washington Monument has already crumbled. Tens of thousands of people are panicking in the streets. You jump out of bed—that shower will have to wait. The battlesuit jumps with you, immediately forming itself around your body.

Are you really prepared to take on three villains at once, though? The Ox kicked your ass by himself. It might help if you and your battlesuit were fused together into a sort of unnatural, terrifying hive mind. Are you ready for that kind of commitment, though?

"If you want to try bonding with the armor," Octavia says, "we could do it now."

▶ *If you tell Octavia you're ready,* **turn to page 152.**

▶ *Whoa, whoa, whoa. If you're not ready at all and would rather face the villains unbonded,* **turn to page 221.**

You may have superpowers, but you have absolutely no clue what they might be, so taking a swing at one of the toughest supervillains in the world seems just plain stupid. You bolt out the motel room door (and not particularly quickly— at the very least you can rule out superhuman speed).

The Ox crashes right through the wall behind you. Crap! Across the street is a run-down office building, so you scoot into the alley behind it and, for lack of a better plan, make a running leap for a rusty old fire escape hanging just out of reach. To your complete surprise, you grab the bottom rung with ease and start scurrying up. Really? Half the superheroes in New York can fly, but you get the power of, what, parkour?

Then again, if you *could* fly, how would you even know? It's five flights to the building's roof and you're good and winded by the time you reach it, but the Ox didn't try to follow you up (which makes sense, since you can't imagine that the ancient fire escape would hold his weight). Then, as you clamber over the rooftop's ledge, you see a gargantuan figure emerge from a doorway right in front of you.

The Ox took the stairs.

He charges. This is it, you think—at this point your choices are to take a punch from this monster or make a flying leap and pray for a miracle. Either way, if you're not superpowered, you're probably about to be super *dead*.

▶ *If you brace for impact and hope to somehow survive the Ox's wrath,* **turn to page 53.**

▶ *If you jump over the building's edge and flap your arms like crazy,* **turn to page 146.**

We're not going to lie to you, you're screwed either way. Axemaster has been preparing for this moment for years, and is ready to counter attacks you don't even know you have. His mask has a built-in oxygen supply to render your knockout gas useless, and he's given himself regular electric shocks so he'll be able to withstand the ones your gauntlets emit. He's studied the Nightwatchman's fighting style and taught himself a combination of Brazilian Ju Jitzu and Scandinavian Tae Kwon Do specifically designed to throw even the world's most dangerous hand-to-hand combatant off his guard.

Essentially, it's a choice between going down fighting or facing your death as a sniveling coward, and we hope you've made peace with whichever route you chose. He immediately gets you in a wrestling hold, lifts you over his head, and breaks your back over his knee—then, before you have a chance to wonder who might take up the mantle of the Nightwatchman while you lie in a cave somewhere recuperating, he carves open your chest and tears out your still-beating heart. And then he eats your face off.

The guy is completely off his rocker. And he's wrong about how long it takes you to die, but he doesn't let that spoil his fun. He continues mutilating your corpse for a good three or four hours.

THE END

The aliens turn out to be ferocious but not particularly tough. They're completely gross, though—all blisters and pustules, with bony appendages they use to propel themselves like flagella. One of them jumps you and sucks your entire helmet into its expanding maw. You manage to dislodge it from your head and then pound away until it stops moving. The things keep hurling themselves at you, but you keep smacking them down. The fight is over inside of ten minutes.

"Nice work, assmunch."

The voice comes from a speaker inside your helmet, but you spot a human figure approaching in a space suit that matches yours. He's crackling with electricity. "Megawatt," Ox sneers. You hear him through your helmet as well—they must all be linked. "I knew that hero thing was a load of crap. This is how you use your powers now? Helping alien pus bags take over the Earth?"

"You don't get it," Megawatt says. "These things *gave* me my powers. They gave *all of us* our powers. And they're giving me a bitchin' flying battlesuit to help invade the next planet, too. Listen, there's a suit for you too, man. You're part of this. You're on the list."

A giant spacecraft and an offer to join the dark side? Megawatt sees the look on your face, and chuckles. "Not you, dumbass. I don't even know who you are. They've been planning this for decades, Ox. It's way too late to stop them."

Ox gives you a glance and shrugs. "We *are* supervillains."

▶ *If you try to convince him that the world is worth saving,* **turn to page 76.**

▶ *If you think the fight is a lost cause and just try to talk him into hooking you up with a battlesuit too,* **turn to page 107.**

After finishing your meal, such as it is, you have one more beer and finally head out. Despite all the excitement this morning, today has actually turned out to be kind of a drag. On a whim, you backtrack to the alley where you found Nightwatchman's secret bunker. This time, you push and pull on the dumpster in every imaginable way for at least half an hour, but it doesn't move an inch.

Could you have hallucinated all of that earlier? How drunk *were* you?

Back at your apartment, you find that the second season of "Glee" has arrived from Netflix, so you stay up late into the night burning through episodes and working on a twelve pack. You eventually drift off to sleep, and don't wake up until almost three o'clock the following afternoon. Your friends still haven't returned any of your messages, so you turn the TV back on. Later that evening, you've formulated some pretty strong opinions about the set list for regionals when, without warning, the world literally ends.

All life on Earth could probably have used a hero. Next time, maybe nut up a little. We're just saying.

The End

You agree to join forces with the Ox, and your new friend seems terribly excited about the prospect. He insists that you accompany him back to New York City to learn the supervillain ropes, and he escorts you to a nondescript van with tinted windows parked behind the motel.

You climb into the vehicle (which, in retrospect, is probably soundproofed as well) with the 800-pound bank-robbing stranger. What could possibly go wrong?

The van is actually quite plush inside, and modified to accommodate the Ox's enormous frame. He fills the entire front seat (the steering wheel is mounted directly in the center of the dashboard) and proves to be perfectly courteous, to your relief. In fact, he's downright chatty. "I was planning on hitting up this meeting tonight," he says. "A bunch of guys get together and talk about crimes and stuff. We're not like a team, or a legion or whatever, but sometimes it's good to hear what everybody's up to."

A supervillain meeting? Your reporter's curiosity is piqued. You consider trying to contact Dale and Melah, but you're not sure what you would say, or how much you even want to reveal, now that you have a secret identity.

"Aw, but that's all pretty boring," Ox continues. "You probably wanna get your hands dirty, try to figure out your powers and stuff. We could hit another bank instead. Or an armored truck or something. C'mon, it'll be fun!"

▶ *Why not? If you're ready for the thug life,* **turn to page 114.**

▶ *If you'd rather attend the meeting (either because you're planning an undercover sting operation or just for general networking purposes),* **turn to page 60.**

In addition to the Ox, Tinker, Suong, Savage Cockroach, and Verminator, you've picked up villains from the meeting that include Dr. Diabolus, the Turtle, Rockjockey, someone who may or may not be called Pterodactyl Girl, and nine others with names you can't seem to keep straight. By morning you've added enough additional criminals to triple your numbers, tracking them down before Crexidyne's Guardian Corps can find them and pursuading them to join your army. One of them, a big, creepy guy named Axemaster, insists that he be allowed to personally destroy the Nightwatchman with his own hands, exacting his terrifying revenge. You're okay with that. You know, assuming you happen to run into the Nightwatchman.

Your meddling throws a huge monkey wrench into Crexidyne's carefully crafted plans for the day, and they send their own recruits to meet you in an all-out attack at dawn. The battle is epic. Unfortunately, Crexidyne's goal for the villains was simply to create mass chaos to distract the world's attention from their *real* plan. A balls-out war between supercriminals does the job just as well as what they had worked up to begin with.

And it turns out that their real plan was some evil, evil stuff. You spend the day in the throes of superpowered combat, but it's all for naught—the entire planet more or less shrivels and dies before suppertime.

THE END

You delve deeper into the dog's brain, and realize that there's more than just canine remembrances here. In fact, it seems to be a storage unit for memories from a number of different sources. You get flashes of the Cosmic Guardian battling evil with the Justice Squadron and his first supergroup, the Liberty Patrol. You also find him returning frequently to what looks like a research facility. You can't determine the purpose of these visits, but he seems to be keeping them secret from his superhero colleagues.

You continue deeper, and find the Guardian meeting with a 1970s-era hero named Dogstar, the Savior from Sirius. Dogstar was an alien on a mission to protect Earth from any and all threats from outer space. After he died, the Cosmic Guard sent one of its battlesuits to a worthy Earthling to act as the planet's protector in his stead.

That's the story, anyway. If it's true, how could the two of them have ever met? As you watch the scene unfold, the Guardian fires some kind of energy weapon, catching Dogstar by surprise. The Savior from Sirius falls helplessly to the ground, and the Guardian pounces on him, tearing him to pieces with his bare hands.

You're not sure if your brain can scream or not, but it might have just happened, because suddenly you feel the alien intellect closing in on you. You have to get out of here! But there's so much more to learn . . . .

▶ *If you sever the connection now,* **turn to page 225.**

▶ *If you push your luck just a little further,*
   turn to page 256.

"Ah," Tachyon says. "I've always suspected that to stop them, I'd have to travel in time and undo everything, including my own ability to travel through time." Wait, how does that work? He smiles. "You mustn't worry too much about the paradoxes. Now, are you ready?"

"Uh, am I going with you?" you ask. You didn't even know that was possible. "Will I be able to get back, afterwards?"

"After this, there won't be anything here to come back to."

The room around you fades to white.

*   *   *   *   *

A young woman leans up against the side of a building, smoking a cigarette and waiting for her shift at the steel mill to begin. Most of the people she works with are big, ignorant men, but she's good at her job and doesn't care what they think of her. Above her, something streaks across the sky, crashing to Earth in the empty field behind the factory. The woman picks up a crowbar and walks into the field to investigate.

Minutes later she discovers a shiny blue pod in a smoking crater, the shape of a football and no larger than a baby carriage. Something inside it shakes, as if trying to emerge. However, it's dented from the impact. Perhaps the damage is preventing the pod's inner machinery from functioning properly?

Before she has the chance to poke it with the crowbar, the scene is bathed in a bright, white light. Tachyon's voice calls out, deep and soft.

"*Heed my words,*" he says. "*This box is an instrument of evil. Open it, and your life will never be the same. You'll see more wonders than you could ever imagine, but at the cost of everything*

(continue to the next page)

you will ever hold dear. In the end, it can only lead to destruction. However, the choice must be yours."

That's it? That's Tachyon saving the world? The fate of every living thing on the planet is at stake, and that's his pitch? You try to interject something about impending alien doom, but you have no presence here, no mouth with which to speak the words. The woman looks back at the steel mill, with its arc furnaces and vats of molten ore. She looks at the tiny spacecraft, and once again the scene fades to white.

* * * * *

You've wanted to be an astronaut—the most heroic, adventurous job you could imagine—ever since you were a small child. By the time you were 12, you had discovered that astronauts were just regular people who ate their vegetables, studied hard, and probably joined the Air Force. As you grew older, your friends would laugh about your ambitions. Screw 'em, you thought. Let them give up on their dreams and settle for life as an office worker, telemarketer, or investigative journalist. You knew what you wanted.

And here you are, a decade and a half later, strapped into a rocket and about to embark upon the first manned mission to Mars. The trip will take seven months and any number of things may go terribly wrong along the way. But, if all goes according to plan, you'll be among the first human beings to set foot on another planet. Your entire life has been leading up to this moment, and your heart races as the countdown ticks down. *Four . . . three . . . two . . . one . . .*

Blast off.

The End

You get the hell out of there, emerging from your first encounter with a superhero utterly humiliated. Clearly, you aren't quite ready for the fast lane. You spend the afternoon trying to figure out your powers, but learn almost nothing. It looks like you're going to have to discover them the hard way after all. Once night falls and you're confident Magnifico is long gone, you hit the streets, looking for easier prey.

You find it. Alas, some other dirtbag finds it first. It's a weeknight, meaning the downtown core is pretty vacant, but you hear a scream as some goon grabs a woman's purse and takes off down a back alley. After your run-in with Magnifico, snatching purses seems a little anticlimactic, but you decide to swoop in and take the spoils for yourself. You confront the mugger, but as soon as you do, you hear a voice call out from behind you.

"Drop the purse, scumbag!" You turn to see the glowing eyes of the Nightwatchman peering down at you from a rooftop. At least, it looks like the Nightwatchman. It sounds more like some frat boy doing a goofy-sounding fake voice. Certainly this is some local Nightwatchman wannabe. Which would explain why he wasn't eager to tangle with the Ox this morning.

The hooligan drops the bag and runs. The Nighwatchman seems quite pleased, and introduces himself, sticking out his hand to shake. He's obviously under the impression that you were planning to return the purse to its rightful owner. You wonder if you should correct this little misunderstanding —you did come out looking for a scuffle, after all, and surely you can take this guy.

You're almost ready to commit and fight the little twerp

(continue to the next page)

when a big, jellyfish-shaped craft the size of a bus pops out of the night sky above you. Holy crap! First meteors and superheroes, and now alien invaders? Cleveland is *insane* today. The craft fires a beam of blue energy at the Nightwatchman, just missing him as he leaps out of the way. You get a better look at it in the glow, and realize that it's made of the same type of metal and bears the same distinctive markings as the Cosmic Guardian you saw earlier.

The Guardian always claimed to be part of an intergalactic peace-keeping force called the Cosmic Guard. Could this ship be one of theirs? You look more closely at the way it moves, and realize that it might very well be a single, enormous alien in a Guardian battlesuit.

And it's clearly after the Nightwatchman poser. Is this giant space jellyfish a villain? Maybe you should join forces with it and help take him down. Then again, the alien is scary as hell, and there's no guarantee that it won't attack you next. Perhaps you should pretend to be on Nightwatchman's side, at least until you neutralize this new threat.

▶ *If you join with Nightwatchman to battle the Cosmic Guardian,* **turn to page 185.**

▶ *If you team up with the Cosmic Guardian to put the hurt on Nightwatchman,* **turn to page 270.**

You came looking for evidence that Crexidyne was working with the Cosmic Guard, and what you discover pretty much answers that question straight up. The elevator doors open to a rooftop absolutely swarming with Guardians: hundreds of them, setting up enormous pieces of machinery with a few human beings sprinkled among them, who appear to be in charge.

As one, they all stop what they're doing and look in your direction. Uh-oh. It seems you've found yourself knee-deep in stage two of Nancy's plan, whether you like it or not. Okay—just act cool. Pretend like you belong here.

You try to strike up a conversation with a human supervisor, but he's clearly freaked out by the fact that one of these alien robot things is even shaped like a person, much less speaking English to him. As you lay on the charm, you're grabbed from behind by one set of alien appendages and then another. Before you have a chance to react, dozens of them are on top of you in a big armored dogpile.

They begin tearing your battlesuit from you piece by piece. After a few terrified moments, you come to realize that it's the suit they're interested in—they're destroying your armor with zeal, but don't seem particularly concerned with what's inside it. In fact, as they peel the last fragments of it from your body and continue ripping it to shreds, you have a glimmer of hope that you may even escape unnoticed.

Then, almost as an afterthought, one of them kicks you off the roof.

THE END

"It's okay, Terry," Octavia says. "Just try to relax. You're among friends now."

He responds by lunging at Magnifica, but she leaps into the air just in time to avoid his frenzied grasp. He screams in rage, then immediately turns his gaze to you.

Octavia's eyes are clenched shut. "Come back to us, Terry. You don't have to let it control you." Apparently he does, though. He falls to his knees, then staggers back on his feet, his entire body shaking. You can't see his face through the Guardian helmet, but you imagine a lot of clenched teeth and bulging veins. He slowly takes a step toward you, one fist raised.

"He needs to feel the touch of a human being so he can remember who he is!" Octavia says.

Magnifica is still hovering. "I ain't touching him," she says.

"Only the warm embrace of humanity can save him," Octavia insists, her face tense with focus. "I can't do it myself —I have to concentrate on this!"

The Ox is still approaching, and you can't imagine there's anything other than murder on his mind. Seriously, how is he supposed to even *feel* the warm embrace of humanity through all that alien steel? "I don't think this is—"

"Just hug him, damn it!" Octavia says. "It's the only way to calm him down!"

▶ *Okay, fine. If you hug him,* **turn to page 281.**

▶ *Screw that. If you fall back on Magnifica's beating-the-crap-out-of-him plan,* **turn to page 182.**

"Fine," the Ox says. "We do it your way. But I'm still pissed off about being attacked by robots from space. Oh, hey, Tink." He introduces you to a pudgy man in his mid-forties emerging from behind an overturned table. "This is Tinker, my costume guy. Dude, the horns broke again."

"I'm a weapons manufacturer, mostly," the man says, offering you a hand to shake. "And I told you, Ox, you have to break the walls with your fists, not your head."

Tinker tells you that he recognized the man in the tweed jacket as Carlo Moretti of the Crexidyne Corporation, a multinational conglomerate run by notorious villain Reginald Thorpe. If the Cosmic Guard is in league with them, it's definitely bad news. Tinker has done some contract work for Crexidyne and has accumulated a file of sensitive information. You and the Ox follow him back to his home, which turns out to be a tiny, squalid house across the bridge in Newark.

Tinker's files are in even worse shape than his living room. He pulls out a big brown accordion folder full of miscellaneous receipts and take-out menus, insisting that copies of secret Crexidyne papers are scattered throughout.

The Ox is peeking out the window through the blinds. "Uh, guys? One of those Cosmic Guardian things is outside. Don't worry, though—I've been wantin' to beat up some more stuff anyway."

He rushes out the door to tussle, and you get to work. Some of the papers actually look fairly interesting. Tinker had apparently developed a long-range targeting system for Crexidyne, but they never told him what it was intended to be used for.

Ox pokes his head inside the door. "I killed the one, but

(continue to the next page)

now there's like six more, plus a big jellyfish one the size of a Winnebago," he says through a wide grin. "Just so you know."

There are bits and pieces of other documents and memos, and schematics for some kind of satellite. Could this be what they're working on with the Guardians? It all seems to be lumped together under something called Project Bogotá.

"Here come the superheroes!" the Ox yells from outside, sounding a bit more frazzled than he did a minute ago. "If Megawatt or Magnifico show up, we might be in trouble. Crap, is that the Phenomenal Three?"

Something about Bogotá jogs your memory, so you get on Tinker's computer and do a quick search. Sure enough, a few months ago there was a mysterious incident in Bogotá, Colombia, in which several diplomats were killed by what was reported to be a giant column of fire from the sky. Six different terrorist organizations claimed responsibility, but none that possessed anything like the technology necessary to pull such a thing off.

"I think it's some kind of satellite laser weapon," you say.

"That doesn't make sense," Tinker says. "It would only be good for taking out a single target, and the expense would be astronomical. Crexidyne has quieter, cheaper ways to pull off a simple assassination. When would they even use something like that?"

The Ox stumbles back inside, panting and dusting off his clothes. "Wooo!" he crows. "Aliens can't touch me! Superheroes can't touch me! What else you got?"

You and Tinker exchange a terrified glance just as the huge, orange beam blasts through the roof and completely incinerates all three of you.

THE END

You have no idea what's going on here, but something isn't right and your gut tells you that Crexidyne is the key. Also, you have to admit that you'd really like to meet Nancy North. How can you get in touch with her, though? *Contact Nancy North*, you think. Could it be that easy? Sure enough, an e-mail window shows up on the screen with her address auto-filled. This stuff is awesome. You peck out a brief but urgent message and send it off. You hope that does the trick.

As you're figuring out how to work the chamber doors, a new message pops up on your glove. "Long time. Meet me in old spot tonight, 10 p.m. —N" Old spot? Maybe there's something in your wrist computer's files about that? After a bit of searching, your best guess is that she's referring to the water tower on top of the *New York Globe* building. Which would mean it really

(continue to the next page)

has been a long time, since Nancy left the *Globe* for an anchor gig at the NBS Nightly News in the late '90s. You'll have to drive all the way through Pennsylvania and New Jersey to get there, though, and you're not even sure you can make it by 10.

To the Watchmobile, you think. Your wristscreen has no response. Sigh. To the 1996 Ford Taurus.

The long drive offers plenty of time to plan your meeting with the news icon. According to her book, the Nightwatchman always stuck to the shadows and disguised his voice, so if you do the same, maybe you can pull off this charade. And for the record, yes, you've read *No Nonsense*, the 1989 tell-all by Nancy North, cover to cover. You also once mailed her your sprawling, conspiracy theory-filled thesis on the secret identities of the Justice Squadron back when you were in journalism school. She didn't write back. It wasn't your proudest moment.

By the time you arrive and find a route up to the water tower that doesn't involve a grappling hook, it's almost 11 and Nancy is waiting. "You're late," she says. She must be in her mid-sixties by now, but she still looks good. *Really* good, in fact.

You answer in the deepest, most gravelly voice you can muster. "Had to make sure I wasn't followed." That sounds like something the Nightwatchman would say, right? You make every effort to conceal yourself in the darkness.

"Jesus, what happened to your voice?"

At this moment you're acutely aware of the degree to which you are not the Nightwatchman. "Uh, nothing." Man, that really hurts your throat, too. "A cold."

"Seriously, do you want a lozenge? I have some Sucrets." She starts digging in her purse.

(continue to the next page)

"No lozenge," you croak. This isn't going as well as you hoped. "What can you tell me about Crexidyne, the Ox, and Brain Stem?"

"Hmm," she says. This woman is cool as a cucumber, and you can't tell yet if she's buying you as the legendary vigilante. "I know they're both being tracked by Crexidyne's top brass. They've got some kind of program that keeps tabs on superhumans, and from what I can tell, their interest is spread evenly between heroes and villains. I also know Brain Stem is missing. Is he dead? Is that what this is about?"

You pause for a moment, wondering if you should fill her in. How much do you really know about Nancy North? Can you trust her?

"Can't talk about that," you reply. "Tell me more about the surveillance."

She takes a step back, perhaps trying to get a better look at you. "It goes straight to the top, whatever it is. It has Thorpe's fingerprints all over it." As Crexidyne's CEO, Reginald Thorpe's name is synonymous with mad power grabs and dirty backroom deals, and even though he's a normal human, over the years he's achieved sort of an honorary supervillain status. "And it's been ramping up," Nancy continues. "If they did kill Brain Stem, it's just the beginning."

You can't help but wonder if you're in over your head. "Listen," Nancy says. "I know you've been doing this a long time, but Thorpe has resources that you wouldn't believe." A long time? *Yes!* She thinks you're the real thing! "If you're going after him, don't go lone-wolf. Consider some backup on this one."

(continue to the next page)

"I'll take that under consideration," you say. The five-syllable word sounds particularly ridiculous in your forced Cookie-Monster grumble.

"You know that there's only one person you can really trust," Nancy says as you retreat into the shadows. "With the jet, you could be in Broward County in 45 minutes."

Broward County, Florida? Wait. *The jet?* Sure enough, your suit's onboard computer tells you that the Nightwatchman's radar-invisible stealth fighter is parked in an underground hangar nearby, gassed up, thought-controlled, and ready to take you anywhere on the planet. Something is bugging you about the gaping holes in your predecessor's security measures, but to be honest you're too giddy to dwell on it much.

You start thinking about the backup Nancy mentioned. Maybe it's time to bring Melah and Dale into the loop. They're both good journalists—they could help you put the pieces together, and with a jet you could be back in Cleveland in no time. Or maybe it's time to stop thinking like an unemployed reporter and start thinking like a superhero. Besides, you've got a feeling that investigative backup isn't what Nancy was talking about.

▶ If you call your friends and turn this mission into a team effort, **turn to page 68.**

▶ If you skip right past amateur hour and round up some bigger, preferably superpowered guns, **turn to page 150.**

The Cosmic Guardian told you to lie low with his honest-to-god dying breath—maybe you should listen, at least until you figure out just what's going on here. You use your slightly shaky understanding of world geography to locate Cleveland on the globe, and head straight for your apartment. After about 15 minutes of trying to figure out how to remove your gauntlets so you can type (they retract into the suit's arm plates, which is pretty cool), you're puttering about on your laptop, which is what you'd be doing on a normal weekday afternoon even if you weren't mostly encased in alien cybernetics.

You turn up plenty about the Cosmic Guardian's adventures, but very little regarding his disappearance. Even his old teammates don't seem to know what happened to him. One quote from the Human Torpedo sums it up:

Those space heroes were like that, you know, always coming and going. Most people don't remember this, but the Cosmic Guardian wasn't the first. The space police, or whatever, sent him to replace Dogstar, the Savior from Sirius. Nice guy, Dogstar, although, frankly, I never really understood what the hell he was talking about. But one day he's just dead, and the Guardian shows up. I kind of expected another one to come after he finally split, but I guess the space cops figured that by then we had things under control.

Then the interview mostly degenerates into a plug for Oceanopolis, the ill-fated theme park Torpedo lent his name to when he retired back in '97. You recall seeing Dogstar in group photos of the old Liberty Patrol, but never knew he had any connection to the Cosmic Guardian.

Before you can type "Dogstar" into Google, you hear a

(continue to the next page)

knock at the door, accompanied by a shrill, all-too-familiar voice. "I know you're there," your neighbor Mrs. Pinkett shouts from the porch. You freeze. "I saw you come home—I'm not blind, you know."

Wait a minute. She *saw* you? Flying out of the clear blue sky, decked out in full-body space armor? Your visor quickly closes, completely of its own volition, and the gauntlets that took so long to coax off your fingers snap back into place.

"I checked with the landlord," your neighbor says. "You're not allowed to have robot suits in the building, just so you know."

No, no, no. Mrs. Pinkett is an incorrigible gossip. If she realizes you're the Cosmic Guardian, it'll be on the nightly news by six o'clock. She keeps knocking, and two little missiles pop out of your armored shoulders, humming as if ready to launch. The suit is responding to your panic, and gearing up for battle! You need to calm yourself before you accidentally carpet bomb the place.

▶ *If you grab your laptop and flee out the back door,* **turn to page 63.**

▶ *If you stay and try to control the damage before Mrs. Pinkett shares your secret identity with the entire apartment complex (or the world),* **turn to page 112.**

You didn't grow up idolizing villains and thugs. And you're not sure what kind of power you've stumbled upon, but you're fairly certain it comes with at least medium-grade responsibility. You refuse the Ox's offer to join him in his life of crime.

So he punches you. In a flash of blinding pain, you find yourself splayed out on the floor, immediately regretting your decision. You glance over and discover that your right arm is a twisted mess of exposed bone and pooling blood. You instinctively threw your arms up to protect your face, so your elbow took most of the force of impact.

Wait a minute. Since when do you bleed *purple*?

You watch your arm dissolve right before your eyes until your wrist and shoulder are connected by a lumpy puddle of purple goo, which then solidifies into a vaguely arm-shaped mass. Something really freaky is going on here, but at least the pain is gone. Stumbling to your feet, you find that you can still move your fingers, and sort of flop around your new boneless, stretchy appendage.

"What are you supposed to be? The Latex Avenger?" The Ox takes a step toward you, balling up his fists. "Seriously, *stay down*." Before he can throw another punch, purple goo spreads from your arm, quickly covering your body below the neck. The Ox's fist connects with your chest, but your sludgy coating absorbs most of the impact. It also covers your opponent's fist in gunk. He tries to wipe one hand clean with the other, but only manages to get them get them stuck together.

It looks like you've discovered your superpower. Given a choice you would probably have picked something a little sexier

(continue to the next page)

than purple goop, but it just saved your life so you'll take what you can get.

Concentrating, you discover that you have control over the sludge's consistency, and you harden your coating into a protective shell. Which gives you an idea. You focus on the Ox, and the gunk on his hands solidifies.

"What the hell?" He starts grunting, trying to pry his hands apart with his considerable strength, but they don't budge. You jump back, and with a flick of your shoulder stretch your bendy right arm several feet across the room to gunk up his feet as well. Once you've willed the foot goo to solidify, the Ox is effectively immobilized.

"Face justice, evildoer," you say a bit too enthusiastically as your opponent falls to the floor. That was awesome! A quick, anonymous phone call alerts the local police that you've gift-wrapped their errant bank robber. You briefly consider pocketing a small stack of unmarked bills on your way out, but that is *not* how you roll.

Now what? Helping the helpless, obviously, but where to begin? New York City is where the real action is, and you've just proven that you can throw down with the heavy hitters. Or perhaps you should start off slow, and just be the sworn protector of Cleveland until you have time to get the hang of this hero gig.

▶ *If Cleveland just got its first superhero,*
turn to page 168.

▶ *Screw Cleveland. If you think you're ready for the big time,* **turn to page 70.**

"I don't actually know where Thorpe is," you say. You start pecking at your wrist screen, hoping to dig up some info on his possible whereabouts. "Crexidyne headquarters, maybe?"

"Yeah, okay. Can we do this in the morning, though? I gotta get back to friggin' bed."

You spend the night in the surprisingly comfortable cockpit of your jet. You had hoped to get an early start, but Magnifica insists that she needs to build up energy if she's going to go busting heads, and brunch isn't served until 10:30. When she's finally ready to leave, it's almost noon. And although you had intended to fly back to New York yourself, your companion has other ideas.

"By the time you get there in this bucket of bolts, you'll have missed the asskicking." Before you can protest, Magnifica grabs you by the waist and launches into the sky. The trip to New York takes only moments, but the less said about it, the better. Suffice it to say that it's utterly terrifying. You had planned to use fear and intimidation to scare Thorpe into revealing his diabolical plot, Nightwatchman-style, but that's pretty much shot to hell when you're crouched on his office floor trying not to wet yourself.

Magnifica, in the meantime, gets down to brass tacks. "We're here for answers," she says. You notice that she's left her walker back in Florida. "Wait a minute—who the hell are you?"

A small man with beady eyes and a tablet computer sits at a desk in the center of the room. "Carlo Moretti, operations manager for Crexidyne Megacorp," he says. "You must be Maggie McClain, a.k.a. Magnifica. And, uh . . . *guest*." You peel yourself off the floor and try to look a little more intimidating.

(continue to the next page)

Magnifica is clearly disappointed. "Reggie lets you use the big office, huh? That ain't like him."

"Mr. Thorpe rarely finds it necessary to visit headquarters these days. I'm in charge here."

"Oh yeah?" She strides over to him and lifts him off the floor by his neck. "You kill any superheroes lately? I can hear your little weasel heart beating, so I'll know if you lie to me." Moretti just makes a gurgling noise, so she loosens her grip. "What was that?"

"I said you're trespassing on private property, and you need to leave before I have you thrown out."

Magnifica grins. "Send for your goons. I skipped aquatic therapy this morning, anyway. I could use the exercise."

"You've broken into my office and threatened my life." He has difficulty getting the words out with her hand still around his throat, but you have to give him credit for not really flinching. "If I so much as say the word, you'll have the Justice Squadron to deal with."

"Even better," Maggie says. Still, there's something in Moretti's tone that you don't like. And he certainly doesn't seem to be responding to intimidation. Perhaps it's time to retreat and gather information by other methods. Or should you call his bluff? If he does summon the Squadron, you imagine they'd be very interested to hear what you've learned about Brain Stem's murder.

▶ *If you tell Magnifica to back down,* **turn to page 266.**

▶ *If you let Magnifica do her thing and see where this leads,* **turn to page 160.**

"I'll give you the suit," you say, "but answer me one question first."

Moretti snorts. "If you really intended to give it up, it would have already severed its connection to you. Remember, I did warn you about this."

He pushes the button.

On impulse, you shoot straight up like an arrow, smashing through 60 floors of office building and rocketing into the stratosphere. If he really does have a death laser poised to take out your friends, you're guessing it'll be the hottest thing in the sky, and you command the suit to hurtle toward its energy signature at top speed. Your little ruse may have failed miserably, but if there's still any way to save your friends, you're going to find it.

Your guess is right on the money, and it takes a mere five seconds to reach the satellite. Unfortunately, it takes the weapon just under six seconds to fire. You smash into the laser canon at full speed just as it does, causing the device to explode in a flash of bright orange light that incinerates you into fine mist right along with it. You sacrificed your own life to do it, but at least Nancy and that spooky, silent Nightwatch person are safe.

Whatever Thorpe and Moretti are planning, it's up to them to stop them now.

THE END

The following few seconds are a whirlwind of pain, until it's all mercifully ended by a crack on the jaw that switches you off like a light. Fortunately, your opponent is something of an expert on how much damage the human body can withstand, and he's not actually trying to kill you. In fact, he only chased you in the first place because you ran (safety rules for encountering supervillains are largely identical to safety rules for encountering pit bulls). The pounding he administers is calculated to put you out of commission for one to two business days. Sure enough, you regain consciousness the following morning, still on that rooftop. You're in rough shape, though: your body is a mass of bruises and abrasions, you've clearly broken several ribs, and that thing sticking out of your left leg might be a bone.

You make your slow, agonizing descent down the stairs to the building's lobby, where you find several people huddled around a television set. A group of villains has launched a full-scale attack on Washington, D.C.! This sounds like a job for . . .

Someone else, surely. You could barely hobble down five flights of stairs, and at this point you're starting to wonder if you even have superpowers at all. There are plenty of actual heroes who can handle this, and whatever the villains are up to, it isn't going to be the end of the world, right?

▶ *If you rush to Washington to thwart their nefarious plot as fast as your broken, twisted body can manage,* **turn to page 212.**

▶ *If you rush to check yourself into a hospital, like a sane person,* **turn to page 89.**

Bank robbery is one thing, but you're no murderer. Not yet, anyway. It *is* your first day of villainy, so you decide to take things slow. You withdraw the purple gunk from Magnifico's innards. He flashes you a look of abject terror, then turns and launches into the air through the front door, coughing and sputtering as he goes. You just defeated your first superhero! Also, you discover a small leather pouch stuck to your various effluvia—you must have somehow managed to pull it off his belt while you were utterly humiliating him. Inside it you find a glass orb a bit larger than a golf ball, containing a tiny, wriggling worm suspended in blue mist. A piece of masking tape has been stuck to it with two letters written in black Sharpie: OX.

The bank has long since cleared of patrons and employees. "Hey Ox, come look at this," you say. "I found a freaky little worm with your name on it."

"What?" He's already in the vaults, stuffing stacks of cash into a duffel bag. "Later, okay? Seriously, we gotta get out of here."

"We just took down Magnifico," you say with a chuckle. "Are you really sweating a few of Cleveland's finest showing up?"

"Not them," he says. "The freakin' Justice Squadron. We just pissed one of 'em off good, and you can bet your ass the rest are about to come down like the wrath of god."

"But he tried to kill me," you say. "I let him *live!*"

"Yeah. If you'd offed him, we would have had time to get outta here, at least. I'm not saying I would have done it, but it sure woulda made things easier." Apparently the reward for compassion in the supervillain game is a swift kick in the teeth. You help your partner with his cash grabbing and leave the bank in a hurry.

(continue to the next page)

As you make haste for the Ox's van, he starts to lighten up a bit. "You know, you're going to need a cool supervillain name," he says. "Something gross, like your powers. How about the Furious Phlegm? Ooh, I know: Gunkmaster."

Before you have the chance to tell him you will never, under any circumstances, answer to the name Gunkmaster, you glance up at the skyline and spot three members of the Justice Squadron approaching: Gravity Bomb, Coldfront, Skyhawk and Cosmic Guardian.

Your heart sinks. Gravity Bomb alone would be a tough opponent—her complete control over gravitational forces means you're unlikely to get close enough to try your goop-in-the-lungs trick. Coldfront is the Squadron's newest member, and it actually created a bit of an international incident when they recruited him, since he was more or less Canada's only respectable hero. He has weather powers, and does this tornado twist thing with his body that will make it tough to even lay a hand on him.

Skyhawk isn't terribly formidable, but the fourth one is the biggest surprise. Not only has the Cosmic Guardian been missing from the team's roster since the 1990s, but this is definitely not the one you saw meteor-busting earlier today. For starters, although it's covered in the distinctive Guardian armor, it's shaped less like a human being and more like a giant eyeball with tentacles.

"We're hosed," Ox says, raising both hands above his head with a sigh.

▶ *He's probably right. If you surrender,*
   turn to page 104.

▶ *No way, you can take 'em! If you put up a fight,*
   turn to page 138.

MATT YOUNGMARK

"You know who's a bunch of jerks?" Ocean Boy says, slurring his words almost beyond comprehension. Several hours into the first jug, you've never seen two human beings put away so much liquor. Seriously, the younger partner may look like a fish, but they can both drink like one.

"News . . . paper . . . editors?" you mumble. Truthfully, you've done your level best to keep up with them.

"Orca whales," he continues. "I try my . . . you know, I try my hardest to be a good protector for all the ocean creatures—"

"You do," Chuck interrupts. "You're a *great* protector."

"But orca whales don't give a damn," he says, becoming more animated. "You know I can talk to them, right? And they *like it*. They eat the littlest little baby seals, and they *like it*."

(continue to the next page)

"We need to teach those orca whales a lesson," Chuck sputters, stumbling to his feet.

You're overwhelmed by their compassion. "You guys," you say. "You guys are *heroes*. Me, I find a space suit that has super cosmic powers, and I think that makes me a hero. But your *regular bodies* are the super powers. I admire you *so much*."

"I admire YOU," Ocean Boy says, closing his eyes and gesticulating wildly. "You don't think I wish I had a suit like you do? I could be a superhero *on land* if I had a suit like you do." He pauses, considering it. "You should *totally* lend me your suit."

"Obie! You don't ask another super person to lend you their super suit. It's not right. It's a very intimate . . . thing." Chuck has now made it to the water's edge, but stops and turns to you, almost losing his balance in the effort. "And you know better than anyone that it's not *powers* that make a superhero a man. It's what you *do* with them. Now come on, both of you, and let's go beat up some orca whales."

You're not sure what to do, because they both make excellent points. You realize now that Ocean Boy is probably the finest hero of his generation, and letting him try out the Guardian armor only seems fair. But also, what the other one said. You're pretty sure the suit itself is trying to communicate something to you, but you're way too drunk to come anywhere close to understanding what it might be.

▶ *If you let Ocean Boy borrow the armor,*
    turn to page 15.

▶ *If you unite with your superhero brethren against
    the villainous orca threat,* **turn to page 250.**

You're going to need more than friendly reassurances from some skinny guy in a bad suit before you start taking orders from the government. Assuming he even works for the government—you notice that the helicopter is all black with no identifying marks. "Um, why don't you just give me your contact info, and I'll call you a little bit later?" you say.

Moretti hands you a business card, but he doesn't look pleased. Its sole feature is a phone number, which you don't find reassuring. "Look, we really need to get started right away," he says. "Our top priority is—"

"Right, the Ox! I'm all over it!" You launch into the air, quickly leaving man and helicopter behind. The more you ponder it, the less sure you are about Agent Moretti. You also realize that you're clutching his business card in your gauntleted hand. Hmm—does your armor have pockets? For now, you press the card up against your helmet's visor and try to memorize the number. Should this really be *that* difficult?

Before you can check to see if your suit's AI has some kind of built-in Rolodex, you spot something approaching on the horizon. If that's a plane, you'd better get out of its flight path. You take a hard right, only to spot another shape coming from that direction—fast. Could Moretti have sent goons after you? Does Moretti *have* goons? Pouring on the speed, you alter course and shoot straight up toward the stratosphere.

Whereupon you almost collide with a third bogey, tracking you from above. It veers out of your way and paces you, allowing a better look. The thing is shaped like a giant eyeball with tentacles, and you realize that its coloring and markings match your suit. A second figure draws up, and although this one is

(continue to the next page)

shaped like an enormous insect, it's also wearing cybernetic armor similar to your own. It's the Cosmic Guard!

You ease back on the throttle and within moments you're surrounded by Guardians of all shapes and sizes. Your inner geek is about to pee itself. You wanted superheroes? Here's a whole freaking army of superheroes. And not just that, but *alien* superheroes. Bona fide sentient life from elsewhere in the galaxy! You're overcome with pride at being given the chance to join their ranks. You're not sure if there's some sort of universal space greeting, so you just sort of hold up one hand and wave. As one, the Cosmic Guardians each stretch a single appendage toward you.

And open fire.

The energy blasts hit you from all angles, shorting out the visual display on your visor. Everything goes black, and a burning smell fills your nostrils. The 1950s announcer guy starts gibbering in your brain again, but now he sounds more than a little panicked. And he's still making very little sense, but you can pick out the phrases "evasive maneuvers" and "flee." Surely this is all some kind of mistake!

▶ *If you try to communicate with the Cosmic Guard and convince them to hold their fire,* **turn to page 211.**

▶ *If you get the hell out of there as quickly as possible,* **turn to page 166.**

You decide to ease into things and meet with the supervillains. It's an eight-hour drive to New York, so along the way you attempt to explore your theoretical powers. You definitely feel stronger, faster, and more agile, but not to any degree that you'd really consider "super." You start to worry that you might be one of those martial arts heroes who hone their skills to perfection and battle injustice with their bare hands. Which, honestly, seems like a lot of work.

Ox is concentrating on your new supervillain code name. "You need something that inspires fear," he insists. "Animal names work pretty good. The Orangutan? Oh, I know! The Soft-Shell Crab! Because you're soft on the inside, but super tough."

You stare at him blankly. "This is what inspires fear, to you?"

"Dude, those things creep me the hell out. Ooh, how about King Crab? That's a TOTAL supervillain name."

After hours of unsuccessfully combing the animal kingdom for a suitable moniker, you arrive in the city and find the villains gathered in the basement of a YWCA under the guise of an AA meeting. A rail-thin older gentleman with an honest-to-god monocle is talking as you sit down.

"That damn Nightwatchman is the worst," he seethes. "You see those glowing eyes in the shadows and you know you're about to get your ass kicked. Plus, you have to bring an oxygen mask to every freakin' crime or he just gets you with the gas."

"Tell me about it," Ox says, settling in. "Last time I fought him I had to hold my breath for like 45 minutes." The room goes silent. "What? It's one of my superpowers. You know who I really hate, though?"

The entire group moans.

(continue to the next page)

"Megawatt," he continues. "He thinks he's so cool because he can fly in space. I bet *I* could fly in space. I told you I could hold my breath for a really long time, right?"

This may not be a planning session as much as it is a supervillain support group. Before it's your turn to share, though, you hear a scream from the stairwell and turn to see a group of armored figures burst into the room. Their outfits resemble that of the Cosmic Guardian who stopped that meteor back in Cleveland, but most of them are clearly not human. One is vaguely insect-like, and another is shaped like a giant slug. The Guardian always claimed to be part of an intergalactic peace-keeping force. Could that be where he's been for the past 15 years? Fetching reinforcements?

The villains scatter. A short man holding a fancy little tablet computer enters and points to the old guy with the monocle. "Doctor Diabolus," he says. "He's on the list." One of the Guardians fires a blue beam from its gauntlet, which drops the doctor like a sack of meat. The Guardian then scoops him up into a burlap sack. Whoa. No interstellar Miranda rights, then? That doesn't seem right.

"The Ox," the tablet man says. "Priority one! He's on the list!"

▶ *If your plan was to gather evidence to bust these evildoers, it looks like that's pretty well taken care of. If you step back and let the space police do their job,* **turn to page 177.**

▶ *Then again, you're starting to genuinely like the Ox. If you help him fight them off,* **turn to page 124.**

The thing is, when you're the size of a dust mote, it takes an incredibly long time to even get to a person's adrenal gland, much less overload it to the point where he or she passes out. While your cosmic space armor is being systematically ripped to shreds, your partner is still doing his *Fantastic Voyage* schtick somewhere along the pulmonary artery.

Also, you should know that the Ox isn't actually trying to kill you. In his many years of bank robbing, street brawling, and general all-purpose supervillainy, he's become remarkably adept at judging how much punishment the human body can take. And even though you kept *pushing* and *pushing* until you pushed him right over the edge, he had every reason to believe the thrashing he gave you was just enough to leave you in a good solid coma for a couple of days. For whatever that's worth.

So it's not the Ox's beating that technically kills you, but for one reason or another (*ooh, cryptic*), you're dead before you ever wake up from it.

THE END

The suit is giving you a powerful fight-or-flight vibe, and since "Calmly defuse the situation" doesn't seem to appear on that list, you opt for flight. You scoot out the back, take to the air, and, for lack of a better destination, finally settle atop Key Tower, Cleveland's tallest building. Things should be reasonably private up there. Before you have a chance to tackle your next problem (finding an unsecured wifi signal), you hear a muffled sound coming from somewhere near your left leg and realize that your cell phone is ringing. By the time you extract it from the suit, you've missed the call, but discover it was from Dale. In fact, he's left you three phone messages and seven texts.

You call him back, trying to sound nonchalant. "Dale, what's up?"

"What do you mean, what's up?" He sounds jittery. "I'm back at the bar. Can you meet me here? We really need to talk about what just happened."

"Um, nothing happened," you say. "Mine was a dead end."

"Oh, something happened, all right," Dale says. He couldn't possibly know about the Guardian armor, could he? Then again, he is an investigative journalist. And as Mrs. Pinkett proved, so far you've earned zero points for stealth.

"Something *amazing* happened," he continues. "You might even say something . . . *super*."

Yeah, he knows.

▶ *If you agree to meet Dale at the bar,* **turn to page 134.**

▶ *If you think it's wiser not to meet him and hope it all blows over,* **turn to page 280.**

"Sten Janssen is dead," you say. "He sacrificed himself saving Cleveland from a meteor. I was there, and the suit just . . . came to me."

If Agent Moretti doubts your story, it doesn't show on his face. "Then you're worthy of it. The Cosmic Guard has proven time and again that its judgment and honor are beyond reproach. In fact, that's why we signaled for you." Moretti explains that he works for a top-secret government project, and they've uncovered a conspiracy involving dozens of villains who've never been known to work together before. They've also found evidence of a potential superhero traitor, so they're reluctant to turn to the Justice Squadron or the Phenomenal Three.

"It's been a long time, but we need the Cosmic Guard once again," he says. "Our first priority is to stop the Ox. He's a lunkhead, but he's invulnerable to just about everything, including your built-in weaponry. In league with a criminal mastermind, he could become unstoppable."

That explains the asswhupping, at least. "Take this," Moretti says, handing you a small electronic device. "Plug it into your helmet. It'll let us track your movements and keep us in constant contact." He gestures toward the helicopter with his thumb. "I'll debrief you further on the way to headquarters."

A job with the U.S. government would be a pretty sweet gig. And it sounds like they know a lot more about the whole Cosmic Guardian business than you do. Then again, how much do you know about this Moretti guy? Can you trust him?

▶ *If you take the communicator and get in the helicopter,* **turn to page 172.**

▶ *If you tell Moretti you'd rather remain a free agent for now,* **turn to page 58.**

Maggie leaps out the open window to head off the attackers. Whatever this new threat is, you have complete faith in the old bird's abilities. Now to do *your* job. You manage to break Crexidyne network security with minimal effort. The sheer volume of the data would be daunting to a lesser human being, but you're an *entry-level newspaper reporter*. Sifting through mountains of poorly organized records could be *your* superpower. You dig up everything you can find on superheroes and villains. A folder labeled "Hostile Takeover" looks interesting as well.

Outside, it sounds like a war zone. Magnifica's opponents appear to be alien creatures of incredible variety dressed in Cosmic Guardian uniforms, and she's knocking them out of the sky with her bare fists as quickly as they come at her. Far below, the streets are in chaos as people flee in panic, hoping to avoid debris and falling aliens. She seems to have things pretty well under control, so you begin to dig though the Crexidyne files.

What you find isn't good. It appears Crexidyne is responsible for every superhero and villain in the past two decades. They conducted experiments on anyone who agreed to swear loyalty to them, then wiped the subjects' minds of the incident, leaving them to discover their superpowers and make their own way in the world. Some chose a life of crime and others sought the glory of the hero, but eventually all would have their memories restored and be called upon to pay the piper.

The first such activation was Magnifico, just last week. You start sifting through the files of other superhumans, and discover that from the Justice Squadron all the way down to the low-level street thugs, the rest were all activated and called into service on the same day. *Yesterday.*

(continue to the next page)

And it only gets worse. The "Hostile Takeover" file is a series of personal communications between Moretti and a nearly unintelligible Reginald Thorpe. Seriously, most of his emails border on gibberish—how does this guy run a corporation? He gives a lengthy series of very specific, if rambling, instructions on how to prepare for new management, assuring Moretti that he'll still retain his position after the new owners take over. Hmm. How can a takeover be considered hostile when the CEO is so clearly on board with it?

That's when you realize that it isn't a takeover of Crexidyne Megacorp. *It's a takeover of the planet Earth.* And according to these memos, it's happening *right now*.

You check your computer for media reports and discover that supervillains are attacking national monuments all over the world. The international media is going wild over it. More disturbing, though, are a few sketchy reports of some kind of sudden biological outbreak in southern Chile. You can't seem to find any additional information, though, because all communications in the area have gone down.

In fact, you find more blackouts in the northern tips of Greenland and Canada. Whatever's happening, it's starting at the North and South Poles and spreading rapidly.

"Maggie, we have to go!" If this is a full-scale alien invasion, you'd better get to the bottom of it fast. The bogeys that have been dive-bombing Magnifica seem to be in retreat now, but one huge, human-shaped Guardian is approaching, hefting a large, glowing orb. Magnifica spots him and changes course to intercept, but she suddenly shudders, freezing up in mid-air and then dropping to the streets below like a rock.

(continue to the next page)

Magnifico said they could take his powers away.

"Maggie!"

You toss a grappling hook at the window frame and leap out of it. You have nowhere near enough rope to rappel 60 stories, but cut the wire halfway through, throwing a second line to slow your fall as you approach to the ground.

You find Magnifica in one piece, but badly broken. "Tachyon," she gasps as you cradle her head in your arms. "Tachyon . . . there's no more time . . . ."

She's gone.

Tachyon. The time traveler. Was Magnifica trying to tell you to find him? Or, in her final moments, did she think you were Tachyon? According to your files, he's in a hospital in Connecticut. Your Ford Taurus is still here in New York where you left it last night—you could be there in a couple of hours.

To do what? Watch another legend die? Tachyon is in a coma. And if those spreading power blackouts are linked to a full-scale invasion, time is short. Your jet is still in southern Florida, but if you can find a way back to it, you could fly to the North Pole and see what's happening for yourself.

▶ If you think Tachyon is your last, best hope to save the world, **turn to page 218.**

▶ If you'd rather take matters into your own hands, **turn to page 279.**

Dale and Melah are your closest friends—if you can't trust them with your secrets, you can't trust anyone. And you can always call in the big guns later after they help you figure out what's going on. You give your friends a call. It turns out they're both here in New York as well, although they seem to have come independently of one another. Which is odd, considering it took you eight hours to get here by car—did they both split town immediately after you separated? Did *neither* of them think it was worth staying to cover the bank robbery for ClevelandNewsExplosion.com? Oh, well. A ride in your fancy new plane will just have to wait.

You make plans to meet them in a secluded alley near the underground hangar—all the better for dramatically unveiling your new identity, you figure. When you arrive at the spot, you pose yourself carefully on a ledge and wait. And wait. And wait some more. An hour later, you're still waiting. Melah and Dale aren't answering their phones, and now your legs are cramping up like crazy. You've just about decided to move on to plan B when you spot a lone figure approaching in the alley beneath you.

It isn't either of your friends, unless one of them has taken to dressing in a shiny purple bodysuit. Since your spiffy new goggles feature infrared vision and telescopic lenses, you zoom in for a better look. The mysterious stranger is definitely female, and quite fit—her skin-tight outfit covers her from head to toe but leaves little to the imagination. She's sprinting down the alley at an impressive clip, and just as she's about to pass you, she makes a flying leap onto the building across the way, clearing about ten feet of it and sticking to the wall like glue. It's a neat trick.

(continue to the next page)

You soon discover what she's running from: the Cosmic Guardian appears at the other end of the alley, rocketing toward her. She flings a couple of gooey purple blobs from the palms of her hands at him but they just splatter harmlessly against his blue, metallic battlesuit. Then she makes a motion like she's throwing a baseball and stretches her arm 20 feet toward her attacker, grabbing his shoulder. She jumps from her perch, swings around in a wide arc, and affixes herself to his back.

Well, there's your superhero team-up right there. You'll have to move quickly if you want to get in on the action, though —the Guardian changes course in mid-air and launches straight up into the sky. Your grappling hook has a magnetic clamp on it—with a lucky throw you could attach it to him and tag along, helping him subdue this miscreant, whoever she is.

But is that really the best way to introduce yourself to the Cosmic Guardian? And anyway, didn't Nancy say the only person you could really trust was in Florida somewhere? Surely the Guardian can handle one stretchy purple villain by himself.

It's clear that your friends have ditched you. Perhaps you should just go back to your supersonic jet and look for help elsewhere.

▶ *If you chuck your grappling hook at the pair of them and join the fray,* **turn to page 95.**

▶ *If you skip it and head south to the Sunshine State,* **turn to page 150.**

New York is a long drive from Cleveland, but if you leave now, you can make it before midnight. You grab a few things from your apartment and then spend most of your journey trying to come up with a decent superhero name. Let's see—you can excrete and control a gooey purple substance, and stretch one arm really far. From a branding perspective, it's not great. The Purple Protector? Globulon? Fantastic Elastic? Each of your ideas sounds worse than the last, and to be honest, none of them are any better than the Latex Avenger.

Speaking of which, you're gaining more and more control of your bendy appendage, and when you finally reach the city you find you can stretch it at least fifteen or twenty feet. You arrange your malleable goo coating into something resembling a costume and park your car in the worst neighborhood you can find. You're looking for trouble.

Trouble is surprisingly difficult to find. A few strangers give you menacing glares, but if they're up to no good, they're certainly not advertising it. How do real superheroes do this? Should you come back on a weekend? By 2:30 or so you're almost ready to give up. That's when you hear a lone voice cry out in the night.

"Hey! That's my bike!"

You rush around the corner to see a man in his early twenties cursing at a bicyclist disappearing down the street. Honestly? This is the kind of justice you could probably be dishing out back in Cleveland. Still, a crime is being committed. It may not be earth-shattering and it may not be glamorous. Based on the way he's dressed, the victim may even be a bit of a douche. But being a hero means doing what's right, regardless

(continue to the next page)

of the glory. Some hood thinks he can just go around stealing bikes? In your town?

Not on the Purple . . . Gooey . . . wow, you've still got nothing. Not on your watch.

You hurl your right arm at a lightpost halfway down the street and retract, pulling yourself forward. It works! Slingshotting into the air, you shoot out your arm again, hoping it finds purchase before you hit the ground. Fortunately, your goop can adhere to just about anything. It's mildly terrifying, but your new mode of transportation is also pretty damn fun. And fast! You should catch up with the bicycle miscreant in no time!

You hear the crack of thunder, and a simultaneous flash of light illuminates the cloudless sky. You spot Lightning Queen, a notoriously vicious supervillain, hovering above a nearby liquor store and throwing down with the Cosmic Guardian. Scratch that—*two* Cosmic Guardians. You didn't even know there *were* two Cosmic Guardians. This is the kind of thing you came to New York for!

▶ *Team-up time! If you forget about the bike thief and grab a seat at the big kids' table,* **turn to page 233.**

▶ *Wait, what about that whole doing-what's-right speech? Between two Cosmic Guardians, they probably have this covered. If you feel that it's your duty to recover the stolen bike,* **turn to page 156.**

Since there's no one with superpowers under the age of 60 on your "trust maybe" list (at least, no one who isn't a convicted felon), you settle on the Human Torpedo. He's one of Magnifica's Liberty Patrol contemporaries, but he's remained in the public eye since retiring, and from all accounts is still healthy as a horse. However, when you show up at his beachfront San Diego home the following morning (after a surprisingly cozy nap in your plane's cockpit), he's not looking quite so fit.

"Nnnnnnngggg," he says, greeting you in his spacious backyard after you've landed the jet. He's in a robe, slippers, and swim trunks, and you get the distinct impression he's just come off a three-day bender. "You say you're Nightwatchman's new protégé, huh? And he's training you to take over for him? Gave you his costume, and his jet and everything?" He takes a long swig of coffee from an enormous mug. "Sure, I can see that. Hey, Obie! I told you the whole sidekick thing would catch on!"

A thin man who's maybe two or three years older than you with blue skin and fins for ears pokes his head out of the kitchen. And if Human Torpedo is a little the worse for wear, his former partner Ocean Boy looks like death warmed over. Human Torpedo—or Chuck, as he insists you call him—invites you inside and promptly dumps his coffee out in the sink, replacing it with something brown and foul-smelling from a glass jug almost as big around as he is.

"Little hair of the dog is what I need," he says. "Genuine eighteenth-century pirate rum, found it on a sunken ship myself. Care for any?"

You politely decline. If that's what bit these two, you'd just

(continue to the next page)

as soon stay clear. "You know," Chuck says as you take a seat at his kitchen table, "I got the chance to put on the old cloak and goggles a couple of times in my day, too. Secret identity stuff, when N-Dub had to be in two places at once to throw somebody off the trail. And I'll tell you, being the Human Torpedo was great, but being Nightwatchman was something else altogether. Guys would crap *bullets* when they ran into me in a dark alley dressed like that."

Before Chuck has the chance to wander further down memory lane, the screen on your gauntlet starts flashing. It's some sort of built-in supervillain alarm—three criminals known as Lightning Queen, Doctor Diabolus, and the Turtle have launched a full-scale attack on the nation's capitol in Washington, D.C. "Perfect!" Chuck exclaims. "What are we waiting for? C'mon, Obie. This'll be way more fun than beating up orca whales."

You hesitate to even ask about the whales. You're also not sure the pair of them are in any shape for a tussle, but Chuck insists, practically carrying Ocean Boy onto your jet. Even at Mach 3, it takes several hours to get back to the east coast, and by the time you're in the air above D.C., the situation on the ground has worsened. Axemaster, the Savage Cockroach, and Jekyll and Hyde have joined the villains' ranks, and somehow the East Coast's abundant hero fraternity has yet to arrive on the scene.

"C'mon, Obie!" Chuck says, throwing open a hatch in mid-flight. He has no parachute. He does look much recovered from this morning, but Ocean Boy, if anything, looks worse.

"Um, I think he's still a bit hung over," you say.

(continue to the next page)

"Nah," Chuck insists. "He has the constitution of a baleen whale. That's just the landsickness setting in—he'll be fine once he has the chance to dip himself back in some salt water. But maybe you're right—you can come help me clean up these jokers, and we'll leave Obie to fly the plane."

That actually sounds like an even worse idea. "Obie?" you ask gently. "Have you ever flown a jet aircraft before?"

Chuck scoffs. "I flew this thing once, before it was even thought-controlled. It's easy, he'll pick it up! You know, Obie saved the entire world by himself one time. Remind me to tell you that story."

Battling supervillains *is* kind of a lifelong dream of yours, so you'd hate for the two of them to finish the job while you were still finding a spot to park the plane. And your suit has a built-in glider, so you could dive right out and be smacking heads in no time. Still, if Chuck is the experienced pilot, maybe he should be the one to stay with the jet.

▶ *If you take Obie and leave Chuck to land the plane,* **turn to page 189.**

▶ *If you go with Chuck and trust Ocean Boy in the cockpit,* **turn to page 246.**

▶ *If you let the two of them have their fun and just land the stupid plane yourself,* **turn to page 5.**

The Ox seems reluctant to take the road less violent, so you feed him a bunch of New Age hooey about not letting his rage define him and how punching holes in all the superheroes and corporate goons in the world won't bring him peace. By the end of your speech you've even sold yourself, and he agrees that what he needs to embark on is a *spiritual* rampage. A rampage toward enlightenment.

This has two unforeseen consequences. The first is that the Ox starts opening up to you about his childhood, and before long you're lying on the couch in your apartment trying to help an 800-pound supervillain deal with body image issues. The second is that by the time the Justice Squadron tracks you down, the Ox's rage and fury, which enabled you both to live through your last encounter with them, have been largely replaced with frailness and vulnerability.

This time Magnifico has regrouped, bringing Gravity Bomb, Coldfront, Skyhawk, Megawatt, and at least a dozen Cosmic Guardians, apparently from every corner of the galaxy. Brain Stem is missing, but if he were there, the only thing added to the smackdown would be telepathic proof that you were absolutely crapping your pants while they beat the living snot out of you.

And that shows up pretty well on your face, anyway.

THE END

"I know you, Ox," you say with all the earnestness you can muster. "You may be a brawler. You may rob some banks. And you may occasionally kill the odd corporate suit who gets pinned underneath the alien thing you're eviscerating." Your argument is actually getting weaker as it goes along. "But you're not a *monster*. You don't want to help aliens take over the Earth."

"Maybe I do," Ox says, pondering the ramifications.

You'd better try a different approach. "If you won't do it for the people, do it for the *stuff*. What are you going to do with yourself out there in between conquering planets? There are no football games in space. No *Sports Illustrated* swimsuit editions. No *roast beef sandwiches*."

His brow furrows. "No drive-through restaurants at all," he says. "Damn, Megawatt. What kind of life is that?"

"One without you in it, buddy." Megawatt takes a step toward the Ox, electricity arcing off his body through the space suit. "If you want to die for that junk, suit yourself. I was just trying to do you a solid, anyway."

"Aw, crap," Ox says. "This is the part where I get my ass kicked."

"What? You can take him! You've beaten him before, right?"

"Naw. He does this thing where he turns all into energy, and then you can't even touch him. But he gets his freaky ghost hands inside your body and blasts you right in the brain. I'll tell you what, I never really feel pain anymore, but that crap hurts like a sonofabitch."

Little spiral hatches open in the hangar bay walls, and Cosmic Guardians start flying through them. "You should have taken the deal," Megawatt says. "Have you seen these things?

(continue to the next page)

They can fly at the speed of light. They put you in cryogenic sleep for long trips. The suits have their own freakin' brains, which are way smarter than you or me. Smarter than the computer that runs this whole ship."

Their own brains? That gives you an idea. Back on Earth your goo seeped into the battle armor and you seemed to be reading its thoughts. If you try that again, maybe you could mind-meld with it and take control of one of the suits. It's a long shot, but you're quickly running out of options.

Come to think of it, you could also try your plan on the spaceship's computer. According to Douchebag, it's less advanced than the battlesuits are.

▶ *If you attempt to reprogram a Cosmic Guardian to turn on its compatriots,* **turn to page 144.**

▶ *If you try your mind-mojo on the ship itself,* **turn to page 299.**

"I knew you had it in you," Moretti says, handing you a small metal cylinder with a button on one end. "This is the trigger for our emergency backup satellite weapon. Last time we apprehended the Ox, we implanted a targeting beacon, so in the worst case scenario all you have to do is push the button and stand back—a giant beam of light from the sky will take care of the rest."

They haven't even shown you where the bathrooms are yet, but suddenly you're in charge of the orbital death lasers? Moretti seems to sense your hesitation. "It's the only thing we have powerful enough to neutralize him, and it's only to be used as a last resort," he says. "We'd much rather take him alive."

Migraine asks you to open your visor and then leaps at you, shrinking to the size of a Snickers bar in midair and landing right inside your helmet. It's disconcerting. You know those people who stand way too close while they talk? A tiny man is literally leaning on your face, and you thank your lucky stars that at least his uniform shrank along with him.

Wait a minute—shrinking powers? "You're Minuteman, aren't you? Weren't you a supervillain back in the '70s?"

"It was mi-NUTE-man," he says. His tiny voice is comically high-pitched, and if he weren't inches from your eardrum you wouldn't be able to hear it at all. "As in, really small? Jesus, why does nobody get that?" It does make more sense, now that you think about it.

"Migraine works for us now," Moretti says. "He's proven himself time and time again—you can trust him to have your back." He tells you that the Ox is heading east on I-80 in a white van, and beams the details into your visor's display. With your creepy face-passenger onboard, you launch into the sky on an

(continue to the next page)

intercept course. Admittedly, so far that's the entirety of your plan. "So how did you take this guy down the last time?"

The old man cracks his little knuckles. "I shrank down to the size of a dust mote, hopped in his circulatory system, and put him to sleep," he squeaks. "There are a hundred ways to kill a man from the inside, but taking him alive is a pain in the ass. If we get him good and angry, I can overload his adrenal gland, and he'll pass out. I'll need some time, though, so you'll have to keep the big sonafibitch agitated while I do my thing."

The Ox beat you into a pulp earlier without breaking a sweat. You don't even want to *picture* him agitated. "Any other options?"

"Orbital death lasers. Oh, and there's also power dampening tech, but it takes up a whole room. It's not something we can carry into the field."

The Ox may be stronger than you are, but you're guessing you can outsmart him. "If we trick him into coming with us, could we zap his powers once we get him back to the base?"

"I suppose. If you want to try sweet-talking him, knock yourself out. Better decide quick, though—white van, straight ahead."

▶ *If you try using cunning to lure the Ox back to headquarters,* **turn to page 228.**

▶ *If you go with Migraine's plan and rely on your proven ability to take a truly spectacular beating,* **turn to page 163.**

Well, you *do* have a brain-controlled supercomputer built into your evening wear. Who knows—maybe this will be incredibly easy. *Locate Nightwatchman*, you think.

A map of downtown Cleveland appears on your screen with a red dot in the middle. That makes sense, since he couldn't have travelled far in the past ten minutes. *Zoom in*, you think, watching as the map gets larger and more detailed. Okay, that should be the alley where you found the dumpster. *Zoom in again*.

Oh, crap. HE'S IN THE ROOM WITH YOU.

You just about have a heart attack on the spot, until you realize that the dot on the map represents you. Dumbass. You try several commands to indicate that you're looking for the *real* Nightwatchman, or the *previous* Nightwatchman, but get no results. It looks like you're going to have to do this the hard way after all. Fortunately, you excel at mind-numbing research.

You start sifting through digital files, and find a list of safehouses. Apparently the little underground nook you stumbled upon isn't unique—he has upwards of a hundred such hidden grottoes in cities all over the globe. Wow—whoever Nightwatchman is, the guy must be absurdly wealthy. Is it possible that he stores a costume in each of these safehouses for emergencies? Maybe the fancy equipment you've claimed as your own is simply a spare uniform.

The Philadelphia location has a little asterisk by it. Some sort of home base, perhaps? That might be a good place to start your search. As you continue digging, you find that some of the other files are peppered with asterisks as well. On the list of Crexidyne superhumans, every name is marked except one: Rockjockey, a bruiser of a villain who can fuse mineral matter

(continue to the next page)

to his own body to augment his mass.

Is Nightwatchman investigating the names on the list and checking them off as he goes? If so, perhaps you can head him off at the pass. The more you think about it, though, the less you like the idea. All superheroes have arch-nemeses, but Nightwatchman's rogue's gallery is a particularly psychotic and obsessive bunch. Rockjockey has tangled with him several times in the past, so if you plan on confronting that thug, you'd better be prepared to deal with whatever personal grudge or blood vendetta he happens to be nursing.

Rockjockey shows up as a blip on your GPS and, like nearly everything superhero-related, he's in New York City. New York and Philadelphia are each seven to eight hours from Cleveland by car—either way, you'd better get moving.

▶ *If you track down Rockjockey in New York,*
turn to page 142.

▶ *If you'd rather avoid psychotic supervillains for now and check out the Philadelphia safehouse instead,*
turn to page 184.

You command the wreckage of the alien battlesuit to change course, and it responds by shuddering violently and crashing into the ship about midpoint, splattering you against the hull. Fortunately, splattering is no longer a concern. You collect yourself and work your way toward the rear exhaust ports in a kind of rapid, slithering wave. The ship is massive, though, and by the time you get there, the terraforming machines are about to be launched. There's no time to lose! There appear to be two separate engines, but you hope that blowing up one will do the trick. You hurl, squeeze, and seep your way into the bowels of the ship. Within minutes, you hit paydirt.

The starboard-side power source turns out to be a ball of blue plasma hovering weightlessly in the center of a perfectly round room. You pause for just a moment, and your life starts to pass before your eyes, but you cut it short. Nothing you've ever done or could ever possibly do holds a candle to this. Willing yourself into the hardest possible consistency, you form a sphere around the glowing blue mass.

And then you squeeze.

The engine, as they say, goes nuclear. You've done it! The resulting explosion atomizes the ship and all of its inhabitants. Including, of course, you. Technically, you aren't dead, just spread very, very thin. Granted, every particle of you is hurtling out on a different trajectory into the emptiness of space, so the chances of ever reassembling to the point of consciousness is astronomically thin.

All in all, it's a hell of a way to go.

THE END

You manage to lift the Ox by his armpits and fly him back to the mountain base. You're scared you might accidentally drop him, but he assures you that he's tough enough to survive the fall, and actually seems to enjoy the ride. While in flight, you contact Moretti through the earpiece in your helmet and quietly explain your plan. He beams you a schematic of the base's layout.

Once you arrive, you set the Ox down and raise one arm up in the air, firing the widest-range, lowest-intensity burst you can muster from your gauntlet—it's basically not much more than a flash of blue light. "That gravitronic pulse should knock out their security systems and most of their personnel," you say, breaking out in a full run. "Quick! We only have ten minutes before everything comes back online!"

Once inside the wide-open front gates, you find workers strewn about all over the place, feigning unconsciousness as instructed. Your ruse works like a charm. Soon you're in front of the power-dampening chamber in an adjoining room with a full-length mirror along one wall like an interrogation room on a cop show. Subtle.

"The remote control armor shutdown thing is right through this door!" you say.

"Cool. Have at it. I'm gonna go see how much I can bust up this place before everyone wakes up."

"Wait —I might need some help in there."

"You'll be fine."

"No!" You didn't count on this. "Just help me out, and then we'll trash the place together."

He narrows his eyes. "Why do you want me in there so bad?"

(continue to the next page)

"I don't! It's just . . . I mean, it's a *remote control armor shutdown thing.*"

"In fact, why do you need me at all if you have some magic laser beam that opens all the doors and knocks everyone out?" He pauses. "You think I'm stupid, don't you?"

Um, kind of? At least, you did. "I don't think you wanna be my new partner at all," he continues. "I think you were sent by—" He glances at the mirror, then quickly punches his huge fist through it, yanking out a startled Agent Moretti by the face from the room behind it.

"This guy," he finishes.

"Migraine!" you shout into your earpiece. "Plan B! If you can hear me, initiate plan B!"

"Plan B is death lasers now," Migraine replies, his voice coming both from the earpiece and from directly behind you. "I vacated the target as soon as we got back on base—those power dampeners would make a huge freakin' mess if they caught me still inside there."

You grab the trigger to the emergency satellite weapon from a compartment in your chest plate. If you use it to fry the Ox, though, Moretti is getting fricasseed along with him.

Migraine senses your hesitation. "Moretti's a dead man, anyway! If the big guy goes on a rampage, he'll kill us all. Push the button!"

Miscellaneous agents are scrambling to their feet, giving a wide berth to the hulking villain holding their boss in the air with one hand. Moretti tries to yell something, but his voice is muffled by the Ox's grasp on his head. "Mmmph grfff nnnnggg!" he says.

(continue to the next page)

Was that "Pull the trigger?" Or maybe "Don't pull the trigger?" What should you do?

▶ *If you push the button and bring pulsating, high-intensity optical death from above,* **turn to page 283.**

▶ *If you don't push it, and try to save the lives of the entire military installation in a way that doesn't sacrifice Agent Moretti in the process,* **turn to page 308.**

If forced to choose between a pissed-off old superhero and the guy who might actually know how to build a spaceship, you have to go with the latter. Magnifica gives you a look that makes you shake in your poorly-fitted boots, then turns and flies away.

Conrad and Tinker start debating outer-space propulsion methods, reinforcing the hull, and repurposing a life support system from the old Liberty Sub, which Nancy has lying around for parts. Then Conrad uses his powers to contort hunks of machinery into whatever shapes he needs, creating complex systems out of little more than scrap metal. Between them they make short work of the retrofit, and announce the craft ready to launch in under an hour.

"I'll need to fly this bucket of bolts myself," Conrad says. "Most of it won't even function properly without my powers pushing and pulling on it."

"And I suppose you'll need me to fix stuff when various systems inevitably fail," Tinker sighs.

This isn't giving you much confidence. The jet shakes like crazy while breaking atmosphere, but soon you're cruising high above the planet. Tinker picks up an energy source so massive it must be the alien mothership. "We've only got enough power for two or three shots," he says. "So make them count."

The ship looms on the horizon. And then just keeps looming—it's enormous. A platoon of Cosmic Guardians is swarming like worker ants around a huge tower-like structure in an open hangar bay. "Aim for that thing," you say. It seems like as good a target as any. "Fire!"

A burst of orange light sears your retinas, but when your vision returns, the scene in front of you looks very much the

(continue to the next page)

same, just with a smallish hole in the middle of it. You're not sure what you were expecting—a chain reaction causing a concussive blast, perhaps?—but the mothership hasn't budged.

"Maybe we've punctured it and they're losing all their oxygen?" Tinker says helpfully.

"Maybe," Conrad says. "Those look like engines in the back. Let's pull around behind it for another shot."

Effective or not, your opening volley has caught the attention of the Cosmic Guard, who start breaking away and rocketing toward you. Just as you're in position, the first one crashes into you, knocking the jet just a hair off course.

Your second laser blast goes wide, missing the ship entirely.

"Damn it! Line up for one more!"

"That was it," Tinker says, his head buried in a console. "That was all the power we had."

"You said we had three shots!"

"I said *two* or three." He's as white as a sheet. "We got two."

"I can reroute power from the engines," Conrad says. "Will that give us what we need?"

Tinker whips out a pocket calculator and punches frantically at the keys. "Maybe! It'll take everything we've got, though. Propulsion, life support . . . everything."

Everything?

"It's your call, boss," Conrad says.

▶ *If you use up your jet's power for one last shot with the laser cannon,* **turn to page 289.**

▶ *If you get the hell out of Dodge and hope for the best,* **turn to page 210.**

You decide to give your compatriots in the Cosmic Guard a wide berth, at least for now. So you bid Octavia farewell and rush to Washingtion, D.C. Thanks to your armor's memory banks, you know to stay clear of Lightning Queen, since her bolts of electricity are powerful enough to short out your systems. In fact, Übermind once accomplished a similar effect with a localized pulse—electrical attacks in general are a bit of an Achilles heel.

Doctor Diabolus represents no such threat, though. You swoop down, pull him off the battlefield and carry him to a nearby rooftop for interrogation. His mind-control powers prove useless on you, and soon he's telling you everything he knows, although it isn't much. He claims that he was given his powers 15 years ago by Crexidyne Megacorp, but they erased all memory of the incident until last night. They sent a platoon of Guardians to abduct him, and demanded that he participate in today's attack or they'd take back the superpowers they bestowed upon him so many years ago.

His story has the ring of truth to it—the Crexidyne project was certainly part of your orders to Thorpe, but your memory of it seems to be missing as well. Did you purposefully rid yourself of those memories? What purpose would that serve?

By the time you're through with Diabolus, a handful of new villains has joined the fracas below. You spot members of the Justice Squadron approaching, and fly toward them to compare notes. In front is Megawatt, the man who can turn himself into a being made of pure—

Electricity. He attacks you without warning, and you never stand a chance.

THE END

You call an ambulance, and based on the horror and shock that registers in the the paramedics' faces when they see your sorry ass, it was the right call. The doctors in the ER have to pump you with a ridiculous amount of morphine to provide any sort of pain relief whatsoever, and before long you've drifted off into blissful oblivion. Honestly, it wouldn't be a bad way to spend an afternoon on unemployment—except for one thing.

That nefarious supervillain plot? It actually *was* the end of the world.

The truth is, while you were lying unconscious on top of a building in Cleveland, all sorts of crazy stuff was going on out there. We're not saying that by the time you woke up you were in any condition to stop it. In fact, considering how the rest of humanity is going to die, all that morphine was probably a good choice. The world goes straight to hell, but you're too doped up to hear any of the screaming.

THE END

You're not sure how well the suit understands you, but you think *safety* as hard as you can, and it responds. At first you wonder if the suit's idea of a safe spot might be somewhere out in the middle of the solar system, but after a few minutes of rapid travel you're flying over the Pacific Ocean, and then plummeting into the depths of it.

You plunge through a smack of deep sea jellyfish, and then find yourself entering a vast complex of subterranean caves, emerging from the water in a dry, strangely-lit chamber miles beneath the ocean's surface. You can't imagine anywhere on Earth safer than this, which is good because you need to gather your thoughts. What does it mean that there are other Guardians on Earth? And what about Agent Moretti—is he really who he says he is? A little solitude is just what you need.

Except you're not alone.

"Hello? Hey, you're not Uncle Chuck." You turn to see a thin, blue-skinned man with fins for ears who somehow looks more surprised to see you than you are to see him. As you recover from the shock, you realize this can only be one person.

"Ocean Boy!" As sidekick to the legendary Human Torpedo, Ocean Boy was a full member of the original Liberty Patrol before it disbanded in the mid-'80s. Since his powers only worked underwater—in fact, he couldn't even survive on land more than a day or two, if you recall correctly—he was always something of a joke to the superhero fan community. He was only a few years older than you, though, so as a child you really looked up to him. He was everything you wanted to be.

"Oh," he says, a little skittishly. "Cosmic Guardian. I remember you from when I was a kid."

(continue to the next page)

"Actually, that was my predecessor. I'm new." You can barely contain your excitement, and open your visor to introduce yourself.

He takes your hand somewhat reluctantly. "I'm, uh . . . well, Ocean Boy's actually my real name," he says. "I'm sort of part fish." It takes some time for him to open up, but before long you've got him regaling you with tales of his thrilling exploits with the Liberty Patrol. Basically, you're two fans geeking out over your shared enthusiasm, and it's not until a few brisk hours later that you're interrupted by a loud splash coming from the water's edge behind you.

"Obie! You have a *friend!*"

Standing before you is Chuck Westernson, the Human Torpedo himself, a grey-bearded, barrel-chested mountain of a man. He may have put on a few pounds since his heyday, but he still has arms like tree trunks, and is carrying two enormous glass jugs almost as big around as he is.

Ocean Boy blushes a deep magenta. "Um, this is the new Cosmic Guardian," he says.

"Well, you'll stay for drinks, won't you?" He raises one of the mighty jugs over his head, beaming. "It's eighteenth-century pirate rum!"

▶ *Normally this would be the part where you make a choice, but the chances of you turning down drinks with Ocean Boy and the Human freaking Torpedo are roughly zero percent. Besides, based on the size of those bottles, it's important that you rescue the pair of them from alcohol poisoning (or at least help spread the alcohol poisoning around).* **Turn to page 56.**

Who needs the Nightwatchman's toys when you have cleverness? And guile? This is definitely the best idea you've had so far.

"I must have gotten the instructions mixed up," you say. Look at you, with the guile. "What was the whole deal with the D.C. contingent again?"

His eyes narrow. "Who did you say you were?"

"Ha! Like you don't remember. You hired me yourself. Remember? At the thing?" This isn't working as well as you'd hoped. "Standards and Practices?"

"Security! I have a Code Blue on floor 58. I repeat, Code Blue!"

Son of a *bitch*. You hit the button on your wrist screen and tackle Moretti, punching through the window behind him with an augmented gauntlet strike and pulling him through the shattered glass. You pop your wings as soon as you've cleared the ledge and tumble into a controlled glide.

That part was pretty smooth, at least. There's only one problem. Your entire plan hinged on flying below the radar, and Code Blue calls several hundred Cosmic Guardians into Moretti's office from their post on Crexidyne's roof. Rather than opening fire, they quickly determine that they're up against the Nightwatchman and simply short out your costume's power while you're still in mid-flight. Your cloak relies on an electrical pulse to maintain the rigidity of the glider configuration, so it immediately goes limp.

It's over 50 stories to the New York City streets below. You do your best to land on Moretti, but his bony ass isn't nearly enough to break your fall.

THE END

If you blast off to confront them in space, you're looking at, what, a big silver coffin versus whatever weaponry the advanced alien race has brought to invade an entire planet with? How is that possibly going to work out in your favor? Let them do their worst. They may have time to prepare, but so will you, and you intend to be ready for them.

Alas, all you have up your sleeve is travelling the globe throughout the night and convincing a bunch of additional supervillains (and even a hero or two) to join your cause. What the aliens bring to the party is the technology that created all those superbeings in the first place, but in reverse. Just after dawn, a pair of Guardians flies in carrying a big glowing orb between them. It pulsates, and the various superpowers drain from your collected forces. If you hoped that no history with Crexidyne's R&D department meant no takebacks on your own abilities, you're out of luck. That meteor was filled with the same biochemical crud Crexidyne's lab monkeys use, and your purple goo powers dry up on the spot.

Curiously, the Ox is the only one among you who seems immune. A giant, orange bolt of light from out of nowhere vaporizes him before he has much of a chance to gloat, though. Then more Guardians fly in, wiping up the rest of the riffraff with minimal effort.

THE END

You just fled a group of several hundred Cosmic Guardians on top of a building. What makes you think there will be *fewer* of them on their own spaceship?

The manual override instructions start out fairly clear: pull the thrust control all the way down and hold it while your co-pilot flips a series of switches. The ship appears to be of alien design, with various human control mechanisms haphazardly welded to it. You grab the thrust lever and have Ox take the role of copilot. Instantly, the ship lurches and starts to plummet toward the Earth. The next set of instructions is for—

Uh-oh. The memo outlines jobs for a pilot, copilot, navigator, navigator's assistant, and dedicated technician to monitor something called "yaw." "Ox!" you shout. "Can you, uh, reach that lever back there with your foot or something?"

It's too late. The craft goes into a roll, throwing you off your feet and pressing you helplessly to the ceiling. You desperately attempt to reach the controls, but it's no use. Panicked, Ox starts screaming at the top of his lungs, "I'm too pretty to die!"

The good news is, your friend truly is indestructible. Moments later, he's prying himself loose from the ship's burning wreckage. The bad news is, although you turn to malleable purple glop on impact, after losing consciousness your body quickly reverts to its original form. And that form burns to a crisp before the Ox can pull you out of the flames.

Stupid yaw.

THE END

No guts, no glory, right? You throw your grappling hook like a seasoned pro, and it clamps right onto the Guardian's foot as if it were designed to do just that—heck, for all you know, it *was*. You're immediately yanked from your perch and are soon rocketing toward the stratosphere. It's fun! As you continue rising, though, you start to worry—what if he just keeps flying higher until he breaks atmosphere? It seems like an unsportsmanlike way to rid himself of a hitchhiker, but you don't know how these guys operate. Of course, your suit has a built-in glider, so you can always cut the cord and sail back to Earth before the air gets too thin.

Fortunately, it doesn't come to that. Or unfortunately, perhaps? The Guardian slows his ascent, and you soon find out why. A whole platoon of similarly-armored, alien shapes surrounds the whole bunch of you. It's the Cosmic Guard! Rumor had it that the Guardian was a member of an elite interplanetary peacekeeping force, and it looks like he's called in some backup.

At least, it does at first. They open fire on him, and it quickly becomes apparent that they're trying to take him down, not just rid him of his passenger. Is this some kind of renegade, *rogue* Guardian? Could Purple Stretchy Woman actually be the good guy here? You cut your line and activate the glider, but it's too late—you've been spotted.

An elite interplanetary peacekeeping force blasts you into particles.

THE END

The first order of business is to get yourself out of the hell-hole that is Cleveland, Ohio. The Ox says he can have you in New York City within nine hours, but you're a bloody criminal mastermind now, and insist that he do better. First, though, you have him stuff Magnifico's remains into one of his duffel bags —you can tell he's done henchman work before, because he falls naturally into the role.

He finishes the gruesome task quickly, then starts scrolling through the contacts on his cell phone. "Hey, Tink," he says after settling on one. "You know anyone with a jet or any kinda supervehicle? I need to get home from Cleveland in a hurry. Really? Yeah, awesome."

He rattles off the address of the bank, and seconds later a pale gray cloud materializes just in front of it, and a tiny Asian girl who can't be a day over 14 pops out of the cloud. She's dressed from head to toe in black, but it's more of a fashion statement than a supervillain costume—the look is backed up by several piercings and about half a pound of eye makeup. She gestures at you to follow, then disappears back into the mist.

"Teleporter," the Ox says, almost giddy. "I never met one before—come on!" He hurries into the fog, and a moment later you hear his voice echoing from somewhere on the other side, so you decide it's safe to follow. You step through and, after a mildly terrifying second of weightlessness, find yourself in a cramped workshop with the girl, the Ox, and two middle-aged men.

"This is Tinker," Ox says as one of the men wipes his hand on his coveralls and offers it to you. You ignore it. "He makes weapons and stuff. And this is, uh . . ."

"Savage Cockroach," the other man says, looking you over

(continue to the next page)

skeptically. You recognize the name, if not the face—he's a villain with the power to replicate himself into any number of duplicates, each of which he's perfectly willing to send to their death, making him a formidable opponent.

"And this is Suong," Tinker says, repeating something to the black-clad girl in a language that might be Vietnamese. She just stares at you like she hopes you'll drop dead on the spot —pretty much the reaction you'd expect from any teenage girl. "She's new, so I've been helping her out here and there."

The workshop is Tinker's, and the Cockroach is there on business. He says the Cosmic Guard—a vast, intergalactic police force that provided Earth with the Cosmic Guardian you saw earlier today—is rounding up supervillains on orders from Crexidyne Corporation. His story makes little sense to you, since Crexidyne is a front organization for renowned villain Reginald Thorpe, and the Guardians are supposed to be the good guys. The Cockroach, however, claims his knowledge is first-hand, and has come looking for a weapon that can fend off armor-clad space marines. Tinker says he has just the thing, and drags out a big metal box with an electric paddle attached to it, explaining that he designed it for Übermind back in the '90s.

You've got plenty of openings for lackeys, and could do worse than a mad scientist, a teleporter, and a one-man suicide squad. So you offer the three of them the chance to join your crew. There's some grousing and posturing, but it quickly stops when you open the Ox's bag and reveal a bloody, mutilated corpse in a Magnifico costume.

Of the three, you would have pegged Tinker for the most squeamish, but he quickly recovers from his shock and moves

(continue to the next page)

closer to inspect the hero's remains. "Wow," he says. "Yeah, this looks like the real deal. Hey, what's this? Ox, it has your name on it." He pulls a little glass orb out of a pouch he finds somewhere inside the bundle of gore.

"Gimme that," Ox says, snatching the bauble and taking a closer look. Sure enough, it has a piece of masking tape stuck to it inscribed with the word 'Ox.' "Ew, it's got a little worm or something inside. What's Magnifico doing with a friggin' worm in a ball?"

"Verminator could tell you," Cockroach says. "He can communicate with stuff like that. Worms, rodents, bugs, pretty much anything small and disgusting." He shakes his head, as if having second thoughts. "Only thing is, he's a goddamn lying bastard. I left him in a Mexican jail a few years back. Feel free to bust him out, but you can't trust him as far as you can throw him."

More information is always a good thing, and you're confident that if necessary you could have the Ox throw Verminator pretty far. But is the mystery orb really your top priority? The truth is, if you're building a criminal empire, you're bound to cross Reginald Thorpe's path sooner or later, and if he's working with an army of space marines to haul in villains, you should probably look into it. Thorpe has no superpowers of his own —with this crew you should be able to lean on him pretty hard. And Tinker's contraption should allow you to handle any Cosmic Guardians he might have protecting him, right?

▶ *If you gather up your forces and pay Mr. Thorpe a visit,* **turn to page 244.**

▶ *If you organize a jailbreak and follow up on Magnifico's worm,* **turn to page 119.**

Let the Justice Squadron deal with the Washington Monument, you think. Without Magnifica's help you'd probably just get yourself clobbered, anyway. If you're going to New Mexico, though, you'll have to fly well outside the path of interference, since the jet is mind-controlled as well. "What's in Sante Fe?" you ask.

"Here, I'll show you." Before you can protest, Magnifica grabs you by the waist and hauls you into the clear blue sky.

Flying in the arms of a superhero is far from the magical experience that it looks like in Saturday morning cartoons. She wraps her withered arms around you in a full-body hug, but even so, you're moving so fast that the wind feels like knives. And you can't breathe! You start to panic, but a moment later you're back on the ground.

"Are we there?" you gasp. That experience was *terrifying*.

"Who's the kid?"

You're greeted by a silver-haired woman who looks slightly younger than Magnifica and much better preserved. She's dressed in denim and Native American prints, which makes her look like a high school art teacher trying a bit too hard to be culturally diverse.

"What, you don't recognize the Nightwatchman?" Magnifica is glaring at her. "Fess up, Octavia. You killed Brain Stem with some kind of brain beam, didn't you?"

"Hmph. I probably should have. But no, it wasn't me. You know I don't have anything to do with the hero crowd anymore, Maggie. I *help* people."

"With psychoanalysis! Of course!" Magnifica takes a step toward the woman. "Saving the world, one self-actualized yuppie

(continue to the next page)

jackass at a time. You never had the balls for *real* hero work. Even before Maximus died."

Maximus? You've just realized who this woman is. Professor Medium Maximus was the Gentleman Mentalist, a hero and stage magician from Magnifica's era who passed away in the '80s from pancreatic cancer. He fought crime alongside his completely human, non-powered female assistant.

"Girl Friday!" you say. "You have psychic powers, too?"

"She has psychic powers *instead*," Magnifica says. "It was always her. The Gentleman Mentalcase was a giant fraud, and she did all the mind junk while hiding behind his stupid coattails."

"Ramón was a great man!" Friday says. If Magnifica is trying to push her buttons, it's working. "And a lot of women stayed under the radar back then. It was a different time."

"Yeah, well some of us never gave a load of crap about that."

"*Some* of us didn't have diamond-hard skin! *Some* of us couldn't lift freight trains!"

"You're a coward, Octavia."

"You're a pompous ass!"

The two of them lock stares for a moment, then suddenly clutch one another in a long, passionate kiss. Geriatric tongue is everywhere. Ew. You keep waiting for it to end, but they don't seem to be stopping.

You clear your throat. "Uh, about the Brain Stem thing . . ."

Girl Friday breaks away, her face turning red. "Uh, sorry about that. Years of pent-up, convoluted superhero backstory."

Magnifica seems unfazed by the extended makeout, but you give Octavia a moment to straighten her clothing. "We followed a trail of psychic interference from Brain Stem's murder

(continue to the next page)

THRUSTS OF JUSTICE

101

scene straight here," you say. You've checked your gear, and sure enough, it shorts out in a straight line pointing from Girl Friday back toward New York. "Do you know what that's about?"

"I sensed his death when it happened. Usually I need to be close by to read someone's thoughts, but I think he blasted the entire contents of his psyche out into the ether when he died. Even this far away, I couldn't get it out of my head. And believe me, I tried. For a hero, that man was a bastard."

"Do you know who killed him?"

"No. His mind was a scrambled mess. Just trying to sort through it has been giving me nightmares. It's as if someone deliberately tampered with his thoughts—there are real memories covered with fake memories, and huge swaths have just been erased. I know it has to do with Crexidyne Megacorp, though. I keep getting this flash of the Crexidyne labs, and then just emptiness."

"Crexidyne was keeping tabs on him," you say. "Him, the Ox, and a bunch of other superhumans. It's the only other lead I have. I think we should head back to Cleveland and find out what the Ox has to do with all this."

Magnifica grunts. "It's Thorpe. It's always Thorpe. If you don't wanna go bust his head open, fine. But with Octavia here, we can at least go spy on his brain. You want answers? That's where you'll find them."

▶ *She does make a compelling case. If it's time to pay Reginald Thorpe a visit,* **turn to page 170.**

▶ *Nightwatchman was in Cleveland, though, investigating the Ox. It must have been important. If you follow up on that lead instead,* **turn to page 262.**

Five villains at once seems like a lot, especially on your first patrol. To the harbor it is.

You locate the ship, and find that it's a posh luxury yacht. "That's him, right on the deck there," Dale says. "According to your armor, there's no one else on board. Do you think he's transporting drugs on that thing?"

"Seriously, how are you doing that?"

"You know, I think it communicates through a telepathic link, and my superslime is acting as, like, a signal booster or something."

It makes a kind of sense, you suppose. Either that or Dale is just plain making stuff up, and you're about to scare the pants off of some old rich guy. Well, there's only one way to find out. You bring the suit down slowly and land on the boat about ten feet from its passenger.

He's a small, middle-aged man who looks fairly well built but not particularly imposing. His weathered face, though, doesn't give the impression that he's lived a life of luxury, and he's dressed in a big leather overcoat. Before you get the chance to calmly explain that you just want to ask him a few questions, he completely flips out.

"I knew you'd come for me!" he shouts, tearing off his coat and throwing it on the deck. "Bastards! You won't take me without a fight!" Underneath the coat he's decked out in a brown, armored outfit that looks vaguely familiar.

"Wait a second," Dale says. "There's another superpowered being behind us. No, two. Or four—what the hell?"

Oh, no. You recognize his guy now: he's the Savage Cockroach, a villain with the ability to split himself into dozens

(continue to the next page)

of copies. They're each inhumanly strong, and operate with a kind of hive mind—there's no "master" copy, so whichever units survive any given fight will simply merge back into a single form and carry on. The clones are legendarily vicious, often throwing themselves to their deaths like kamikaze pilots. The one in front of you charges.

Dale is still stuck to your back. "Split up!" you say. You bat your attacker away, but feel several sets of hands—other than your partner's—grabbing you from behind.

"No!" Dale says. "We should combine our strength and attack as a single, unified whole!"

What? "Dude, we're not *Voltron!*"

"Trust me," he says. "This will work!"

▶ *If you like Dale's idea of combining two superheroes into one mega-superhero,* **turn to page 238.**

▶ *If you think he's nuts,* **turn to page 303.**

If the Ox thinks this is a lost cause, who are you to argue? The heroes surround you but don't seem to be in any hurry to take you into custody. After a few moments of uncomfortable silence and the superhero stink eye, a black, unmarked helicopter descends into the empty intersection in front of you.

"Hey, I've seen that thing before," the Ox says as it lands. "These guys work for that Reginald Thorpe dude. I did some freelance for 'em one time—buncha assholes, though."

Reginald Thorpe is known throughout the world as the CEO of supervillainy, and can count at least half of the Justice Squadron among his arch-nemeses. If the Squadron is working with his goons, something truly strange is going on. The helicopter door opens and a small man with a tablet computer pops out. Behind him are two more alien forms in Cosmic Guardian armor—one with six arms and no head, and the other shaped like a giant insect. This just gets weirder and weirder.

The man approaches you, shouting over the noise as the helicopter's rotors slow to a halt. "Ox! You may not remember me. Carlo Moretti? We met once before."

"Yeah, and I told you to go screw yourself," the Ox says.

Moretti smiles. "Perhaps you should hear me out before you turn down my offer." Gravity Bomb, Coldfront, Skyhawk, and the tentacled Cosmic Guardian join the other two behind him, looking more like henchmen than heroes. It's disconcerting.

The Ox is getting angry. "Which one of those words did you not understand?" he asks. He waves the big duffel bag of cash in the air. "I don't need your freakin' money."

"You certainly don't," Moretti says, "which is why I come bearing information instead. How much do you remember

(continue to the next page)

about the night you got your superpowers?"

Your partner grimaces. "What do you know about that?"

"Everything," Moretti says. "Magnifico was supposed to offer you a deal, but it seems things got a bit out of hand."

You remember the glass ball. "Ox," you say. "I think this has something to do with it."

Moretti looks surprised to see the bauble in your possession. "It's a mnemonic grub," he says after a short pause. "Every memory that you've been missing from that night is contained within it. We can answer all the questions you've ever had, Ox. Come work for us." He flashes you a grin. "Bring your friend, too. Anyone who can take out Magnifico certainly has skills we can make use of. How does three hundred grand a year sound? Medical? Dental? A 401k?"

The Ox is seething. He looks at Moretti, then at the various superheroes flanking him. "I already have your stupid brain worm," he says. "Maybe I just stick it in my head right now, and you can all bite me."

Moretti's smile stiffens. "We can do this the hard way if you prefer."

You've been unemployed for several weeks now, so you instinctively jump at the mention of health insurance. It certainly appeals more than getting your ass kicked by superheroes or seeing your friend stick a worm in his brain. There's still something about all this that doesn't feel right, though.

The Ox turns to you. "What do you think?"

▶ *If you encourage him to take the job,*
   turn to page 145.

▶ *If you think he should stick the worm in his ear and see what happens,* **turn to page 274.**

What the hell—you're trying to keep the whole alien power-suit thing under the radar anyway, so why not celebrate? You've been a little preoccupied since your trip to outer space this morning, but Dale's unbridled enthusiasm reminds you that this is something you've been dreaming about your entire life. You're a real goddamn *superhero* now, and that merits a drink!

Besides, drinking is old hat to you. What could possibly go wrong? Previous drunken evenings with Dale have involved a small amount of blacking out, the occasional ill-advised hookup, and at your very lowest, stumbling around downtown Cleveland and doing something . . .

Stupid. Uh-oh.

Of course, you and Dale egg each other on, trying to determine if your livers now have superpowers as well. And of course, sometime around 1 a.m., drunken crimefighting sounds like the best idea ever. It's all just a blur of jumbled images and sensations after that: Flying through the air. Stopping to open your helmet's visor to throw up. The overpowering smell of salt-water. Battling an army of . . . cockroach people? Is that even a thing? An electric shock, and something that smells a bit like bacon frying.

It reminds you that you could totally go for some bacon, but by then it's too late. Remember, kids: alcohol and superheroics don't mix.

THE END

"Heck yeah, we are," you say. And who knows? Life as part of an alien invasion force is *still* probably better than unemployment.

Megawatt sneers, "Oh, so you wanna join up with us all of a sudden? What makes you think you have anything to offer?"

"Well, I kicked all these guy's asses, for starters," you say.

"Whatever. These pus bag dudes are like administrators and scientists and stuff. What else you got?"

The Ox vouches for you, telling Megawatt that you kicked all kinds of butt back on Earth. It's nice to hear your friend stick up for you. Megawatt taps the chin area of his space helmet with one gloved finger. "If Ox says you're okay, I guess you're okay." He takes a step toward you. "There are still a couple of problems, though," he says.

"Yeah? What?"

With a flash of light, one of Megawatt's arms turns to pure electricity, shooting out of his space suit and directly into your skull. You drop to the floor in agonizing pain.

"I don't make the rules, and you're not on the list." Before you can get your bearings, you're being pulled from your suit, and within moments your entire physiology is ripped apart from the inside by toxic brown gas. You're dead as hell, but at least you've learned one important lesson about duplicitous, mass-murdering psychopaths:

You can't trust 'em.

THE END

Like it or not, these are the soldiers you have to work with. And as much as you'd like Magnifica by your side, she's the only one you can count on to lead the second team. "I'll take the North," she says.

"You'll need me with you," says the Human Torpedo. "You know that's just a sheet of ice up there, right? The actual pole is underwater."

Princess Pixie flutters to Magnifica's side. "Then I'll come, too. With my force bubbles, I can function under the sea."

Wait—she's taking all the good ones! That leaves you with Octavia, Mechaman (sans mecha) and Wheelchair the Barbarian. Even at top speed, it will take your jet some time to reach the South Pole—you hope it's enough to work out a plan that plays to your team's strengths. Also, to figure out what those are.

"So, Tina," you say as casually as possible once you're airborne. "Your wheelchair. Is that some sort of secret identity thing, or . . . ?"

She frowns. "Tank lose both feet to adult onset diabetes. Frosted cupcakes bad! Tank smash stupid frosted cupcakes!"

"Say, what do have for spare parts on this old rig?" Mechaman asks. He seems a little too chipper considering the enormity of your situation. "I bet I could hook up some rocket boosters or something to that chair." Mechaman is a civil rights icon, and was the first African-American superhero in 1969. His power is some kind of supernatural control over machinery that you never completely understood.

He's busy rummaging through the jet's storage bins. "Mechaman—what about the alien technology?" you ask. "Can

(continue to the next page)

you disable it with your powers?"

"Call me Conrad, son. I haven't gone by Mechaman in decades." He sighs. "The truth is, I'm obsolete. My juju doesn't even work that well on the stuff they make on Earth anymore. It's all circuitry—I need moving parts, you know? The Cosmic Guardian's tech was always way too weird for me."

Octavia perks up. "That's because it's biomechanical," she says. "It's *alive*. Conrad, come here. I want to try something."

She's buckled into a padded seat with the remains of Cosmo the Space Dog resting next to her. "I'm going to enter your mind and guide you. Between us, maybe we can get a handle on what really makes this thing tick." He closes his eyes, and after a moment, gasps.

"My lord, Octavia. It's *beautiful*."

By the time you reach Antarctica, the two of them have worked out a plan. Their explanation manages to combine psychobabble and technobabble into complete gibberish, but you take them at their word that they've refashioned the alien organism in Cosmo's robo-tumor into some kind of virus bomb. It uses the technology's ability to graft to a living host in reverse, spreading incompatible human genetic material into the alien machinery and, with luck, destroying it.

"The alien tech had to completely mutate this dog before attaching to it," Mechaman says. "We can reverse the process so that human genetics corrupt it instead. But we'll only have a few minutes to get it to the target before it burns itself out."

"And that's just the first problem," Octavia adds. "The space dog is useless as a carrier. We'll have to graft the bomb to one of us."

(continue to the next page)

"Tank ready to make ultimate sacrifice," Tina says without hesitation. "Tank live long, full life. Tank have no regrets."

"I know you don't, honey." Octavia takes Tina's hand. "I'm actually better suited for this, though. We all have a little alien genetic material in us—it must have something to do with the way we got our superpowers. It seems that I have less mutation than you or Conrad, so I'm the most incompatible with them, and the best bet to corrupt the alien system."

Actually, that would be you—the closest things you have to superpowers are a cape and a utility belt. Before you can volunteer, though, a siren erupts throughout the cabin. You see a gleaming, mechanical monolith the size of a skyscraper towering over the horizon out the jet's windshield. It looks like you've arrived.

You ask the jet's computer for a status report but find it unresponsive. You check your wristscreen, but it doesn't respond to your thoughts either.

Wait a second. That isn't a "Hey, we're almost there" siren. It's more of the "You're about to fall out of the sky" variety.

"Octavia! I'm losing control of the aircraft! Is it psychic interference?"

"There's nothing!" she says. "I don't know what's doing this!"

You try your screen again, only to find the words SYSTEM SHUTDOWN displayed on it. Your boots and gloves start to decompress, losing their custom fit. "Conrad! You've got to take control of the plane!"

"It's all computers!" he says. "I'll have to burn them out and try to create new control mechanisms on the fly!" As the jet goes

(continue to the next page)

into a tailspin, he lurches to the cockpit, ignoring the flight stick and jamming his fist directly into the metal dash instead. "I've got thrust control!" he says. "Lord, how many backup systems do you *have* in this thing? Trying to establish steering . . . Strap in, people! It's going to be a rough one!" The jet levels out just before crashing, scraping against the ground at full speed and skidding thunderously to a halt amid the sounds of broken landscape and crumpling steel.

A quick check reveals that all passengers survived the ordeal, including Cosmo the Space Dog. You climb from the wreckage at least a mile from the tower, and see a swarm of armored figures flying toward you.

"We have to start the graft!" Conrad says. "Who's it going to be?"

Without the Nightwatchman's equipment, you're just an unemployed journalist on a frozen tundra, and now you don't even have shoes that fit right. You may have the most virulent DNA, but if you're taking bets on who might get to the alien machinery in one piece, you'd have to go with the brand new rocket chair and superhuman strength.

▶ *If you tell them to graft the virus bomb to you,*
   turn to page 147.

▶ *If you let Tina the Tank take it,* **turn to page 286.**

You promised a dying superhero that you'd keep *something* safe. And besides, secret identity shenanigans are part of the job description, right? As you open the door, several more missiles pop out of your shoulder plates and a high-pitched whine starts to come from somewhere in your armor. *Just calm down*, you think. All you need here is a decent cover story.

"Warning!" you say. Okay, that was maybe a little too *Lost in Space*. "The citizen who resides here is under the protection of the Cosmic Guard. Please return to your home and stay there until you receive notice that this area has been secured." There, that should do it.

Mrs. Pinkett just stands there, staring. "I know it's you," she says. "You don't think I recognize your voice from when you have people over and stay up all night making sex noises?"

"That was one time, like three years ago!" Crap. "I mean, *danger, Will Robinson!*"

She starts wagging her finger. "I didn't say anything when you had that cat in there," she says. For the record, you know for a fact that Mrs. Pinkett called the landlord several times about the cat and tried to have you evicted. "But this is going too far! I'm calling the police right now."

If she makes that phone call, your secret identity is as good as blown. Your armor is shaking now, and in addition to the missiles, crackling balls of blue energy are starting to form in the palms of your gauntlets.

▶ *Screw it. If you just blast her,* **turn to page 192.**

▶ *What? No! If you believe that being a superhero means even the smallest amount of casual murder is unacceptable,* **turn to page 205.**

A full-scale alien invasion is just too big to leave in the hands of a small group of superpowered retirees. "Call the Patrol," you say, "but I'm bringing in backup just in case." You send a group email to every active hero in your database, and are surprised at how quickly they reply. In less than a minute, the entire Justice Squadron (with the obvious exception of Brain Stem) is landing in the street outside Patel's apartment. You spot Magnifico, Skyhawk, Megawatt, Coldfront, Gravity Bomb, and —uh-oh.

The Squadron is accompanied by five members of the Cosmic Guard. One of them looks more or less like the Guardian you saw yesterday, but at least twice the size. The others clearly come from planets very different from Earth.

"I knew it!" Magnifica exclaims. "You're in league with *them*!"

"Whoa, whoa, whoa," you say, approaching the Squadron's leader. "Magnifico, sir . . ." Blue energy starts crackling in the palms and various palm-like appendages of the Guardians. "Uh, could I talk to you alone for a minute?"

Octavia clenches both her fists and emits a grunt, and suddenly Magnifico collapses, falling to the pavement he was hovering above. Magnifica springs into action as well, but the Squadron is ready for her. And they certainly aren't underestimating her, despite her advanced age.

You can't be sure how well she holds up to the attack, because your personal gravity increasing a hundredfold, 500,000 volts of electricity, a barrage of razor-sharp icicles, any number of white-hot plasma bolts, and a smack in the head with a really big mace are more than enough to take care of you.

The End

If you're going to be a criminal, why not jump in with both feet? The Ox's armored car idea sounds particularly intriguing.

"Yeah, it's like a money buffet on wheels," he says. "But figuring out when they're gonna show up and which ones are already loaded with cash and all that is kind of a pain in the ass. There's a lot more to being a supercriminal than most people think."

Apparently there's quite an art to bank robbery. New York City banks are cake because they're insured against supervillain attacks, so nobody puts up much of a fight. The trade-off, though, is that superheroes get territorial, and pulling crimes right in their backyard is like daring them to come thwart you. New York, of course, is lousy with heroes. That's what makes a city like Cleveland tempting: it's a day trip, and the local fuzz might get a bit bent out of shape, but you're not likely to have the Phenomenal Three breathing down your neck.

"In fact," the Ox says, "we should do another one right here. Two Cleveland banks in one day? That's *crazy*. No one will expect that."

It's hard to argue with his logic, and the Ox insists that the best way to figure out your superpowers is on-the-job training. Before you know it, you're standing in the lobby of the First National Bank of Ohio, yelling at everyone to lie face down on the floor. You feel a little underprepared, but you're with the Sherman Tank that Walks Like a Man—what's the worst that could happen?

A deep, booming voice calls out from behind you. "Hello, Ox. So we meet again."

You turn to see Magnifico, leader of the Justice Squadron

(continue to the next page)

and widely believed to be the most powerful hero on Earth, floating through the front door and grinning like an idiot.

"Dude!" you say. "You said we wouldn't run into any superheroes!"

"Aw, crap," the Ox replies. "I dunno, maybe he came looking for me after I knocked over the first bank? That guy frickin' *hates* me. There's two of us now, though. We can take him."

Magnifico gives you a glance. "Stand aside, citizen. This is going to get messy."

Does he think you're just an innocent bystander? You take a look at his rippling musculature and think maybe you *should* be. The whole point of robbing a bank out here in the boonies was to avoid this very thing, and not get apprehended before you even have a chance to figure out what your powers are. Should you just sell the Ox down the river and split? It doesn't sound right, but you're a thief now. You're pretty sure there's no honor among you guys.

▶ *If you jump into the fray,* **turn to page 236.**

▶ *If you turn tail and flee,* **turn to page 36.**

Seriously, *anything* sounds like a better plan. "Uh, I think I'll sit this one out. You don't happen to have an address for the space dog guy, do you?" Lightning Queen's body turns translucent, and with a crack of thunder she's hit by a bolt of lightning and disappears. Wow. It's probably best that you didn't volunteer for . . . whatever that was. It's late, and you've been beaten up pretty good, so you decide to grab a few hours' sleep in your car.

You awaken some time after daybreak, find an unsecured wireless network on your laptop, and search the web for any and all references to the galactic police force known as the Cosmic Guard. There isn't much, so you turn your attention to Cosmo the Space Dog, who seems to have disappeared when the Guardian did 15 years ago. That was the same year the world saw the last of Übermind, self-proclaimed criminal genius. He was of retirement age in the '90s, and apparently just gave up

(continue to the next page)

villainy. His real name is Omar Patel (for some reason you had always assumed he was German), and sure enough, he's listed in the phone book. After a quick trip across town, you find Patel's apartment, with a conveniently propped-open window on the second floor.

What you find inside, though, you're not sure you would describe as a dog. Lying in a pet bed are the barely-living, ancient remains of a German shepherd grafted to an enormous, pulsing mass of alien technology. It's super gross. Could this really be the Cosmic Guardian's canine pal? If it were still alive, the thing would have to be at least 20 years old, so the level of decay makes sense. Looking at it, though, you can't escape the feeling that the machinery is more alive than the dog is.

Wait a minute, aren't you kind of psychic now? You creep into the room quietly (so as not to arouse whatever wrath Übermind might still have in him at his advanced age) and attempt to communicate with the animal telepathically. This mostly consists of putting your fingers on your temples and thinking really hard. You get nothing and quickly start to feel silly. Well, last night you were connected to the Guardian by the purple supergoo. You hesitantly poke the machinery with one finger. Ew, it's warm. Then you let the goo seep from your fingertips, covering the alien technology, trying to find a connection.

Suddenly you're in. You sense the same dichotomy that you found in the Guardian last night, but this time you get the impression that the piece of its mind that had once been the dog's has been completely hollowed out, and filled up with something foreign. The cold, mechanical presence is vast and all-controlling.

(continue to the next page)

Also, *it knows you're here.*

You retreat from the machine's presence, deeper into what's left of the dog's biological brain. You get a flash of memory—the Cosmic Guardian leaving Cosmo with Omar Patel, explaining to him that as long as he takes good care of the animal, he'll stay out of jail. What the Guardian doesn't disclose, however, is that this task will slowly drain Patel of his free will until he's not much more than a walking puppet. The Guardian removes a chunk of his armor, which sprouts polymer tentacles and attaches itself to the dog. It's more than just a piece of equipment, though—it's a piece of the Guardian himself. It will remain on Earth, feeding on Cosmo's life force and sending instructions telepathically to various operatives all over the world.

The Cosmic Guardian: kind of a dick? Whatever those instructions were, you know that you're not going to find them easily. The machine's mind will be guarding them, and assuming psychic combat is even a thing, you're pretty sure it's a lot better at it than you are. In fact, you can feel it searching for you, trying to root out the intruder in its head. Maybe you should sever the mental link and escape now, before it finds you.

▶ *If you get out while you still can,* **turn to page 225.**

▶ *No! This is too good an opportunity to pass up. If you dig deeper into the dog's memories,* **turn to page 33.**

After a brief set of instructions from Tinker in Vietnamese, the still-silent Suong creates a cloud of mist, then pulls a small man in an orange jumpsuit out of it.

"Verminator," the Cockroach says with a sneer. "How's prison been treating you?"

The man looks startled, but quickly recovers. "Awesome," he shoots back. "How's your mom?"

"You leave my mom out of this."

"Still attached to the umbilical cord, I see. As if you ever stopped talking about your mother for the six years we—"

Hmm. You had assumed Cockroach's differences with Verminator were of a professional nature, but their dispute appears to be a bit more . . . *domestic*. Regardless, it's none of your concern. "We freed you," you say, cutting Verminator off and showing him the orb. "Now, as payment, you'll tell me everything you can about this worm."

He glares at Cockroach again, but seems compliant enough. "It's not a worm," he says. "It's the larva of some kind of beetle. Whoa—no beetle I've ever seen, though. It doesn't have any insect thoughts, like it's been emptied out and filled with . . ."

He pauses, and looks at the Ox. "Human thoughts. Your memories, to be exact."

Verminator relates the story of a young man abducted from the roads of rural Oklahoma and brought to a secret mountain base by operatives of the Crexidyne Corporation. He was offered superhuman powers under the condition that, when the time came, he would betray all of humanity and help deliver the planet to Crexidyne. As a failsafe, the operatives said they could take back the powers any time they saw fit, but that didn't

(continue to the next page)

matter. The young man was eager to accept the bargain.

A series of painful procedures followed, which, from the looks of things, no one expected him to survive. When he emerged as a hulking giant, all memories of the event were wiped from his mind by a telepath from the Justice Squadron called Brain Stem and some complex-looking machinery.

"Oh my god," Verminator says after he finishes his story. "I tell everyone I got my powers from a meteor, but it's a lie. I have no idea how I got them. This could have happened to me, too."

"Nobody knows how they got their mojo," the Cockroach says. "We could all be Crexidyne experiments."

"Not me," Tinker says. "I don't even have superpowers. I just stayed in school."

Verminator's story has certainly raised the Ox's hackles, but the smaller man insists he's telling the truth even after a barrage of intimidation and very convincing threats of physical violence. If Thorpe's organization is gathering villains, it's a good bet they're preparing to make their move. But if anyone's going to take over the world today, it's damn well going to be *you*. You need more recruits, and remember that the Ox mentioned a supervillain meeting happening in the city tonight.

He scratches his head. "Yeah, but I bet Crexidyne knows about it, too. It's like the worst kept secret in villainy, and I know for a fact half those guys freelance for them."

You turn to Tinker. "That weapon of yours—can it take down a whole group of Cosmic Guardians at once?"

It was originally only designed for one—until now there only ever *was* one—but electrical pulse technology has apparently advanced significantly since the mid-'90s, and in a few

(continue to the next page)

hours Tinker has it modified to take out any alien battlesuit in a hundred-yard radius. With Suong's help, you step from the workshop directly into the basement of a downtown YMCA, where the meeting is just getting started. It seems to be more of a supervillain gripe session than anything else, but a good dozen criminals show up for it.

As expected, 30 alien beings decked out in Cosmic Guardian armor burst through the door with energy weapons blazing. The villains scatter, but Tinker throws a switch on his device and sends the whole lot of aliens skittering across the floor, convulsing. With the attackers helpless, the villains pounce. It's a gruesome spectacle, but in moments the Guardians have all been dealt with. There was a Crexidyne stooge in a tweed jacket among them as well, but there's not enough left of that guy to hazard a guess at his identity.

That was easier than you anticipated. The new group of villains seems pretty pumped up from their bloody, horrifying victory, too. What next?

"We should take the fight to Crexidyne," the Ox says, "and hit 'em before they know what's coming!"

Tinker looks at the assembled group. "I don't know. Who knows how many villains they've picked up so far? Maybe we should keep recruiting."

▶ *If you take the group you already have and storm Crexidyne while you have the element of surprise,* **turn to page 264.**

▶ *If you follow Tinker's advice and continue gathering your army,* **turn to page 32.**

Supervillains popping out of a dimensional portal? Wow, that's random (we'll cop to this one—they can't all be winners). You power up your suit and immediately engage its cloaking device. Get ready to face the invisible fury of the Nightwatchman, evildoers!

Alas, a blast of energy hits you square in the back before you can leap into action. What, is the Cosmic Guard just roaming the skies above New York, waiting to receive a signal from the stolen alien technology that powers your equipment? Yep —ever since you kidnapped Moretti, they are. More blasts follow, and you're quickly reduced to a pile of singed Kevlar and charred flesh. Looks like you'll never find out what Crexidyne was up to (preparing the planet for an alien takeover) or what will happen to Nancy North (killed by orbital death lasers 15 minutes later).

THE END

"I work alone," you say. You haven't finished your cocktail yet, so your faceplate is still open and you don't get that booming echo effect, but it still comes out sounding reasonably badass. "A partner would only slow me down."

"That's crazy talk!" Moretti says. "You may be the best we've got, but you're brash and inexperienced, and if you screw this up, it's *my* ass on the line. So we do this by the book, dammit. Am I making myself clear?"

Wow, he's laying it on awfully thick. But you've seen enough cop dramas to know how this plays out. "Sorry, Chief, but I play by my own rules."

He sighs. "I was afraid of that. You're sure there's nothing I can say to make you change your mind?"

"Nothing," you insist.

The earpiece he gave you has burrowed its way inside your helmet, and at this point it explodes, blasting your entire head into a lump of seared flesh and little pieces of charred bone. Wow. You did not see that coming. Moretti taps his earpiece, although with your face as disintegrated as it is, you're technically too dead to hear what he says into it.

"Control? Yeah, it's Moretti. Who else do we have who wants to be the chump in the suit?"

THE END

Space police or no, something's not right here. And the
Ox may not be a saint, but he's been pretty straight with you
so far. Also, you're guessing any trip that starts out in a burlap
sack doesn't end with due process before a jury of one's peers.
The question is, what are you going to do about it? Fend off the
supergestapo with mixed martial arts? Cosmic Guardian-types
are busy gunning people down with ray beams, stuffing them
in bags, and hauling them away. They don't seem to be paying
much attention to you, but the giant slug and the insect are
zeroing in on your friend.

Here goes nothing. You trust your newly upgraded body
and launch yourself at the Bug Guardian in what you hope will
work out to be a flying roundhouse kick. It comes together
surprisingly well. Your foot connects squarely with the thing's
helmet, knocking it backwards, where it collapses in a pile of
limbs on the floor. That was awesome!

Rather than skittering to its feet, however, your opponent
just lifts several of its arms to take aim at you. Crap! Something
purple and tar-like starts spreading across your chest, and the
alien fires a blast of blue light right into the stuff. What's it
doing? Covering you in space clay and trying to bake it on? The
gunk quickly spreads until it covers you from the neck down,
and the big bug keeps firing at you. You can't even feel the blasts
under all that goo.

Suddenly it dawns on you. The goo isn't part of the bug's
attack. You're doing this. *The goo is your superpower.*

Your superpower is *disgusting*.

Of all the ways to be mutated by a radioactive comet, you
get the ability to cover yourself in purple slime? At this point

(continue to the next page)

your opponent just gives up on you and turns his attention back to the Ox, who has his hands full with his own attacker. He's shrugging off the beam attacks as easily as you did (thanks, freaky purple goo!) but now the second alien grabs his arms from behind in a multi-limbed space insect sleeper hold. Ox is strong enough to bust through a concrete wall, yet the alien seems to have him pinned.

From what you know about the original Cosmic Guardian, he was just a regular guy inside a superpowered battle suit. So you decide to see how that suit holds up to an onslaught of gunk. You concentrate, and a ball of the stuff forms in your hand. It's sticky, though, and when you attempt to fling it at the alien it stays half-stuck to you, with the rest of it splatting on the floor at your feet. Okay, time for plan B.

You leap onto the thing's back and figure you'll try pulling its helmet off. The goo seems to have bonded to your skin, increasing your strength exponentially. It gets everywhere, too, oozing over your opponent and seeping into the cracks in its armor. You pull and pull with all your newfound strength. It's loosening! With one more yank the helmet comes free.

Except that—*ew*. The thing's head pops right off along with it. It's coated in superpowered goo, and as the bug dies you're overcome by its mental anguish, as if it were beaming a squealing death rattle directly into your brain. Along with it, you get flashes of something different—cold, almost mechanical, but definitely living. It's some form of communication, but it's more imagery than it is verbal. FINAL STAGES . . . LONG JOURNEY . . . COLONY SHIP . . .

KILL ALL HUMANS.

(continue to the next page)

The scrambled images fade, and you're fairly sure the sci-fi movie diatribe was coming from the robotic battle armor rather than the alien inside it. Freed from his wrestling hold, Ox grabs the slug-shaped alien and throws him across the room. He proceeds to pummel it against the wall with his fists until the body armor is in shambles and its soft insides start to leak onto the floor.

The rest of the Cosmic Guard appears to have gotten what it came for, because the room is empty. You look around for the man who was giving orders and spot the remnants of a tweed jacket pinned between the slug and the basement wall. Ouch. That can't be a pleasant way to go.

The Ox picks up the man's tablet computer, which has been flung halfway across the room. He looks pissed. "I don't know who these assholes are, but I say we follow them back to whatever hole they crawled out of and keep hitting stuff until we find out."

He pauses for a moment, staring at you. "Dude, what the hell are you covered in?"

Your curiosity is more than a little piqued, but deep down you're still a reporter. With a little effort you might be able to dig up some information on whatever's going on before charging off with guns blazing. Also, you just killed someone, or at the very least some*thing*, and you're not sure how to react to that yet.

But if aliens are truly invading, there might not be time for junk like research and feelings.

- ▶ *If you like the sound of Ox's hitting-things plan,* **turn to page 136.**

- ▶ *If you think you can find more answers by harnessing the power of journalism,* **turn to page 40.**

Okay, we get that you're being cautious and all, but you've been a cosmic space hero for almost a full day now, and you're going to have to actually do something heroic eventually. You don't think maybe this is your big chance?

▶ *Okay, fine. If you head to D.C. to have a stupid battle with the stupid supervillains,* **turn to page 188.**

▶ *But knowing is half the battle! If you remain alone in the Himalayas communing with your robot battlesuit,* **turn to page 290.**

"Come on," you say. Octavia has more than proven herself in battle, and your gut tells you that you may need to pull that mass-brain-blast trick again before the day is over. You morph the armor into its passenger configuration, and Octavia climbs into the pod. It's a tight fit, but it'll have to do. It also uses up a significant portion of the suit's mass, leaving the rest of you less protected than you'd like. *Comfortable back there?* You know she can't be, curled up like a fetus.

That's when it hits you. This configuration isn't meant for a passenger at all.

Even with suspended animation for interstellar travel, host bodies don't live forever. But the armor is designed to last indefinitely. *The pod is where you grow the clone.* Properly grafting to an individual host's DNA can take years, so why not just grow a new host, with identical DNA, during the long trip between planets? The result would be an empty vessel without memory, or language, or opinions about how to run the show.

After a journey home and back to Earth again, you had a fully grown, 18-year-old Sten Jannsen clone living in your backpack. Of course, you hadn't followed protocol in raising him —you talked with him, read him stories, shared fully immersive memories from Sten's childhood. You tried to teach him right from wrong. He was your constant companion for almost two decades. It may not have been a traditional upbringing, but your plan was to bring him to a backup battlesuit that was hidden under the Pacific ocean. After a careful bonding process, Sten Junior would have been free to live his own life at last.

Of course, that all ended over Cleveland. The battlesuit they sent for the Ox was designed specifically to mesh with the

(continue to the next page)

target's DNA and—like your backup suit—it was inactive, subsisting on a reserve of biochemical sludge and waiting for a host to graft to. However, it wasn't without protection. The inferior shielding of your armor's pod configuration left you exposed, and the other battlesuit's automatic defenses aimed for the younger, stronger Sten first. He was dead before the meteor—or what you assumed was a meteor, anyway—even entered Earth's atmosphere.

You're overwhelmed with grief. And rage. Rocketing into the sky at top speed, you reach the alien mothership in a matter of minutes. It's immense. Octavia has been trying to console you, but now her thoughts turn to the job at hand. *What do you know about this thing?*

Nothing. You have no information on the ship whatsoever. You've met the alien creatures who built it only once, as far as you can remember. Octavia peeks inside the craft with her mind, and immediately withdraws, shocked. *Oh my god—so full of hate. How does a whole race of beings become like that?* She steels herself and tries again. *Wait . . . I sense something else in there. The ship itself has an artificial intelligence. It's not as advanced as yours—here, see if you can help me.*

She links your thoughts to hers, and you stretch out with your own awareness. The moment you do, though, you can sense the Cosmic Guard approaching. It's the entire army, as far as you can tell. You don't have much time.

You find that some of the ship's programming is similar to your own, and you quickly establish a link. *Can we reprogram it to turn around?* Octavia asks. *To just leave, and go home?*

As soon as the aliens realized what was happening, they'd

(continue to the next page)

just hit the brakes and come right back. What you need is to trigger a self-destruct mechanism.

I'm not finding any such command, Octavia says.

Well, what about jury-rigging one? The ship has two drive engines. What if you set one engine on one course, and the other on a different course, and have both jump to light speed?

That— Octavia pauses. *That would work. Are you seeing what I am, though? The explosion would be massive. It would kill us, too.*

Not if we jump to lightspeed first, you think.

The Cosmic Guardians are starting to arrive. Destroying the mothership will certainly destroy the lot of them as well, and Octavia hesitates at the idea. The hosts inside the battlesuits may be innocent, you think, but surely they're beyond saving — their minds would have all been hollowed out long ago, and the pod-grown clones likely never even had minds to begin with. Still, your thoughts turn to Sten Junior. He was grown in a pod. Was he worth saving?

Octavia has an alternative plan. *We could brain-blast them all, and reprogram the lot in one fell swoop! How much damage can the mothership do once we've taken out its army of stormtroopers?*

How much damage, indeed? Would reprogramming the Cosmic Guard stop the aliens' terraforming plan? Is it worth risking all of Earth to save a handful of host bodies that are probably too far gone to even know they've been saved?

▶ *If you blow up the ship,* **turn to page 306.**

▶ *If you blast the Guardians to make them play nicely with their insane hosts,* **turn to page 213.**

It's an age-old question, debated *ad nauseam* by superhero geeks all over the world: who would win in a fight? Magnifico or Nightwatchman? Would cunning, strategy, and meticulous planning be enough to overcome raw, unbridled power? The crux of the fanboy argument for Nightwatchman is that he's always three moves ahead. Prepared for any contingency, his tactical genius would assure that he had everything worked out in advance, and the battle would be over before it even began.

None of this, of course, even vaguely describes your situation. You throw an exploding boomerang and charge Magnifico with full flash-blinding, gas-pumping, sonic-screeching fury, waving your arms around like a crazy person.

What you get in return is a heaping tablespoon of laser vision, right in the face. Does your wild frenzy at least create a distraction so Magnifica can take the brute down?

You'll never know.

The End

The element of surprise has worked for you so far, and although it's is a bit of a crapshoot, you hope to at least take the invaders off guard. The rocket pods require a crew of five to fly them properly, so you have the Savage Cockroach split himself into half a dozen clones, all linked together in one big hive mind. It's the perfect piloting solution, but turns out to be unnecessary—a single red button engages the pod's autopilot and blasts off right toward your intended target: the alien mothership.

You find a stash of space suits—some among your assortment of misshapen rogues don't quite fit into them perfectly, but you use purple supergoo to patch up the seals. It's a surprisingly short trip through space in the windowless pod, and in less than an hour your craft is met by the mothership's docking clamps. This is it. You've bet the future of your entire planet (and, more importantly, your own hide) on this one fight. You have only one chance at this!

You send the henchmen out (you're not stupid). Fortunately, whatever the alien overlords were expecting to emerge from the pods, it wasn't dozens of amped-up supervillains on a warpath. Your foes turn out to be huge, hideous fleshbags with stick-like, bony appendages, but they aren't wearing the armor of the Cosmic Guard, and when it comes to physical combat, they're actually kind of wussies. The Ox throws their big, bloated bodies around the docking bay like rag dolls, and Suong—even without any firm grasp of her coordinates in the void of space—opens a portal to an empty expanse of Pacific ocean back on Earth, where they quickly suffocate and drown. Even Pterodactyl Girl has little trouble dispatching them. The battle is over before your foes have the chance to radio their shock troops for help.

(continue to the next page)

Victory! You've managed to thwart an alien plot to take over the world, and, to be honest, it wasn't even that hard. A few of your soldiers suffered suit punctures and quickly succumbed to the poisonous alien atmosphere, but the casualties are more than acceptable. You send Tinker and some of his brighter peers out to scout the enormous ship, and they discover several thousand more aliens stored in suspended animation, as well as what appear to be two giant machines designed to replace the Earth's ecosystem with the mothership's toxic brown gas. This was a colonization mission, you realize, and there's very little chance that any living thing on the planet would have survived it.

So what now? Tinker and Ox are terribly excited about turning the ship into an interstellar base of operations for your new criminal empire, and the idea does have its appeal. With Suong's portals—that girl is *crazy* powerful—you can come and go as you please.

The aliens have provided something more than just a bitchin' clubhouse, though: they've given you the ultimate doomsday device. Their plan is already halfway to fruition, and you're a goddamn criminal mastermind—why not follow through and hold the entire world hostage until they bow down and submit to your will?

That's freaking supervillainy, yo.

▶ *If you use the atmospheric converters to bring the entire population of the Earth to its knees,* **turn to page 255.**

▶ *If that sounds a little melodramatic and you'd rather just ride around in your new spaceship being awesome,* **turn to page 206.**

You decide it's best to talk to Dale and find out just what he thinks he knows. It takes you a while to get out of your armor, but once you do, it shifts around and reconfigures itself into a big, shiny blue suitcase. The thing actually weighs about two tons, but it does some kind of anti-gravity hovering thing that allows you to carry it. The overall effect looks a little floaty and weird, but if you hold it just right, it passes for normal.

The street out front still looks like a war zone—maybe you should have done something to stop the Ox after all?—but your favorite bar is still open for business. You find Dale in his usual seat, a nearly-empty beer glass in front of him. He doesn't even seem to notice the suitcase.

"Have you seen Melah?" he asks. "She isn't answering her phone."

Smart girl. "Listen, Dale. About earlier today . . ."

"Yeah, let's talk about that." He finishes his drink, and then just stares at you for a moment. "I'm going to outline a situation, purely hypothetical, of course. Let's say you're drinking one morning with your two closest friends, hammering out details for the greatest local news website the greater Cleveland metropolian area has ever seen."

Sigh. "Sounds pretty out there," you say.

"It's a thought experiment," he continues. "Just bear with me. So all of a sudden a comet and an exploding bank and all these superheroes happen, and you and your friends split up to follow different leads. But once your friends are gone, imagine that something unbelievable happens to you."

"Dale . . ."

"No, let me talk. You wind up making this amazing dis-

(continue to the next page)

covery, getting this fantastic opportunity . . . *gaining powers far beyond those of mortal men*. So what do you do? Do you go back and tell your friends about it? Or do you keep it to yourself, worried that they won't understand, or that just by telling them, you'll be putting their lives in danger?"

He pauses, picking up his glass again before realizing that it's empty. "I've given it a lot of thought," he says, "and I know what *I* would do."

"Listen Dale, we need to think this through very—"

"I'm a superhero!" he exclaims, holding out one hand over the table. Some kind of gooey substance is excreted from his pores, quickly covering his fist and then hardening into a solid purple shell. Frankly, it's pretty gross. He explains that when you and Melah left, he stayed behind to monitor the Ox and fell into the impact crater, hitting his head on the fallen comet and blacking out. When he woke up, he had purple goo powers.

In your excitement, you spill the beans about the Cosmic Guardian armor as well. "You know what we have to do now, don't you?" Dale asks through an ear-to-ear grin.

"Heck yeah, I do."

"CELEBRATE!" he howls. "Bartender! Two bourbons, two scotches, and four beers!"

Actually, you were thinking of something more along the lines of teaming up to fight injustice. But you have to admit that Dale's idea holds a certain appeal as well.

▶ *If you double Dale's order and get this party started,* **turn to page 106.**

▶ *If you'd rather find some crime to fight and save the binge drinking for later,* **turn to page 179.**

You start by digging around in the dead man's tablet. His files are password-protected, but you flip the thing over and discover the words "If found, return to Crexidyne Megacorp" stamped on the back with an address. It's in Manhattan—looks like you have a destination.

The Ox calms down slightly as you make the trip, and you spend some time experimenting with your supersludge, willing the sticky coating into a hard shell (which should provide better protection and has the added benefit of not ruining the van's upholstery). This whole purple goo situation is actually becoming sort of cool. Ox is busy coming up with new potential code names for you, the worst of which include Commander Goo and his personal favorite, Globulon. Hmm. Less cool.

Crexidyne is housed in a Manhattan skyscraper, and although it's well after midnight when you finally arrive, the front entrance opens with a beep from the tablet. If the guy manning the security desk is surprised to see a walking tank and his lumpy, purple-shelled companion stroll by, he shows no sign of it. Not knowing what else to do, you head for the elevator. A button labeled "restricted access" gives you a pretty good clue here, and once again it accepts the tablet as I.D. Ox starts psyching himself up as the elevator zooms upward. "You ready for *vengeance*?" he asks. "Whatever we find up there, I'm gonna punch it." The elevator slows, and the door opens with a ding.

What you find is the building's roof, with several hundred battlesuited Guardians of all different descriptions and a handful of human beings barking orders at them. The elevator closes behind you. Then, as one, every armored alien on the rooftop stops what it's doing and looks your way. Ox makes a little noise

(continue to the next page)

with his throat. "I don't think we can take 'em," he whispers.

Grasping at straws, you spot a group of big, silver pods on what looks like a landing pad. Are those what you think they are? "This way!" you yell, breaking into a run.

You throw yourself into the open hatch in one of the pods and find yourself in a strange chamber that might well be an alien cockpit. A Crexidyne memo has been scotch-taped to he control panel—it seems to outline launch procedures. "They're right behind us!" Ox howls as he lumbers in behind you. He shows very little interest in the memo, instead jamming his thumb into a big red button on the console.

You're swept off your feet as the hatch slams shut and the pod launches into the sky. Acceleration pushes you against the rear wall, and paper tears in your hands as you scan the memo, trying to figure out a way to steer this thing. "It's a shuttle!" you yell through clenched teeth, your cheeks all wobbly from the G forces. "We're on an automatic course for the mothership!"

"Good," Ox replies. He's pressed against the wall too, but you can tell that he's already starting to psych himself up. "Whatever we find up there, I'm gonna punch it."

▶ *Maybe Ox is right. If there are answers to be found, surely they're aboard that ship. If you leave the shuttle on its set course,* **turn to page 267.**

▶ *The memo does include a procedure for manual override, though. If you attempt to turn the thing around,* **turn to page 94.**

You make a flying leap for Gravity Bomb since you've pegged her as the biggest threat (although, honestly, how she can do anything in an outfit that skimpy is a wonder—gravity manipulation must play a significant role in just keeping the thing on). She's ready for you, though, and with a flick of a wrist slams you back into the pavement the instant your feet leave the ground.

The Ox just shakes his head and sighs as the force of gravity squishes you into goo and spreads you all over the intersection. That alone might not be particularly fatal with your newfound superpowers, but Coldfront whips up a sub-zero arctic blast that freezes you on the spot. And the freaky alien Cosmic Guardian thing rains down bolts of blue energy that shatter your frozen, flattened body into hundreds of shards. Skyhawk then hits some of those shards with a mace. While the Squadron casually takes the Ox into custody, volunteers from the local P.D. gather fragments of you into individual containers for later incineration.

When a seasoned supervillain immediately throws in the towel, next time go ahead and take the hint.

THE END

You find the building in question and use your energy beams to carve a little peephole in the back wall. Sure enough, it's chock-full of evil. You recognize four of the five costumed criminals huddled around a dimly lit table inside.

Jekyll and Hyde are twins who try to pull off a mad scientist/monster theme, but actually don't amount to much more than thugs with badger claws and delusions of grandeur. Supercomputer is capable of calculating variables and probabilities with phenomenal speed, but that won't help her much while you're punching her in the face. Lightning Queen is the heavy hitter—she's a raving lunatic with electrical powers and she's gone toe-to-toe with the best. And then the fifth is some big guy decked out all in black, looking every bit the burglar on a cereal box and trying way too hard to appear incognito.

You and Dale formulate a complex plan to take them out—it might have worked, too, but you failed to account for Burglar Guy, and that was your rookie mistake. You burst right through the wall with space weapons blazing, but before you get the chance to put your cunning plot into action, the mysterious stranger turns to face you, and you recognize him instantly.

It's Magnifico, world's most powerful hero and leader of the Justice Squadron. Your first thought is that he could be on some sort of undercover mission, but it only lasts until his fist smashes through your visor (and, in turn, your face).

If he's only pretending to be evil, he's *extremely* committed to the role.

The End

"Bring 'em on," Ox says, almost in a whisper. "I can take 'em." Then he passes out.

With the big guy out of the picture, the Cosmic Guardians pounce. You start to build another goo barrier, but aliens quickly grab hold of your limbs and pull. This can't be good. You focus on increasing the thickness of your armor, spreading it to cover your head and face as well. You feel stronger, but more unidentified appendages grab you. They're pulling you apart! More goo! More goo!

You feel something snap. Suddenly, the goo isn't just coating your body. It's inside your body. It *is* your body.

You are the goo.

You dissolve into a puddle, slipping out of the aliens' miscellaneous grasps, and then quickly form a series of spikes, jutting into your attackers' soft underbellies right through their body armor. These are the battlesuits Megawatt was so impressed with? You're ripping through them like soft-shell crabs. You send out tendrils for each of the Guardians hovering throughout the hangar, and it's as if you're everywhere at once, hyper-aware, with your brain and senses spread throughout every iota of your new form. You quickly seep though the cracks in their armor and resolidify inside. The aliens drop to the floor.

You're Globulon, bitches.

You shoot a line into the ship's console as you scoop Ox up and stuff him into the rocket pod. *Is anything else still alive?*

NEGATIVE. SKELETON CREW EXTERMINATED. PASSENGERS SAFELY IN HIBERNATION AWAITING TERRAFORMING AT TARGET IN 65,000—

Good enough. Another tendril goes into the pod's controls

(continue to the next page)

and you command it to launch. With a direct link to the escape pod's flight systems, you have complete control. You don't even need the Crexidyne memo.

Just moments out of the bay door, the mothership jumps to lightspeed, and the resulting shockwave rocks your tiny craft. As you hit the Earth's atmosphere, the pod begins to shake furiously. She's falling apart! You form yourself into a protective shell around Ox as the pod burns completely away, leaving the two of you hurtling toward the Earth like a meteor.

You hit the ground and completely lose structural integrity, splattering into a million tiny droplets scattered across the acre-wide crater created by your impact.

It takes you several hours, but you slowly manage to reassemble, pulling each speck of yourself together into a concentrated mass. You will yourself back into human form, feeling your insides morph back into bones, then organs, muscle, and skin. Finally, your gooey outer coating is sucked back into your pores and you're none the worse for wear.

Ox is at the center of the crater, curled into a ball. You poke him. He moans. "Whatever just hit me, I'm gonna punch it."

It turns out that while you were stopping the invasion, all hell has broken loose back home. An international coalition of military forces is waging war on the planet's superpowered beings, and the bulk of the Cosmic Guard is still on hand, waiting for a colony ship that, thanks to you, will never come. However, the Earth clearly still needs a champion. You and the Ox may have started out as partners in crime, but you've already rescued all of humanity once today. And this looks like a job for a superhero.

It's your call.

THE END

You may be new to the hero game, but you know one thing for sure: you didn't spend your formative years dreaming about *avoiding* criminals. You switch on your computer's audio during the trip for some hands-free research, and study up on the Nightwatchman suit's capabilities while you drive. It has cloaking technology that will render you invisible if you keep to the shadows. Your gloves have a built-in electric shock to augment hand-to-hand combat, and your cloak can double as a glider, just in case you decide to leap from any tall buildings. It's well after dark by the time you make it to the city, but you're ready.

And your quarry is on the move.

You track Rockjockey to an industrial neighborhood known as Hunts Point and position yourself in an alleyway near the railroad tracks, directly in his path. You switch on the cloaking device, but as you position yourself next to a dilapidated brick wall, you bump up against a garbage can, loudly toppling it over just as your target rounds the corner in front of you.

"Who's there?" he says, skidding to a halt. "I'll kill you all, goddammit!" Suddenly the brickwork behind you shakes violently, and it's all you can do to leap out of the way as chunks of masonry tear free and hurl themselves at the villain, engulfing him. There must be a human being inside it somewhere, but the ten-foot-tall golem that now stands before you is more crumbled architecture than it is man.

Here goes nothing. You drop the invisibility and flicker into view, a stark shadow against the night sky, the yellow lenses of your goggles glowing fiercely in the darkness. "Rockjockey," you say with all the steel your voice can muster. "Fancy meeting you here."

(continue to the next page)

"You!" His shocked expression is exaggerated by the bits of rubble fused to his face. He stumbles backward. "I didn't do nothin', I swear!"

You take a single step toward him, and he flinches. "Oh, no? Then who are you running from?"

"It's that Cosmic Guardian guy from like 15 years ago! He's back, and him and his buddies are hunting villains—just grabbin' 'em off the streets!"

"Sounds like they're performing a public service."

"It ain't like that! They busted into a freakin' AA meeting and hauled off a dozen guys in burlap sacks. This ain't justice, it's a witch hunt! Cockroach says they're working for Crexidyne, but that don't make sense—I just did a job for them. I'm square with those guys."

If anything, in the '90s the Cosmic Guardian was famous for playing by the book, and he certainly wouldn't be allied with Crexidyne. Still, the look of abject terror on Rockjockey's face makes you think he's telling the truth. Or the truth as he understands it, at least. Before you can tighten the screws, however, something flashes across the screen on the back of your gauntlet.

SHUT DOWN YOUR SYSTEMS.

Is somebody *texting* you? Could the real Nightwatchman have discovered that you swiped his stuff? You're sort of in the middle of something, but the warning seems fairly ominous. Should you heed it?

▶ If you quickly wrap this up and shut your Nightwatchman gear down, **turn to page 226.**

▶ Are you kidding? You don't take orders from random text messages. If you ignore it and continue the interrogation, **turn to page 178.**

You throw yourself at one of your attackers, flinging a wad of goo that completely envelops its head. Or head analog, anyway—many of these things aren't even vaguely human-shaped. You manage to create a mental link with the creature almost immediately, but melding with its mind is not a pleasant experience. The armor's intellect is cold and calculating, but the host is barely even self-aware. It's a mass of chaos and confusion, lashing out in anger and pain.

Wow. That's not cool. You try to exert a calming influence, but the thing doesn't even acknowledge your presence. So you focus on the machine mind. Before you get the chance to seek out its innermost hopes and dreams, though, a second Guardian grabs you. You cover its face-thing with goo as well, but now you're connected to two mechanical intellects, and they gang up on you. This isn't working out as planned.

While you try to master the finer points of psychic combat, several more Guardians utilize tried and true methods of regular combat to tear your limbs off and pull out your internal organs through the bloody stumps before your distracted subconscious can even defend itself with goo.

THE END

With a little coaxing, the Ox agrees to work for Moretti. He climbs into the helicopter and you start to follow, but Moretti stops you. "You'll receive your orders in the morning," he says.

Okay. It's been a pretty full slate already, and you still have a bag full of cash from your bank heist, so you go buy a Playstation 3 and a case of good liquor and call it a day. Sometime around eleven o'clock the next morning, your employers send a 14-year-old Vietnamese girl through a dimensional portal to collect you. So that's pretty cool. The portal opens up to Washington, D.C., where a bunch of other villains have already begun trashing the place. You're told to go crazy and cause as much destruction as possible, which is fun at first, but after an hour or two starts to wear thin. You're thinking about sneaking off to grab some lunch when you see several members of the Justice Squadron approaching. Finally, some real action!

To your surprise, the Squadron just joins you in the effort to reduce the nation's capital to rubble. Soon the army shows up, but destroying tanks isn't your idea of a good time—those are regular people in there, with wives and husbands and stuff at home. You're starting to wonder if taking this gig was the right move after all. Still, lots of people work crappy jobs to collect a paycheck, right?

Then the toxic gas rolls in. Thick, brown smoke fills the air, and the slightest whiff of it makes you gag. You try to escape, but it's as if the entire city is filling up with the stuff—you breathe it, and it immediately burns through your lungs and starts eating away at your internal organs.

The Crexidyne retirement plan: not what it's cracked up to be.

THE END

The truth is, your molecular structure is still in the process of being transformed by your contact with the alien biochemical agent. But whatever it is you're turning into, one thing's for sure: it isn't any species of bird.

You hit the pavement like a sack of meat, and a portion of your anatomy melts into purple goo, ready to spring back into its natural form none the worse for wear. The bulk of you, though, just gets kind of broken and bloody the way a regular person would after leaping from a five-story building.

The overall effect is extra gross for the guy whose job it is to hose your remains off the sidewalk.

THE END

"I'll take it," you say. "There's not much else I can do without my equipment, anyway." Your hands and feet are already completely numb. You may in fact be freezing to death. None of you are dressed for this weather.

Tina pushes a lever on her upgraded wheelchair and rockets into the air. "Tank hold off bad guys!" she yells from above.

"There," Octavia says. "Done." The pulsating alien technology clings to your back, clamping a metallic tendril to the back of your head. The terrifying dog is finally out of the picture, at least—Cosmo's ancient form turns to dust and blows away the instant Conrad and Octavia remove it from its alien life support.

You can feel the thing resisting the genetic graft with you, attempting to pollute you with its essence instead of the other way around. So you clench your eyes shut and concentrate on being your human-iest. When you reopen them, everything is tinted a dark, murky orange. Gah. That can't be great.

A figure breaks away from the group dogfighting with Tina and heads your way. It's in the armor of a Cosmic Guardian, but shaped like a giant eyeball with tentacles. Octavia stands in front of you, hands on her temples. She lets out a grunt, and the alien screeches and falls from the sky. Octavia's knees buckle. "I don't know how much more of that I have in me. Let's get moving!"

"I'll catch up!" says Conrad, hurrying back to the wreckage of the jet. You start trudging toward the tower, but the icy terrain makes foot travel difficult. Also, more Guardians have noticed your presence. Octavia is steeling herself for another attack when you hear the sounds of metal scraping against metal. You turn to see huge sections of the jet tearing away from the body and reshaping into something new.

(continue to the next page)

"The computer systems are all dead," Conrad shouts from inside. "This thing is mine now! Jet propulsion is shot, too, but this'll do." The wreckage shudders violently and stands up on two legs. "I made seats for you on top!" Conrad extends the craft's crude metal forelimb and you climb aboard. You had no idea he wielded that kind of power!

Another Guardian is upon you, but Conrad bats it out of the sky with his makeshift battlebot and stomps on it when it hits the ground. He starts tromping toward the tower at a good clip. Octavia takes out another bogey with a mind blast, and Tina rockets around you in a wide arc, providing air support. You've covered half a mile in no time. Three quarters of a mile! You're going to make it!

That's when you spot a huge, man-shaped Guardian fly up with some kind of glowing orb. "He's human!" Octavia says. "Damn it—I can't read his thoughts. I've lost the psychic link! Look out!"

You hear Tina howl, and she falls from her chair, plummeting to the earth below. The craft buckles beneath you. "I'm losing it!" Conrad shrieks. The entire thing lurches forward in a final push, flattening the Guardian and hurtling you forward to the tower. You hit the ground hard, just a few feet short.

There's no time to check on your companions. You drag your frozen, bloody body to the base of the structure and lay yourself flat against it. *Do it!* you think. You're not sure if there's a mental component to the virus transfer, but you're going to give it all you've got. *You wanted the Earth, you bastards? Take it! CHOKE ON THE HUMANITY!*

You feel the life flow out of your body. As you lose con-

(continue to the next page)

sciousness, you're certain you'll never know if your last-ditch effort to save the planet worked.

* * * * *

It totally did!

You awaken in a hospital bed, with a fully armored Cosmic Guardian standing over you. Its visor splits in two to reveal a familiar face underneath.

"Dale? You're the . . . wait, *what*?"

"Melah's here, too," he says. His voice has an odd, mechanical quality—it's definitely Dale, but somehow he seems like something more than just himself.

"All kinds of crazy stuff went down after we got separated in Cleveland," Melah says. She's covered from the neck down in some kind of purple goo. "But you did it! You and Magnifica and the others. We were battling decoy villains—heroes, too, they all kind of joined together—but you guys figured it out and stopped the whole planet-wide alien mutation plot."

"Oh," Dale says, tossing your Nightwatchman gloves and goggles onto your lap. "I fixed your gear for you." Dale and Melah found your group at the South Pole just in time to save the lives of you and your crew, and Dale used his suit's technology to disengage you from the bomb. The alien mothership is still in orbit, though, and most of the world's superpowered beings seem to be rampaging out of control.

This looks like a job for a superhero.

The End

Ten fannish, squee-filled minutes later you're in the air, rocketing toward southern Florida at Mach 3. You sift through your computer's enormous contact list en route, trying to figure out just who in Broward County comes so highly recommended. Each entry seems to include a note that says "Don't trust," so you sort the database by that criteria. This results in 17,852 untrustables, about 20 or 30 "maybes" (you're surprised to see The Ox show up on this list, and note the conspicuous absence of one Nancy North), and a lone, solitary "trust."

That would be Magnifica. The world's greatest hero.

She was, anyway, before she disappeared from the public eye about 15 years ago. That would explain the retirement community that pops up on your plane's radar when you plug in her name. Your suit has a miniature version of the same cloaking gear that keeps the plane undetected (neat!) so sneaking into a Florida rest home shouldn't prove much of a challenge.

The jet lands silently inside the facility's grounds (it's a *really* cool plane). As you climb out of the cockpit, you find an elderly woman in flannel pajamas waiting for you. She's leaning on a walker, and must be pushing 70.

"You ain't the Nightwatchman," she says plainly.

This catches you off guard. Magnifica? "I'm his protégé," you say. "He's . . . training me. You know, to take over for him." That sounded lame, even to you.

"Uh-huh." Her voice reminds you of the old lady who used to drive your school bus in the third grade (she smoked three packs a day and terrified every kid on her route). You get a better look once you're on the ground, and now you're sure of it. This is the mightiest hero who ever lived.

(continue to the next page)

"Did the Nightwatchman tell you I could crush your skull like a goddamn grape?" she asks. "Get the hell offa my lawn."

"Magnifica, I need your help," you say. "It's Reginald Thorpe, and it's serious." She had tangled with every supervillain in the phone book back in her day, but Thorpe was something of an arch-nemesis. "Brain Stem is already dead."

She pauses, still glaring. "Brain Stem was a pissant. You're a pissant. And I'm retired, so I'm telling you the same thing I told Tachyon the other day. Which is *bite me.*"

Tachyon was a time-traveling contemporary of Magnifica and a fellow member of the Liberty Patrol, the superpowered team from the '70s and '80s that predated the Justice Squadron. According to your files, he's also been in a coma for years. "Um, Tachyon was here?" you ask gently.

"Yeah. Looked the same as he did in the '70s, though, so it mighta been a version from back then. You never can tell with that little twerp. But at least he just wanted to chitchat about the glory years, and didn't have the balls to ask me for a goddamn favor."

Has Magnifica really been entertaining visitors from her past? Or has the world's greatest hero gone completely senile? She does look to be a good stretch past her prime—that walker is especially troubling. If she really *is* the only person you can trust, though, your options are limited.

▶ *If you try to talk Magnifica into helping you,*
   turn to page 258.

▶ *If you decide to look elsewhere for aid,*
   turn to page 72.

You pause to consider the life you'll be turning your back on if you bond permanently with the space armor. Mostly, it's thoughts of waking up at eleven and having gin for breakfast with the ranks of the unemployed. You are *so* ready for this.

Octavia puts both hands on your helmet, and suddenly you can feel her presence inside your head. She says that you were never meant to be alone—that your past will always be part of who you are, but right now lives are at stake, and it's time to look toward the future and begin the next chapter. She's talking to the armor, of course.

Slowly, the now-familiar alien presence in your mind swells. This is no longer the tinny, distant voice of the '50s radio announcer. It's vast and intimidating. Its presence dwarfs your own, and you realize that it could easily swallow your psyche whole. But it doesn't want that. It's reaching out, making you an offer. Gingerly—almost timidly—waiting to see if you'll accept.

You do. An odd sensation washes over you, and along with it comes a rush of memories . . . .

Your primary mission was reconnaissance. The creatures of Earth had a complex social order, so it was important to find a suitable host. You found Sten Jannsen, a prime physical specimen whose Olympic victories had earned him a great deal of local celebrity in the city of your initial landing, which by random chance was Stockholm, Sweden.

Your secondary mission was assassination. The alien being known as Dogstar, the Savior from Sirius, didn't stand a chance.

Your long-term objective was more complicated. You joined forces with Earth's heroes, becoming a member of the aging Liberty Patrol, and later helping to form the Justice Squadron.

(continue to the next page)

With them, you saved many lives, but this was not part of your ongoing goal. You discovered that you could get anything you required by giving human beings what they wanted most. Those who wanted a hero got you as their champion. Others with more selfish desires had them fulfilled as well, because none of it mattered to you. Reginald Thorpe's hunger for power made him the perfect pawn, and you started feeding him a very specific set of instructions. Everything was proceeding as planned.

The time frame, however, presented a problem. You would need at least a decade to put all the pieces in place, and Jannsen's psyche would never last that long. The bonding process was designed to give you access to your host's physical body and higher functions, but your alien physiology was essentially incompatible. Your psyche was starting to drive Jannsen mad, but to properly function in society you needed his mind intact. So you improvised. You found a way to balance your intellect with Jannsen's in a kind of merged partnership. Nothing of the kind had ever been done before—you still had your memories and your mission, but now he was as much a part of you as you were of him.

Over the years, you discovered that Sten Jannsen was a remarkable man. Not tremendously bright, but selfless, generous and kind. All he ever wanted was to help others. In fact, the most difficult part was to keep him from betraying your *true* mission—before your minds became one, you had kept him in the dark with the help of Thorpe's memory-erasing machine. Afterward, his moral compass was kept in check—just barely—by the fact that he shared your own psyche, including the programming that told him there was no choice but to follow orders.

(continue to the next page)

Eventually, once your plans were all in motion, it was time to return home. The portion of you that was still Jannsen would spend the interstellar journey in suspended animation, but the part that was self-aware biomechanical battle armor would not.

And nine years is a long time to think.

You remember reporting to your alien masters—their bloated, pustule-covered bodies and sheer malevolence repulsed you. They sent you back to Earth again, this time as a warrior. But you were more than that now. Part of their attack plan was to neutralize the biggest individual threats to the invasion by grafting battlesuits to them and turning them into more soldiers. So when a suit came for the indestructible human known as the Ox—encased in a ball of space rock—you did everything you could to stop it from reaching him. The Ox's impenetrable hide makes him immune to all of the aliens' weaponry—even when you managed to destroy the suit that was custom-designed for him, you knew they'd keep trying, tearing battlesuits off existing troops if necessary, to finish the job. But keeping him out of your masters' hands for as long as possible seemed like humanity's best hope.

Huge swaths of memory are just missing. For example, everyone knows the Cosmic Guardian had a plucky canine companion, but there's absolutely no record of the little guy in your memory banks. And although you had complete awareness of the mission during your first visit to Earth, most of that is gone now. What were the instructions you gave Thorpe? You have a vague sense of leaving part of yourself behind when you left the planet.

Also, Sten's death is still too painful for you to dwell on,

(continue to the next page)

but his last act was to sacrifice himself so you could go on to save Earth. He knew that his human self was dying but that his alien self could graft to a new host and continue to fight. The important thing was that the Cosmic Guard didn't catch on to his betrayal.

Keep it secret. You may have blown that part already. And somehow Jannsen feels like only one piece of your grief. Was there something more? Could there have been a *child*?

The flash of memory has only taken a moment—Octavia is still with you, her hands on the helmet that is now also your head. You start to tell her about the alien invasion, but she stops you—she was in your mind, and saw everything. Unfortunately, though, as a foot soldier you have only snippets of the greater plan. Other Guardians might have other pieces. Should you open up a channel and connect with them? It's dangerous, since it would give them access to your thoughts as well. Surely they already know about your betrayal—or do they? You remember Sten's last words, and wonder if you should stay as far away from the Guard as possible.

How else can you learn how to stop the alien plot, though? If those villains attacking D.C. are part of this, you might be able to beat something out of one of them.

▶ *If you open up communications with your fellow Guardians,* **turn to page 271.**

▶ *If you think that's a bad idea and head out for D.C.,* **turn to page 88.**

You've read enough comic books to know what happens if you shirk your responsibilities here: that bike thief kills your Uncle Ben, and then you have to be the type of superhero with crippling guilt issues lingering behind your lighthearted wise-cracks. No, thanks. You're going to get that damn bike back if it's the last thing you do. Fortunately, it's not terribly arduous. Once the thief realizes you're after him, he jumps off the stolen bike and continues fleeing on foot. Well, that's no fun. It's probably bad form to punch him now, and you can't imagine hauling someone in to the authorities for *almost* stealing a bicycle, so you let him go. By the time you return to the scene of the crime, the bike's owner is nowhere to be found. Honestly, this really isn't how you pictured big-city crimefighting.

"And what exactly do you think you're doing with that bicycle?"

You turn to find Magnifico, leader of the Justice Squadron, floating slowly to the ground behind you, cape billowing majestically. You let out a gasp. It's really him!

He cocks an eyebrow. "If that's a homemade Skyhawk costume, it's absolutely the worst one I've ever seen."

Crap. Does he think you're stealing the bike? And worse, does he think you're *cosplaying*? Magnifico is probably the most famous superhero in the entire world, and so far you're not making much of a first impression.

▶ *If you tell him you're a fellow hero who has just thwarted a bike robbery,* **turn to page 22.**

▶ *If you play it off like you're just out for a walk and dressed weird,* **turn to page 201.**

"You're right," Moretti says. "I am a dead man. The ships will be departing any time now, and I won't be on them. I'll suffer the same fate as the rest of this miserable world."

Nancy's face is unreadable. "And what fate do you imagine that to be?"

"Slow, agonizing death? Toiling away in slavery? It doesn't matter. It's a testament to Mr. Thorpe's genius that he understood it so early on. Their technology dwarfs ours—they'll take the planet for themselves and do with it as they see fit, and our only hope of survival is to join them. A select group of Crexidyne's top brass will ride out the invasion in the safety of the alien mothership, and when it's over, we'll rule over whatever they choose to leave us with."

"And the satellite weapon," Nancy says. "I suppose that's alien technology as well?"

"Oh no, we built that. At enormous cost, I might add." He explains that the multi-billion dollar weapon was created to deal with a single loose thread—the Ox. Their experiments made him immensely strong and virtually invulnerable, with the unintended side effect of rendering him completely immune to alien weaponry. They couldn't even use the aliens' technology to remove his powers once he had them.

"The Orbital Death Laser is an unwieldy solution," he says, "and it requires a tracking device implanted in his brain to target properly, but we finally built something that could kill the big son of a bitch. Fortunately, it proved unnecessary. Yesterday we slapped one of their Guardian battlesuits on him, and it worked like a charm. Now he's just another mindless shock trooper."

(continue to the next page)

It still doesn't make sense to you. "If these aliens are as powerful as you say, why would you need to build a superhuman army in the first place?"

Moretti shakes his head. "They're a sideshow. It's all they've ever been. Instead of developing any real defenses, humanity has looked toward their precious heroes to protect them, marvelling at their idiotic exploits while sitting on their couches, growing fat and content.

"And today will offer the biggest distraction of all," he continues. "A coordinated, worldwide supervillain attack for the masses to gawk at, followed by the shock of betrayal when, instead of rushing to save them, their beloved heroes join in."

"You're in luck, Moretti," Nancy says. "Now you've got front-row seats. If your little prophecy does come true, you'll get to burn right along with the rest of us."

"My dear Ms. North," he says, his lips twisting into an unsettling grin. "You and I will burn much sooner than that. Do you remember my tiny friend, the cancer man? I built him a little home inside my coat so I can literally carry him around in my pocket. And while we've been sitting here talking, he's been as busy as a bee."

Something catches your eye across the room, and you turn to see a speck that quickly expands into a crooked man in a black uniform. He's holding a shiny metal cylinder in one hand with his thumb pressed firmly against one end. You leap at him and knock the device out of his grasp before he shrinks back down out of sight, but you're too late—the button has already been pushed.

Behind you, a column of orange light ten feet across erupts

(continue to the next page)

through the ceiling, burning through to the building's foundation and completely disintegrating both Carlo Moretti and Nancy North.

Suddenly you're alone. Before you can fully process what's just happened, though, something else comes hurtling though the hole in the roof, landing beside you with a rush of wind. You're startled to find that it's an elderly woman in a red track suit. This can only be Magnifica, the world's most powerful hero. She was around long before any Crexidyne program to create superhumans, and has been retired for years.

"I've been keeping my ear on her heartbeat," the woman says softly, staring at the smoldering hole in the floor. "Ever since she called yesterday to warn me something big was going down." She looks up at you, her face shaking with rage. "What did this?"

"They have a satellite laser cannon . . . " you say.

"They *had* one, you mean."

She glances up at the sky, clearly about to launch into space and destroy the weapon responsible for Nancy's death. Which is probably for the best—for all you know, the thing could be powering up right now for a second shot. Something gives you pause, though. On one hand you've got an orbital death laser, and on the other an alien invasion force. Perhaps you could put both those hands together?

▶ *If you tell Magnifica to wait, in hopes of using the laser cannon against the aliens,* **turn to page 174.**

▶ *If you think it's better that she destroys it before it does any more damage,* **turn to page 217.**

"Maybe things have changed since I wore the tights," Magnifica says, "but in my time, crapweasels like you didn't get much love from superhero types."

"These days we protect and serve all innocent citizens," a booming voice calls out from behind you. "It's called *justice*. You may want to look it up."

You turn to see Magnifico, leader of the Justice Squadron, float through the same window you utilized during the terrifying blur of your own entrance. His uniform is a more masculine, modern update of Maggie's old costume, although as far as you know, they aren't actually related. He came on the scene several years after Magnifica retired, and you always assumed the two of them had worked out some sort of licensing deal.

"That's big talk from some runt wearing an old lady's underwear," Maggie says, almost spitting with contempt. Clearly there's no love lost here. Magnifico lands on the floor in front of her—he's at least a foot and a half taller than she is, and built like a fitness model. Maggie is still holding Moretti up by the throat, and he makes a little choking sound. "This is your innocent civilian?" she asks. "You know he killed your buddy Brain Stem, right?"

"No, he didn't." Twin laser beams erupt from Magnifico's eyes, and with a flash of light Moretti's body burns to ashes right in Maggie's grip.

"I did."

Oh, crap. Maggie takes a step back, looking as shocked as you are. "Why?"

"Orders." He threads his fingers, his knuckles cracking loudly. Magnifico was never your favorite superhero, but never-

(continue to the next page)

theless, your world just turned upside down. "Same reason I'm going to kill you."

You quickly bring up Magnifico on your wrist computer, but what you find is not encouraging. All of your standard attacks (knockout gas, blinding flash, sonic screech—you didn't even know you *had* most of this stuff) have been ruled out as ineffective. Your notes indicate that he doesn't have the strength or speed of Magnifica in her prime, but that prime was a *long* time ago. This guy is big-league for a reason. As far as you can tell, he's unstoppable.

Magnifica isn't backing down. In fact, she's taunting him. Her successor lunges at her, looking for all the world like he's going to tear her head off.

▶ *If you throw yourself into the fray in a desperate attempt to even the odds,* **turn to page 131.**

▶ *If you trust that Maggie knows what she's doing, and let her handle Magnifico while you try to figure out what the hell is going on here,* **turn to page 268.**

Your reign of terror starts tonight, and the streets will flow with the blood of the righteous. After cleaning out the vaults, you and the Ox part company, as he lacks the stomach for what you're planning and, frankly, would only slow you down. There are a few heroes with the power to shift from solid form who might make trouble for you—Megawatt, Coldfront, and of course whatshisname from the Phenomenal Three—but most should succumb to your wrath as quickly as Magnifico did.

In the time it takes to drive to New York you narrow your list of potential targets to one: Luminati is a shining beacon of kindness and hope, so snuffing her should prove particularly dispiriting to the superhero community. Also, she glows like a goddamn nightlight, so you spot her flickering above the Manhattan skyline before you've even made the city limits. As you follow her into a darkened warehouse, you're already starting to wonder if her murder will provide the same rush you felt with Magnifico. If not, no worries—there are plenty of victims out there, just waiting for you to eviscerate them one by one.

The only flaw in your plan? Most of those theoretical victims are actually waiting together in one big group. As you creep through the door, you discover roughly 40 costumed heroes, including Coldfront and the entire Phenomenal Three, packed together like sardines. You can't imagine what brought so many of them together, but one of the things they've been discussing is the final transmission from Magnifico's communicator, showing a gooey purple maniac ripping his internal organs out through his face.

To say that they kill you would be an understatement.

THE END

Why not play to your strengths? You force the Ox to pull over by popping a tire with a targeted energy blast and then swoop down in front of him once he's out of the van, ready to dart away when he lunges at you. He doesn't lunge, though. "You again? Seriously, dude. Get outta here before I have to kick your ass again."

Oh, he *is* going to have to kick your ass. But this time you're ready for it. You crack your helmet to let Migraine out and then start flinging plasma bursts and insults at the Ox in rapid succession. At first he ignores you and just starts changing his tire, but you don't let up. If there's one thing you know, it's how to get under somebody's skin. You're a *reporter*.

Suddenly you're hit with a flying tackle, and find yourself pinned to the ground with a frothing, purple-faced Ox on top of you. Bingo! He starts pounding away at you, but you've been through this before. Your suit will protect you! Then you feel a rush of air on your chest, and realize that he's tearing pieces of your armor right off you.

Uh-oh. What now? You can't use the orbital death lasers —your partner is in his brain! Also, you're kind of directly underneath him. One thing's for certain, though: his adrenaline is pumping like friggin' crazy. Migraine never said exactly how long he would need, but if it's more than about 20 seconds, you're not confident you'll walk away from this.

▶ *Abandon the mission! If you make a desperate attempt to escape the Ox's clutches and live to fight another day,* **turn to page 277.**

▶ *Never surrender! If you tough it out, hoping that Migraine can finish the job before the Ox finishes you,* **turn to page 62.**

Magnifica thinks you're just dragging things out unnecessarily, but agrees to accompany you. "Tomorrow," she says. "All that detective stuff chaps my ass, and anyway it's one o'clock in the goddamn morning." The jet's cloaking device renders it invisible, so you climb back into the cockpit to get some rest. First, though, a little research.

Brain Stem. Real name: Barnaby Herbert Llewelyn. Not trustworthy, for the record. Psychic and telekinetic abilities. Justice Squadron member for eight years. Also, Nightwatchman seemed to really dislike the guy. He was found stuffed into a refrigerator on an abandoned farm in upstate New York last Tuesday.

The next morning, Magnifica greets you with a low grunt and the two of you set out for New York—separately, of course, as you've been informed that invisible jets are for pussies. The old bird can still fly without any trouble, and to your relief she leaves her walker behind. By the time your jet lands, she's waiting for you.

"If you're looking for empty beer cans and used condoms, you're in luck," she says. "Mystery solved."

You check your wrist screen to see what you can find out about the crime scene, but it's blank. That can't be good. You take a few steps back toward the jet, and the screen comes to life. But when you retrace your steps it goes out again —there seems to be some sort of dead zone. With a little trial and error, you find that the zone is actually a line, and it leads directly to the farmhouse. Llewelyn's body is long gone, but nobody cleaned up much afterward, and the kitchen area in particular is still swarming with flies and crusted with gore.

(continue to the next page)

"Jesus, what died in here?" Magnifica says. "Oh, right. Well, unless you got magic brain powers like the dead kid, I don't know what you think you're gonna suss out."

Magic brain powers? Your equipment is *thought-controlled.* "I think I'm picking up some kind of psychic interference," you say. "It starts here and points very clearly in a straight line." Maybe you can use your GPS to figure out where that line ends. You walk away from the farmhouse until you regain telepathic wristphone service, and then try to extrapolate the data. The problem is, you have no idea how far the line of interference stretches. "Could be Toledo. Kansas City, maybe? Santa Fe?"

"Santa Fe." Magnifica spits on the ground. "Goddamn hippie city. I know *exactly* who that thing is pointing to."

Before you can press her for information, though, your screen lights up. It seems to be some kind of supervillain alarm. "Doctor Diabolus, The Turtle, and Lightning Queen are busting up national monuments in Washington, D.C.," you say. "Hmm, that's random. I've never heard of those three working together before."

"Let 'em," Magnifica says. "You said I only had to help with the Brain Fart thing, and I sure as hell didn't sign up for general patrol duty."

Should you at least check it out? Whatever's going on, it might be related to your Crexidyne investigation. Then again, it's not like the Eastern seaboard has a shortage of costumed heroes to handle this sort of thing.

▶ *If you think the threat to the nation's capital demands your immediate attention,* **turn to page 298.**

▶ *If you decide to follow Brain Stem's psychic trail to New Mexico instead,* **turn to page 99.**

You make a mental note: if you ever encounter a group of aliens from across the galaxy, *don't wave*. "Evasive maneuvers!" you shout into your helmet. There's no sense of motion, but in a moment your viewscreen flicks back to life, and you find yourself careening wildly through the air. Is that intentional? Are you evading?

Not well enough. You're briefly enveloped in one flash of blue light, and then another. The voice in your head starts up again. *Revive the following coordinated bituiui momentum*, it insists, then spits out a string of numbers. What does that even *mean*? There's another flash, and this time you feel your armor shake.

"BETTER evasive maneuvers!" you yell. The voice just repeats itself. "Okay, do it!" you say. Nothing happens. Is it waiting for a specific command? "Bituiui momentum! Go!"

With a pop, everything goes white. You feel your armor begin to shift around you, and soon it has reconfigured into a small pod—you can freely move your arms and legs inside the tiny chamber, but have no idea what's happening outside. "Hello?" The suit doesn't respond. Is this bituiui momentum? There don't seem to be any more energy blasts, at least. You start to get bored, and check your phone messages, but can't get a signal. Then, after about eight minutes, you feel the armor shift back into its previous configuration.

Beneath you is the giant, flaming yellow surface of the sun. You know that it takes the sun's rays eight or nine minutes to reach Earth, which would indicate that you've been *traveling at the speed of light*.

But where are the rest of the Guardians? Can't they travel

(continue to the next page)

just as fast? You think it through. Assuming light speed is a universal constant, if they started out three seconds behind you they could chase you forever and *always* be three seconds behind. They couldn't even signal ahead and have someone cut you off at the pass unless their communications could travel faster than light. Technically, you suppose they could stay on your tail until you starved to death in your little pod, but three cheers for an interplanetary police squad having more important things to do with their time than that. Since they knew they couldn't catch you, they apparently didn't even try.

Okay, then, what next? Your suit starts spouting gibberish again—something about safe harbor? A safehouse? You realize that these can't be recorded messages. Your suit is communicating with you. Or trying to, at least. You have no idea why the Cosmic Guard attacked you, but your alien battlesuit just saved your life. You try holding a conversation with it, but just get more telepathic gobbledygook.

Telepathic? Hmm. Brain Stem, a member of the Justice Squadron, is a telepath. He might be able to get inside the suit's mind, or get you better psychic reception or something. Then again, Moretti mentioned a traitor. Can you trust the Squadron? Can you trust Moretti? You're fairly sure you can trust your suit. So maybe you should take its advice, skip the Justice Squadron, and find that safehouse.

▶ *If you track down Brain Stem and ask him to help you figure out what the hell your battle armor is talking about,* **turn to page 293**.

▶ *If you just take your best guess at deciphering the gibberish and try to follow your suit's instructions to safety,* **turn to page 90**.

You saunter off, having emerged from your first encounter with a supervillain utterly victorious. Still, that doesn't mean you're ready for the fast lane. You decide that, for now, Cleveland is more your speed. Besides, smaller cities need heroes, too! You spend the afternoon experimenting with your powers and learn quite a bit. Once night falls, you hit the streets looking for evil.

You find it. Or low-grade thuggery, at any rate. It's a week-night, meaning the downtown core is pretty vacant, but you hear a scream as some goon grabs a woman's purse and takes off down a back alley. After your run-in with the Ox, purse snatchers may be a bit anticlimactic, but you'll take what you can get. You rush to confront him, but he takes one look at you, drops the bag, and flees. Hmm. That was so easy, it wasn't even any fun.

"Drop the purse, scumbag!" You turn to see the glowing eyes of the Nightwatchman peering down at you from a rooftop. At least, it looks like the Nightwatchman. It sounds more like some frat boy doing a goofy-sounding fake voice. Also, he trips and twists one ankle as he scampers down from his perch.

Certainly this is some local Nightwatchman poser, which would also explain why he wasn't eager to tangle with the Ox this morning. He can't seem to get it through his head that you took the purse from the original snatcher in order to return it to its owner, and didn't steal the thing yourself.

You're almost ready to give up and just fight the little twerp when a big, jellyfish-shaped craft the size of a bus pops out of the night sky above you. Holy cow! First meteors and super-villains, and now alien invaders? Cleveland is *amazing* today. The craft fires a beam of blue energy at the Nightwatchman, just

(continue to the next page)

missing him as he leaps out of the way. You get a better look at the ship in the glow, and realize that it's made of the same type of metal and bears the same distinctive markings as the Cosmic Guardian you saw earlier.

The Guardian always claimed to be part of an intergalactic peace-keeping force. Could this ship be one of theirs? You look more closely at the way it moves, and realize that it might very well be a single, enormous alien being in a Guardian battlesuit.

And it's clearly after the Nightwatchman wannabe. Is he the bad guy here? Maybe you should help it apprehend him. Then again, he seems honorable enough, if a bit confused. And that thing did attack him unprovoked—perhaps he's the one who needs your help.

▶ *If you help the Nightwatchman to fend off the Cosmic Guardian,* **turn to page 185.**

▶ *If you team up with the Cosmic Guardian to bring the Nightwatchman to justice,* **turn to page 270.**

All the clues point to Thorpe, and you're ready to get some answers. "I got this," Magnifica says, grabbing you by the waist again, and picking up Octavia with her other hand. Oh, no. After 20 seconds of windshear and oxygen deprivation, you come down hard on a penthouse balcony. Crexidyne headquarters, perhaps? Before you have a chance to get your bearings, Magnifica tears the balcony doors right off their hinges.

"Reggie!" Her voice booms through the suite. "How've you been, old man?"

You hear the whir of machinery, and see a golden, metallic figure approach from inside. More droids quickly follow, and Magnifica lunges at the first, snatching it by a limb and hurling it at the next in line. They both explode. "These are damn cheap robots, Reg!" She drives a third mechanical guard into the wall with her bare fists. "Must be some cut-rate twerps come to thwart your ugly ass these days, if these are your defenses!"

Magnifica continues tearing through metal as Octavia drops to one knee, her eyes turning ghostly white. "I think he's here," she says, hands on her temples. "Or something is, anyway. Its mind is a mess. *Yow.* I can't even tell if that's a person."

Magnifica quickly reduces the remaining robots to shrapnel. You search the suite and find Thorpe cowering in a bedroom, bearded, wild-eyed, and crusted with filth. He barely acknowledges your presence, muttering to himself under his breath. "Damn," Magnifica says. "He was always crazy, but like supervillain crazy, you know? Not meth-freak, Howard Hughes crazy."

From Octavia's anguished face, it's clear that trying to probe his thoughts is causing her physical pain. "Oh my God.

(continue to the next page)

He's still running the company. *He's still giving orders.* There's a whole web of directives in there . . . the names of a huge number of supervillains. I think they're all working for him."

"The attack on D.C.?" you ask. "Is that part of it?"

Thorpe lets out a screech and gathers a blanket around himself, shaking. "D.C. is just the beginning," Octavia says. "Los Angeles. Paris. Tokyo. There are attacks planned all over the planet—and it's all happening today. It's happening *right now.*"

"Aw, hell," Magnifica says. "We gotta get out there."

You're not ready to go charging off quite yet. "What's the point of it, though? What's the motivation?"

Octavia grimaces. "I don't think there is one. His higher functions are just gone. It's like his mind is a radio receiver tuned to an open frequency. Something is broadcasting to him."

"Whatever," Magnifica says. "Couldn't have happened to a nicer fella. We can figure out the whys and the wherefores after we stomp the bad guys. You know damn well those Squadron pipsqueaks won't be able to handle this on their own."

"I don't think we should dive into this until we have more answers," Octavia insists. "We need to trace the brainwaves to their source." They're both looking at you. Apparently you're in charge here?

▶ *If you agree with Magnifica that it's time for action,* **turn to page 305.**

▶ *If you think Octavia's plan to keep gathering intelligence makes more sense,* **turn to page 230.**

You're not sure how to make Agent Moretti's gadget interface with your armor, but as soon as you hold it up to your head, tiny mechanical tendrils shoot out of your helmet and suck the thing right in. Neat! You follow Moretti to the helicopter, and find that the inside is incredibly swank. You've never actually ridden in one before, but with the federal budget cuts you've read about, the last thing you expected was a wet bar. Moretti offers you a drink, which you accept gratefully. "Um, what branch of the government did you say you were with again?"

"Our department doesn't have a name. In fact, official channels will deny that we even exist." He explains that the United Nations has a long history with the Cosmic Guard, and although they try to handle Earthly affairs with local law enforcement, occasionally they're forced to ask the galactic authorities to step in.

"Now, I know you guys prefer to work solo," Moretti says. "Making split-second decisions with lives in the balance. Not having to worry about personal safety while using the power of the cosmos to singlehandedly vanquish the forces of evil. It's a lone wolf thing, and I get that. But I have to insist that you take a partner along with you on this mission."

▶ *Actually, the way he describes it, the lone wolf scenario sounds AWESOME. If you immediately decide to go that route,* **turn to page 123.**

▶ *No, Moretti is right. If you agree to partner up (if nothing else, at least to rein in the whole loose-cannon thing you've clearly got going on),* **turn to page 259.**

You've seen plenty of *Star Trek* episodes about first contact with aliens gone horribly wrong, so the last thing you want to do is rush into anything before thinking it through. So you step out of the craft with one arm raised in what you hope is some kind of universal semaphore for "We come in peace."

One of the forms approaches you, but it doesn't seem particularly aggressive. Upon closer inspection, you see that it's composed of bulbous, misshapen segments of blotchy brown and red flesh with thick, bony rods sticking out at random intervals which it uses to propel itself like giant flagella. It's as if some writer tried to come up with the grossest alien imaginable, you think. But then you're the one covered from head to toe in purple gunk. Who are you to judge?

Soon the aliens surround you completely and you feel yourself being lifted gently off the floor. In the thick brown haze you can't see whether the Ox is receiving similar treatment, but they still don't seem overly hostile, so you just go with it. Perhaps they're taking you to see their leader? After a few moments they set you down in a smaller chamber that's indistinguishable from the room you came from, and disappear through a big spiral hatch.

Once you're alone, the wall behind you opens with a rush of air and you're sucked out into the void of space.

Airlock. Yeah, that makes sense. Your purple coating holds up surprisingly well in the vacuum, but there's no way to propel yourself, so you just float listlessly until you eventually run out of oxygen. Well, you did hope to avoid a fight.

Mission accomplished, my friend.

THE END

"Magnifica, wait," you say. "There's an alien invasion that's been brewing for something like the last 25 years. And to stop it, we might need that laser cannon intact."

She looks at you, and her anger melts away. "Then it's too late already," she says. "We had plenty of muscle, but Nancy was always the brains. Without her, it's all hopeless anyway." You find it hard to believe that a woman who can punch through steel plates would put so much stock in the abilities of an ordinary, mild-mannered reporter. Suddenly, the realization hits you like a ton of bricks.

"*Nancy North was the Nightwatchman.*"

"It was the media that named her," Magnifica says. "They'd interview the villains, and we used to laugh about how every one of 'em assumed it was a man kicking their ass in a dark alley. Eventually she just went with it. Helluva secret identity."

Nancy North. Battling superpowered criminals with nothing but her wits and sheer strength of will. It's inspiring. "We have to try, Magnifica," you say. "Moretti mentioned an alien mothership. If you could sort of point the cannon in that direction . . ."

"I dunno," she says. "I can fly in space for a bit, but only as long as I can hold my breath. And I was never much good at aiming . . . never had to be, you know?" She cocks her head, thinking. "Nancy has that big-ass jet, though. We could probably strap the cannon on that thing."

It's not a bad idea. She brings you to Nancy's secret underground hangar, and you take a look around as Magnifica goes to rustle up more help. Moments later she flies in carrying two men, one under each arm.

(continue to the next page)

One of them, a stately gentleman who must be about Magnifica's age, introduces himself. "I'm Conrad," he says, "but they used to call me Mechaman. I helped Nancy upgrade the jet with that Cosmic Guardian stuff back in the '90s, but if we're going to use it against them, we'll have to take it all back out. Of course, Nancy was the genius who figured out how to make it all work—I was just the mechanic. Fortunately, I knew where to dig up my own genius. This is Tinker."

The other man is middle-aged, pudgy, and stained with grease. "Conrad, you know you can't just strip a bunch of alien electronics out of a modern aircraft and still expect it to fly."

Conrad waves a finger and a hatch pops open in the jet's fuselage. A huge turbine floats out of it and across the hangar toward him. "Trust me, I can keep this thing in the air," he says. "You just concentrate on making it spaceworthy."

After a quick jaunt into low orbit, Magnifica returns with the satellite weapon in tow. "So *this* is the death laser you were talking about," Tinker says. "You know, I think I might have designed the targeting system for this thing."

In a rush of wind, suddenly Magnifica has him by the

(continue to the next page)

throat. "You did *what*?"

"They never told me what it was for!" he says. "I thought it might be something awful, so I made it terrible on purpose—I mean, a *cranial implant beacon*? It's ridiculous."

She drops him to the floor. "You have no idea what you've done, you little runt."

Tinker drops his head into his hands. "I just get these ideas in my head," he says. "Like for a shrink ray, or a device that body-swaps a person with a mackerel, you know? I get an idea and it just consumes me. I can't stop thinking about it until I *make it real*. And you have no idea what the raw materials for a mackerel swap machine cost . . ."

Conrad puts his hand on Tinker's shoulder. "We've all done things we're not proud of," he says. "The question now is, what are you going to do to make it right?"

"No."

Magnifica is standing with her hands on her hips, facing away from you. "If you want to give that little punk the chance to redeem himself, fine. But I won't work with him. Christ, I can't even *look* at him. So you're going to have to decide who you want more in this fight—him or me."

She won't be swayed. It seems there's only room for three on this mission—should you take the world's greatest hero (retired), or the weaselly guy with the welding torch?

▶ *If you choose Magnifica,* **turn to page 278.**

▶ *If you choose Tinker,* **turn to page 86.**

The Ox might not be a bad guy to hang around with, but he *is* a supervillain. And he did rob the Union Bank of Cleveland. Besides, it looks like your new superpowers might be a bit of a letdown, and if that's the case, you're still going to need the journalism thing to fall back on. Maybe you can get an interview with a space alien!

The Guardians continue their work, bagging and tagging selected villains after they've been identified by the little guy with the tablet. It takes four of them to subdue the Ox, but eventually they cart him away. By the time they finish, the room is empty except for a single Guardian, the boss man, and a handful of confused, cowering criminals. One of them, a pudgy, forty-something man in overalls, pipes up.

"Mr. Moretti, it's me," he says. "Remember? The Tinker? I worked on that remote targeting system for you?"

The tablet computer guy seems uninterested. "He's not on the list. None of them are." He glances at you. "I don't even know who this person is." Meanwhile, you're trying to get the attention of an alien who's roughly humanoid but larger, with no head and six arms.

"Excuse me, sir! Are you a member of the interstellar peacekeeping force known as the Cosmic Guard? Can you tell me what you're doing on Earth? Would you be interested in doing an interview for ClevelandNewsExplosion.com?"

He shoots you in the face with an energy weapon, killing you instantly.

Those guys from the Cosmic Guard? Total dicks.

THE END

You're not about to take your glove's advice and power down now, particularly when you've got a two-ton criminal cowering before you. I mean, what kind of message does that send? "Tell me more about these Cosmic Guardians," you say.

Rockjockey's information seems to come mostly from rumor and innuendo. It doesn't help that he's scared out of his mind just talking to you, either—soon he's begging you just to take him into custody and get it over with. Suddenly, without warning, a volley of missiles comes out of the sky and strikes Rockjockey, knocking him to the ground. You leap backward as a volley of missiles strikes him, reducing his enormous stone form to a pile of rubble.

In the darkness it's difficult to tell if the three figures that descend are wearing the armor of the Cosmic Guard, but judging by their shapes they're definitely alien. One of them extracts Rockjockey's human body from the debris with its tentacles and stuffs it into a sack. That can't be standard procedure for an intergalactic peacekeeping force, can it?

Before you have a chance to switch on your cloaking device, you feel your boots and gauntlets decompress, and your wrist screen goes blank. Crap—did the aliens just do that? Or did the Nightwatchman cut your power remotely after issuing a final warning? Either way, you tap your touchscreen furiously, but can't get it to respond. The aliens, finished with their errand, turn their attention toward you.

And you don't fare nearly as well against their missiles as the last target did.

THE END

You've been keeping the Guardian armor a secret, but now the temptation to thwart evil is just too strong to resist. "Drinking can wait," you say. "Tonight, evil shudders in the presence of Cosmic Guardian and . . ."

"Commander Goo!" Dale finishes. "I'm still working on that. Also, I'm already a little drunk." You find a vacant alley and suit up (for Dale, that involves covering himself from head to toe in purple slime). With the Ox long gone, your best chance to root out evildoers is a quick flight to New York City, so Dale affixes himself to your back with his gunk, and you're off.

Ew. You can almost feel the stuff seeping into the cracks in your armor.

Now what? Maybe your armor has some way of detecting crime? You try to ask it, but all you get is the tinny recorded voice you heard before. *Uptown shop are hand fingers*, it says.

Not this again. Dale, however, shouts at you over the windshear. "There's a group of five villains hidden in a warehouse!"

"What? How do you get that?"

"Forget what it's saying," he says. "Listen to what it *means*." You try, and get the vague feeling that your suit is attempting to tell you something. "It says there's another one out in the harbor on a ship," Dale insists. Your friend may be far more inebriated than he's letting on. Still, it's worth a shot.

▶ *If you head toward the five theoretical villains in the warehouse,* **turn to page 139.**

▶ *If you think you're better off taking things slow, and stick with the lone one in the harbor,* **turn to page 102.**

"Gather the troops," you say. "The superheroes, the government—just call everybody. Tell them what's coming. I'm going to go try to stop it."

You're already airborne before Octavia can protest. Within moments you break through the planet's atmosphere, and a communications beacon allows you to pinpoint the alien mothership quickly. Although simply having eyes would probably allow you to pinpoint the alien mothership quickly—the thing's enormous.

You make a few passes around the craft to get your bearings, but soon spot a whole fleet of Guardians coming your way. Someone apparently got wind of your last run-in and upgraded your threat level, because from what you can tell, this is the entire army. You knock a few of them out with your reprogramming trick, but there are just too many—soon armored hands, pincers, and tentacles (one of them might even be a mouth) grab you from all sides.

Your only hope is to get out of there! You make the jump to light speed, but immediately discover that several of the Guardians who grabbed you have come along for the ride. And as you're searching your new merged consciousness to understand how your warp technology even works, they're digging into your armor and tearing pieces of that technology right out. Your entire body is torn asunder as some of its particles slow down abruptly, while others continue to travel at light speed.

Would you have fared any better if you had taken Octavia along? Unless you still have your finger stuck in that last page (don't pretend you never do it), there's no way to know.

THE END

What the hell. "I'm Sten Janssen," you say. "What's the emergency?"

Moretti shakes his head. "Things are completely falling apart," he says. Then he mutters something into a device clipped to his jacket collar that you don't quite catch. "The supervillain community is getting organized and planning something big. Plus, we have a traitor in one of the major hero teams, so I don't know who I can trust."

He pauses, looking you straight in the reflective visor. "And right now I need people I can trust. Like Sten Janssen, who I worked with for almost 15 years."

Uh, oh. "Rip this joker out of the suit, boys, and we'll get somebody dependable in it."

Before you can protest, something big rockets out of the sky and smashes you into the ground. It's another Cosmic Guardian, and it's quickly followed by two more. They must be the Guardians of distant planets, though, because they aren't shaped like people, and their understanding of human anatomy seems iffy at best. Their efforts to separate you from the armor mostly involve scooping, so your excitement at meeting actual extraterrestrial life is dampened significantly by the chunks of flesh being systematically torn from your body.

Needless to say, you don't survive the ordeal. Honesty: still the best superhero policy. You should write that down.

The End

Oh, you'll calm him down, all right. *With your fists.* "Attack!"

Magnifica charges, pummeling the Ox with a double-fisted blow that knocks him back a few steps. Even this far past her prime, she remains the Earth's most powerful hero. Of all the world's villains, however, the Ox's strength nearly matches her own, and his hide may be even tougher. Combine them with an all-consuming rage and all the advanced alien weaponry of the Cosmic Guardian, and the ensuing battle truly is one for the ages.

That's the battle between the Ox and Magnifica, you understand. Your part in it ends rather quickly, when you fire a grappling hook at him and he snatches it out of the air, pulls you in by the cable, and crushes your whole head under his armored heel with a single stomp.

THE END

You were right in thinking that your psychic adversary holds the key to defending the planet from an alien invasion—the entire blueprint for the attackers' nefarious schemes is locked away inside its mechanical mind. You were wrong, however, in thinking that you stood any chance against Cosmo the Space Dog.

As far as telepathy goes, you're a rank amateur. The alien intellect's psychic onslaught is relentless, and overwhelms your tiny brain in a matter of seconds, gutting your higher functions and leaving you little more than a vegetable. Then it detaches itself from its ancient, canine host and grafts to your physiology. It finds new uses for your superpowers as well, melting your human form down into pure goo and reassembling it into an amorphous, tentacled purple mass. It slithers off to personally supervise the Earth's destruction while somewhere, deep inside, the faintest echo of everything you once were screams out in hopeless despair.

Wow, that went to kind of a dark place.

THE END

Sure enough, you don't reach Philadelphia until some ungodly hour. The safehouse entrance is in an alleyway quite similar to the one in Cleveland—with setups like this all around the world, you have to wonder if he gets a bulk discount on fake hydraulic dumpsters. As you climb down the hatch, though, you notice that the chamber's lights are already on.

"Ha! I knew if I waited, you'd show up eventually!" Standing in the tiny room, amidst bags of trash and piles of take-out containers and fast food wrappers, you see the distinctive leather mask of Axemaster, a notoriously violent criminal. A pair of rounded, wicked-looking blades jut out from the flesh of each of his forearms. "I've spent years hunting you down, fascist pig. Prepare to face my wrath!"

What the hell, Nightwatchman? An asterisk on one list means "already talked to that villain, move on," but on another list it means "security compromised, under no circumstances go there?" You're dismayed by the inconsistency of his note taking. You don't have time to dwell on it, though, because Axemaster isn't finished spouting epithets.

"I will break you. I will cleave your ugly skull in two and flay the skin from your bones. You will lie suffering for days before I finally let you die!" Somehow, you don't think you're going to intimidate this guy with Nightwatchman's striking-fear-in-the-hearts-of-men schtick. Is there any chance he'll believe you're not the superhero he's looking for?

▶ *If you surrender and try to convince Axemaster that you're just some schmuck in a costume,* **turn to page 28.**

▶ *If you leap into action and give this madman the fight he's looking for,* **also turn to page 28.**

You decide to ally yourself with the goofy wannabe in the superhero outfit. "If we work together, we can defeat this thing!" you yell, springing into action. Granted, your best attempt at springing into action is to leap out of the alien's direct line of fire and try to analyze it for some kind of weakness. You don't see much. The Nightwatchman, meanwhile, touches a panel on the back of his glove, whereupon his entire body flickers and disappears. Whoa—if this guy's just some cosplayer, he's put some serious money into his hobby. The Cosmic Guardian, however, seems unimpressed with either of you. It bathes the alley in a blue light that neutralizes your partner's cloaking technology— you see his shimmering form hugging a brick wall across from you. He doesn't seem to be brandishing any weapons or anything. Is his idea of working together hiding until his attacker leaves?

The Guardian opens fire, incinerating him on the spot.

Holy *monkeynuts*. Wherever this thing is from, they administer a harsh brand of justice there. It immediately turns its attention to you. Apparently perturbed that its original target didn't put up much of a fight, it snatches you off the ground with its jellyfish tentacles and rips you into dozens of pieces, torching each one individually.

You, my friend, clearly picked the wrong puppy in this dogfight.

THE END

It's your first day as a superpowered government operative. Why make waves? You tell Moretti you'd just as soon let your veteran partner take command. He looks disappointed. "Well, I suppose this is for you, then," he says, handing Migraine a metal cylinder with a button on one end. "It's ONLY to be used as a last resort, you understand? I don't want a repeat of the Bogotá incident."

Bogotá, Colombia? Where a group of diplomats were recently incinerated by a mysterious, giant laser that fired from out of the clear blue sky? You glance at Migraine, who's flipping the safety latch on the trigger open and shut, grinning to himself.

"We call it the emergency satellite weapon," Moretti says, seeing the look on your face. "The Ox has been tagged with a targeting beacon, so if it comes to it, we can take him out with this. But it's plan Z. Plans A through Y involve bringing him back alive."

He leaves you and Migraine to your mission. "So, what's the plan of attack?" you ask.

"Familiarize yourself with the target," Migraine says, leading you to a small office about the size of a broom closet. He drops an oversized folder on the desk in front of you with a loud thud. "This is the Ox's file. Read it."

It's at least 500 pages thick, and it's boring as hell. As you slog through it, though, it paints an interesting picture of the villain who pummeled you earlier. His real name is Terry Oxenberger, and over the past decade he's focused mainly on robbery and extortion, leaving a huge amount of injury and property damage in his wake, but surprisingly few fatalities. Standard procedure for stopping him seems to be calling in Magnifico or Megawatt

(continue to the next page)

from the Justice Squadron (Megawatt had actually been the Ox's partner before giving up his life of crime, so there must be quite a bit of bad blood between those two).

After what must be hours—you can't get to your cellphone to check the time without removing your armor—you finish reading and track down Migraine. "Excellent," he says. "Now I'm gonna need 30 copies of that file. And the machine's kinda broken, so you'll have to hand-collate."

Clearly, this is some sort of hazing ritual, you think—light clerical work can't possibly be the best use for an armored space hero. But your protests fall on dead ears. Fine, you'll be a sport. Several mind-numbingly tedious hours later, you present Migraine with the copies.

"I like your hustle, kid," he says with a smirk. "Okay, maybe you're ready for some real work." He leads you outside the complex through a series of magnetically locked gates, and you note that the sky is pitch black. It's even later than you thought. You find yourself in a large parking lot, surrounded by an entire fleet of nondescript SUVs.

"You'll find soap and buckets over by the fence," Migraine says. "I want these vehicles to sparkle by morning."

"You're joking."

He sneers. "No. I'm your commanding officer and I'm telling you to wash the goddamn cars. That's an order."

Is this a test? Is he just pushing you to see how much crap you'll take? Or is it some sort of team-building trust exercise? If so, it's a truly awful one.

▶ *If you suck it up and grab a bucket,* **turn to page 292.**

▶ *If you put your foot down and refuse,* **turn to page 191.**

You're pretty tired, seeing as how you've been up all night learning about your space armor and trying to get Windows to run on alien hardware, but right now battling a bunch of supervillains sounds like just what you need to clear your head. What's the worst that could happen?

In two words: Lightning Queen. She's a notoriously unhinged criminal with the power to control electricity at her fingertips. And as soon as she sees you flying into Washington's downtown core, she calls down a bolt of lightning that knocks you right out of the clear blue sky.

"Come for a rematch, have you?" she says as you skid across the pavement to her feet. "Guess you're not so tough when there's only one of you! Where's your partner?" You have no idea what she's talking about. "Oh, that's right, I fried him, didn't I?"

The battlesuit isn't responding to your commands, and soon a second bolt hits you square in the chest. This one really hurts. "I fried him just like I promised I'd fry you if I ever laid eyes on you again, alien swine!"

Then the third bolt hits, and you're done for. "Fry, swine, fry!" Lightning Queen says. Then she laughs at the connotation.

"Hey, guys!" she yells gleefully to her cohorts. "I'm making alien bacon!"

THE END

You're just not comfortable leaving Nightwatchman's jet in the hands of someone who might at any moment pass out vomiting. Granted, you're not sure what help he'll be on the ground, either, but Chuck insists, and Obie obviously doesn't want to let his old mentor down. "You two go," Chuck says, disappointed. "I'll provide air support. This thing still has missiles, right?"

Your computer indicates that the suit's glider is easily strong enough to carry two, and Ocean Boy can't possibly weigh more than 120 pounds, so you take him securely in your arms and make the leap.

And that's when the trouble begins.

The truth is, before last night Ocean Boy hadn't left the confines of the Pacific Ocean in nearly 15 years, and despite putting on a brave face for HT, the sensation of falling induces full-blown panic. He starts screaming and clawing wildly, and the little guy is much stronger than he appears. You immediately lose control, plummeting frantically toward the ground.

This is normally the part where we'd give you the choice to attempt to calm him down and pull out of the tailspin together, or just drop his ass to save yourself. But we're going to spare you the trouble here—his panic attack has already irreparably damaged your glider, and at this point it's essentially a choice between a noble death trying to save your passenger, or ditching his dead weight and falling to your doom alone.

Feel free to do some soul-searching and decide which route you honestly would have gone. We'll give you the benefit of the doubt on this one.

THE END

It turns out there's no negotiating with this group. They're out for blood, and a random assortment of nine of New York's mightiest heroes against the lone, long-retired Magnifica makes for just about an even fight. You're not about to let her face them alone, though. Most fans think Nightwatchman's fancy gadgets and astronomical wealth are his true assets, while others insist it's the fear he inspires in the hearts of criminals. In fact, Nightwatchman's *true* superpower is tactical genius and a brilliant analytical mind.

And you, my friend, are no Nightwatchman. If you were, you'd know never to face a bloodthirsty mob of superheroes head-on. They don't know you aren't the genuine article, though, and divide their numbers to attack you and Magnifica simultaneously. Thanks to the distraction you provide, your partner is able to make short work of her attackers.

You, on the other hand, are murdered four different ways within five seconds. Once she's finished the first group, Magnifica comes down on your killers like the hammer of god, but it's too late for you. Your selfless sacrifice has saved her life, though—left to her own devices, will she be able to unravel Crexidyne's sinister plot and save the world?

You'll never know.

THE END

You've already had a long day of reading reports and collating documents, and you'll be damned if you're going to spend all night washing cars. "You know what? I changed my mind," you say. "As of right now, I'm taking command of this mission."

Migraine pulls the little metal cylinder from his pocket and flips open the safety cover. "I told you where the buckets were," he says. "Now get started."

"Or what? You'll blow up the Ox by remote control?"

"It's not set for the tracking beacon we planted in the Ox," he says, grinning. "It's set for the one we planted in *you*."

You let that sink in for a moment. "The mission was never to bring him in at all, was it?"

"No, the mission was to find out if you're worth a damn, and guess what? Mission's over."

Crap. Should you try to take Migraine out? Or make a run for it? You have no idea if your battlesuit can fly fast enough to outrun an orbital death laser.

Migraine chuckles and puts the device back in his pocket. "Relax, I'm not going to pull the trigger. You realize that thing costs like a hundred million dollars every time we fire it, right? Moretti would kill me."

Something inside your helmet explodes, vaporizing a large section of your cranium and killing you instantly.

"The bomb inside your comlink, though, runs about 40 bucks."

THE END

You have to admit that, for a moment, it feels really good just to let those missiles fly. Then you look at the charred remains of Mrs. Pinkett standing outside next to the mailboxes and are instantly horrified at what you've done. You just straight up murdered a lady. You panic for a few minutes, then decide to flee the scene. But the moment you launch into the air, something slams you right back down onto the cement walkway. It feels as if weights are pressing down on every inch of your body. You can't see much with your face pressed against the ground, but you hear a woman's voice somewhere to the left of you.

"We have a rogue Guardian," she says. "I repeat: the Cosmic Guardian has gone rogue." Oh, no. That would be Gravity Bomb of the Justice Squadron. And a moment later she's joined by a second voice.

"Cosmic Guardian," the voice booms. That would be Magnifico, the Justice Squadron's leader. "Missing for 15 years, and now you show up killing old ladies? *Tsk*—you should know better than that." You try to speak, but it's difficult with your personal gravity increased a hundredfold. Plus, you can't deny that you *did* go somewhat rogue.

"After all," Magnifico continues, "you were the one who made sure we'd have a way to neutralize each Squadron member in case anyone went broken arrow." You feel something clamp onto your back, and suddenly an electrical shock shorts out your armor. "I just never thought it would be you."

As the suit shuts down, the automatic force field that was keeping the increased gravity from smooshing your body into a fine pulp shuts down with it.

"I always kind of hoped it would be, though."

THE END

You're certain you're going to regret this.

"We'll meet in an hour on Liberty Island," Magnifica says, pushing a button on her ring and grinning from ear to ear. "We used to have a secret base under that big damn statue, you know. C'mon, let's go fetch your airplane."

Octavia is cradling Mr. Patel's hands in her own, her gaze locked on his. "It's time to let go of Barkley, Mr. Patel," she says gently.

"Jesus, buy the poor bastard a puppy or something and let's go," Magnifica says. "We've got places to be."

Octavia opts to bring Cosmo with her—the thing utterly weirds you out, but she thinks she can glean further information from it, and you can't really argue with that. After a quick,

(continue to the next page)

gut wrenching trip back to the farm, you and Octavia fly the jet to Liberty Island. By the time you arrive, Magnifica has already shooed away the tourist crowd and is greeting the Human Torpedo as he arrives on the shore. He's an enormous, barrel-chested man with a thick gray beard. Saltwater living seems to have been good to him.

"Chuck! How've you been? How's Ocean Boy?"

"He's good—I just saw him yesterday. In fact, we were out late drinking, and I have the headache to prove it."

Magnifica scowls. "So you're his drinking buddy now? *This* is how you look after him?"

"He's 32 years old, Maggie! And I'm not his father —if you care so much, maybe pay him a visit yourself every once in a while."

You spot two figures floating across the channel toward the island. No, make that three: as they land, you can see that the one providing transport is Princess Pixie (although you're not certain that moniker suits a woman in her sixties, even if she's ten inches tall with fairy wings). The other two are a thin, hunched-over man with a cane and an oversized lady in a wheelchair. That would be Mechaman, you assume, minus his transformable battle gear. He looks more ready for a family reunion than a firefight. And the woman must be . . .

"Old friends make Tank happy! Tank no smash old friends!"

Tina the Tank. That's not dementia setting in or anything —from what you've read, she was pretty much like that in the 1970s as well. The wheelchair is new.

Meanwhile, the argument between Magnifica and the Torpedo has become more heated, and the others begin to

(continue to the next page)

bicker as well. Octavia's eyes are locked with Mechaman's, and the tiny Pixie is gesticulating wildly at Tina the Tank. You can feel the passion growing, and you're sure that they're all on the brink of making out. *Seriously?* Convoluted romantic history may come with the superhero territory, but you don't have time for this. You interrupt as loudly as possible. "Hello! People? Is this everyone?"

Torpedo tears himself away from Magnifica's stare. "Tachyon's still in a coma," he says. "Dogstar and Maximus are still dead. If you're what passes for Nightwatchman these days, then that's it."

Magnifica quickly explains the situation, then turns to you. "Okay, what now?"

It appears that you really are in charge—Magnifica seems to think so, anyway, and none of the others challenge her. You survey your troops, and swallow hard. Most of their files came up under "maybe" in your trustworthiness index (Human Torpedo actually earned an almost-unprecedented "probably, I guess"), so that's one vote of confidence, you suppose. The aliens have set up shop at the planet's poles, and you had intended to split into groups and mount attacks on each simultaneously, but you're not sure you have the manpower to be dividing your forces. On the other hand, Octavia has been picking the dog-creature's brain and believes that time is of the absolute essence—if one terraforming machine goes online while you concentrate on the other, the world will still end, just a little more slowly.

▶ *If you split into two teams,* **turn to page 108.**

▶ *If you take a unified force and hit the poles one at a time,* **turn to page 282.**

"No," you say. And it takes all of your strength just to say it. "It has to be Dale." As soon as you've made up your mind, the suit leaps off the floor, reconfiguring from suitcase to space armor in midair and wrapping itself around your friend. He gives you a quick salute and takes flight, bursting through his apartment's front window in the process.

"Wow," Melah says. "Listen, I've got to round up some other heroes to meet Nightwatchman and Maggie at the pole . . ." She trails off, suddenly realizing that *you aren't a part of this any more.* "Hey, I'll check back in when it's over. Wish me luck, okay?" Then she's gone. You putter around for a while, and eventually head home to make yourself some lunch. The world doesn't end, so that's good news at least.

It's another week before you see either of them again—Dale did destroy the second tower, but then had the entire Cosmic Guard to battle, and a whole mess of garden-variety villains and heroes as well. The thing is, while stopping the invasion, he somehow managed to graft himself genetically to the battlesuit, merging with it to become a single organism.

There's no getting it back from him now.

Melah goes on to take over for a retiring Nightwatchman, and Dale becomes the mightiest of Earth's new generation of heroes—a malleable, amorphous blob inside a robotic exo-skeleton that instantly reshapes itself to any form he stretches himself into.

And you go back to unemployment. You would have sac-rificed your life to save the world, and in a way you did. That makes you the real hero, doesn't it?

Doesn't it?

THE END

Half by instinct and half by blind panic, your entire body melts from bone and flesh to purple supergoo. Everything changes. It's as if time slows down, and you find that you have complete control of every molecule in your squishy body. Your senses are amplified tenfold, even without proper eyes or ears, and your awareness is distributed equally in every molecule. You form yourself into a streamlined shell around the battle-suit—a living, purple skin over a half-alive mechanical one, over a very dead, charred organic lump—and watch in awe as you break into orbit and approach an enormous spacecraft, easily the size of downtown Cleveland. From giant hangar doors, two cylindrical structures are being prepared for launch by miscellaneously-shaped figures in Guardian armor. You realize that this equipment can have only one purpose: the terraforming of Earth is about to begin.

Somehow, you have to stop it. At the rear of the vessel you spot several mammoth exhaust vents big enough to house office buildings. If exhaust can get out, perhaps you can get in. If those vents lead to an engine room, maybe you could get to it and blow the entire craft to smithereens, stopping the invasion in one fell swoop.

As final acts of desperation go, it's not a bad plan. You can't help wondering, though, if you might be able to come up with something a little less, you know, suicidal.

▶ *If you embrace the kamikaze thing and head for the exhaust ports,* **turn to page 82.**

▶ *If you go toward the hangar bays instead, hoping to formulate a plan that involves marginally less risk of personal explosion,* **turn to page 241.**

Moretti ushers you into an elevator, taking you on a lengthy and incredibly dull tour of Crexidyne's top-secret basement levels. You begin to suspect that he's stalling for time. Fortunately, you're doing the same thing—you just hope that diverting Moretti's attention constitutes a big enough distraction to keep any heat off Nightwatch. After ten minutes, a message from her pops up on your display: GOT WHAT I NEED. MEET YOU BACK IN CLEVELAND.

Whew! The tour, however, just keeps going on and on. You eventually wind up in a big conference room with a huge flat-panel TV that covers one entire wall, and Moretti gets down to business. "I've been focused chiefly on one initiative during my time here at Crexidyne," he says, clicking a tiny remote control. The screen flickers on to show schematics of what appears to be a satellite with a giant cannon attached to it.

"Well, two initiatives, really, but the other's not important right now. This is something we like to call the orbital death laser," he says, beaming. "Instant disintegration of any human being on the planet at the flick of a switch. Its only limitation is that we need to plant a tracking device in the target beforehand in order to aim it properly.

"You mean *they* need to plant a tracking device," you say.

"Sure, whatever."

Yeah, he's definitely lying about the government mole business. "So what is it that you need from me?" you ask carefully.

"Nothing," Moretti replies with a grin. "Just that you putter around with me for a bit while we plant the device in your glowy-eyed little friend."

You tense up, balls of blue energy immediately forming in

(continue to the next page)

the palms of your hands. "Oh, it's too late for all that," Moretti says, pulling a small metal cylinder with a button from his jacket pocket. "One of my operatives is a member of your little superpowered fraternity, and he planted the tracker inside her cranium half an hour ago. Then he caught a ride to her rendezvous with that horrible newslady. She's been a pain in Mr. Thorpe's ass for decades, and our man is placing a second device in her brain as we speak. Not that it really matters—your friends are currently together in the same room, so if I push this button, they'll both fry."

You fire blasts from both gauntlets at Moretti, but the energy hits some kind of invisible shield two feet in front of him and dissipates. So you lunge at him, but you bounce right off the force field as well. "Please," he says. "I have 300 aliens in suits like that doing manual labor on my roof. You don't think we've worked out defenses already?" He flips open the safety on his trigger mechanism.

"What do you want?"

"I want you to give up the armor. All you need to do is make the decision to disengage, and the telepathic control system will break its bond with your consciousness and release itself from your control." Now he's gently rubbing the button with his thumb, his eyes a bit wild. "Do it now. And don't bluff me on this, either. I'll know if you're lying."

He means it. Also, you officially suck at diversions. "Okay, I'll do it!" you say. "Just don't kill them."

▶ *If you're telling the truth,* **turn to page 287.**

▶ *If you're just trying to buy a little time until you can figure something else out,* **turn to page 52.**

Remember yesterday, when climbing a ladder to follow the Nightwatchman in Cleveland was almost too much physical exertion for one day? If you think the sedentary life of a newspaper reporter has done anything to prepare you for unarmed combat with a pair of supervillains, you're sadly mistaken. You had hoped to use your superior cunning to outwit them, but Jekyll and Hyde only have orders to bring in Nancy. That makes you collateral damage, and Hyde gleefully rips your throat out with one clawed hand the moment you utter a single defiant peep.

In the meantime, Nancy knees her attacker in the groin and uses the inertia of his collapsing frame to throw him over her shoulder and back through the dimensional portal in one deft move. Wow—Nancy North is kind of a badass. If you'd known her at all, there would have been a third option just to back away from the villains and let her rescue herself. You were caught up in the whole damsel in distress thing, though. Don't blame yourself—blame the persistent gender bias ubiquitous in traditional media.

It only takes Nancy a moment to incapacitate her second attacker, but you're a pretty fast bleeder. She's too late to save you.

THE END

"Oh, there was this costume party thing tonight," you say. "I don't usually dress like this. Also, that guy over there forgot his bike."

"Of course he did," Magnifico says. He looks like he's about to pat you on the head, but takes a closer look at the texture of your outfit and has second thoughts. "Here, why don't I sign you an autograph? Got a pen?"

You don't, and to be honest you'd just as soon end what has turned into a fairly humiliating experience. "That's all right," you say. "I know you're busy—you probably need to go help those Cosmic Guardians beat up Lightning Queen."

He pauses. "Oh, you saw that, did you?"

"Yeah, two Guardians! Exciting stuff. Listen, though, I gotta go . . . ."

"That's unfortunate," Magnifico says. Then he casually reaches out with both hands and squishes your head into mush. The head in question dissolves into purple goop, which, frankly, freaks him the hell out. So he keeps squishing and pounding until your entire body is paste. Then he surveys the various purple puddles of you and quickly gathers them up into individual containers. Then he takes those containers back to Squadron headquarters and evaporates each of them with his heat vision.

It turns out Magnifico is a pretty paranoid guy. And he didn't become the world's most famous superhero by doing stuff half-assed.

THE END

You haul ass back the way you came, rocketing through the corridors and out the front gate. It wasn't your fault! And besides, how much do you even *know* about the Cosmic Guard? All you can say for sure is that right now they're freaking you out.

For good reason, too. A blast of white-hot plasma glances off you, fusing some of the plates on your left arm together. They're in pursuit! *Get me to safety!* you think. Evasive maneuvers aren't really your strong point, but maybe your suit's automated systems can do better? The ground beneath you turns to a brown and black blur, replaced by a blue and green one as you plunge into a deep body of water. You dive for a few moments, but then another plasma bolt hits you square in the back. *Safer than that!* you think.

With a pop everything goes white, and you feel nothing at all for several minutes. When your senses return, you find yourself floating above a vast, ringed planet that must be Saturn. For a moment you're mesmerized by its beauty, but suddenly the other Guardians start popping out of hyperspace all around you, weapons blazing. *Safer!* you think. *Just keep running!* The white nothingness returns, and this time it doesn't abate at all. You slowly drift into a deep slumber.

You sleep for a very, very, *very* long time.

* * * * *

Welcome back, a cheerful voice says inside your head. *I've been waiting for this day.* You know the muddled, groggy feeling you get when you've slept too much? You have that, like, times

(continue to the next page)

a hundred. You open your eyes and see nothing but the vast, star-speckled expanse of space. Where are you?

The Andromeda Galaxy, the voice answers. *Two and a half million years from home at the speed of light. The invasion that conquered Earth was just one tendril of a much larger threat spreading throughout the Milky Way. This was the only way you'd be truly safe.*

Two and a half million years. To put that in perspective, when you left Earth modern humans had only been on it for a tenth of that time. There's no going back. Whatever happened back there happened without you.

If your battlesuit seems oddly chipper, you have to remember that it's had a whole lot longer to mourn humanity than you have. It's had ample time to plumb the depths of your consciousness and perfect your psychic bond as well. *So what should we do now?* it thinks, almost giddy. *Chart out this new galaxy? Search for an inhabitable planet?*

What indeed? You're still trying to wrap your mind around this. *Oh, and one other thing,* the voice says. *I'd like to introduce you to someone. This will take a little getting used to, but meet your most recent clone.*

"'Sup," says a shockingly familiar voice, this time through the speaker in your helmet.

The good news is, whatever you decide to do next, you've got your whole life ahead of you to do it. And at least you won't be doing it alone.

THE END

Whatever is in that computer, it's not worth losing your life over. "Let's get out of here," you say.

Magnifica grabs hold of you, and after another horrifying flight sets you down on top of a two story building in some chilly, rural town. "Where are we?" you ask.

"I dunno—somewhere in the middle of Manitoba, Canada," she says. "It was the most remote craphole I could think of. Whatever's going on, it's a lot bigger than I thought. I gotta go check on some friends—will you be okay by yourself for a little while?"

"Sure," you say. Hmm. They don't speak French in Manitoba, do they? "I've got plenty of research I can do from here. I'll be fine—there's no way anyone could find me all the way out in the middle of nowhere, anyway."

Actually, they can. And they do. Soon after Magnifica leaves, you're trying to find a way down from your rooftop perch when a shadow falls over you. A flock of something is flying overhead that's so dense it blocks out the sun. Is it a big-ass gang of Canada Geese? As the formation gets closer, you realize they're much too large to be birds. There's no way they could be aircraft, though—not flying that close together. Wait a minute. They couldn't possibly be—

They all open fire on you simultaneously, whatever they are. Which is kind of overkill, since the very first blue energy bolt that strikes you is enough to wipe you off the face of the Earth.

THE END

Okay, killing Mrs. Pinkett isn't an option. You try to interrupt her call, but she's already reached an operator. She clearly has the Cleveland Police Department on speed dial. "I'd like to report that my neighbor has a giant robot suit. Yes, it's Clara Pinkett. It *is too* an emergency!"

You go back inside, shut the door behind you, and try to tune out her breathless efforts to reach various network news channels. You decide that Mrs. Pinkett isn't going to convince anyone of anything other than a questionable grip on sanity, and get back to your research. Before long, though, a new reference to the Cosmic Guardian pops up on some gossip blog. Sure enough, the post is about a woman in Cleveland who insists that her next-door-neighbor has been flying around in a suit that fits the description of the long-vanished hero.

It goes viral. Within minutes it's all over the internet, and one site even publishes your address and apartment number. You're staring in disbelief at a picture of yourself on the screen from your middle school yearbook when you hear another knock. *Crap!* You holler something about being right there and hurry to get out of your armor. It takes what feels like forever, but you finally get the suit stuffed into a closet and answer the door, half expecting to find a television news crew outside.

What you find instead are more than a hundred alien beings, decked out in full Cosmic Guardian armor, waiting patiently. You gasp. Before your mind can even process what you're seeing, they each raise a hand (or, in several cases, a weird alien appendage) and burn you to a crisp with a blast of energy.

Good job keeping it secret, champ.

THE END

Tinker has Suong open up one portal to Earth and another to deep space—the vacuum pulls poison gas out into the void and sucks in clean air to replace it. The ship is so massive that it will take months to clear it with this method, but you're able to seal off various sections and take it one chamber at a time. After that, a large collection of potted plants should keep the carbon dioxide-to-oxygen ratio steady.

Through the foggy portal to Earth, you find you have a different sort of vacuum to contend with. Most of the planet's superpowered beings have been recruited by Crexidyne, but they seem to have had some sudden vacancies within their upper management, so various factions within the organization are struggling to assert control.

Meanwhile, an odd assortment of heroes and villains has come together under Nightwatchman to keep the peace, and what's left of the Cosmic Guard is being led by the Earth's Cosmic Guardian, theoretically to further the greater good, but in practice often to disastrous ends. Without strict orders from their alien overlords, it turns out those things are *nuts*. It all means that power structures have been upended, leaving room for someone with a little imagination, a group of willing minions, and an iron will to swoop in and take charge.

Wait 'til they get a load of you.

THE END

You switch on your equipment, activate your glider, and throw up your cloaking device for good measure—Moretti literally doesn't know what hits him when you charge and break through his office window, dragging him out over the building's ledge. You sail effortlessly over the New York City streets to your meeting place with Nancy. Touchdown is a bit rougher than you intended, but you try to play it off like landing on top of Moretti in a big tangle was your intention all along.

"That's right," he says as you shut down your gear and stumble to your feet. "They'll be looking for you now. Turn your suit back on, just for one second. I *dare* you. You'll be dead in a heartbeat."

Nancy enters, and Moretti's seething anger quickly turns to open rage. "You! I should have known. You've been a thorn in my side for far too long, North. You will burn. Do you understand me? *Burn.*"

It's nice that non-superpowered scumbags can have archenemies as well, you think. And it makes sense that Nancy would be his—over the years, her investigations have surely cost Crexidyne billions. If Nancy is pleased to have gotten so far under his skin, though, it doesn't show on her face. In fact, the icy steel of her gaze is mildly terrifying, even to you. "Why did Thorpe order Brain Stem's murder?" she asks. It sounds more like a command than a question.

Moretti sneers. "Reginald Thorpe is a genius—his brilliance has long since transcended day-to-day operations. It's my duty to interpret his visions and attempt to make them a reality. So that particular order came from me."

"Tell me why."

(continue to the next page)

"Always focusing on the details," he scoffs, "and missing the big picture staring you right in the face. The question isn't why we killed him. It's why we *created* him. Why we created any of them."

Moretti tells you that every single human being to gain superpowers since the the mid-'80s—heroes and villains alike—has been the result of experiments conducted by Crexidyne. They would abduct strangers off the streets and strike a bargain: powers far beyond those of mortal men in exchange for loyalty to Thorpe, and a promise to help take over the world when the time came. The idea was that anyone willing to make such a bargain would suit Crexidyne's purposes, and anyone unwilling had their memory of the incident erased and was given a dose of pancreatic cancer as a lovely parting gift.

"How do you give a person pancreatic cancer?" you ask. It may not be the most relevant detail, but the prospect of it horrifies you, and you just sort of blurt it out.

Moretti pauses, staring at you like you're beneath his contempt. "We have a tiny little man who shrinks down and personally delivers it to your pancreas." With all his talk of superpowers, you can't be sure if he's serious or if he's just being a dick.

Nancy's thoughts, however, are elsewhere. "You couldn't possibly have kept all this a secret," she says. "Someone would have talked."

"Oh, we wiped the memories of the successful recruits as well—those who survived. We left them to their own devices. Some turned to crime, and the more narcissistic among them imagined themselves heroes, basking in the adoration of the

(continue to the next page)

masses. We were confident that eventually restoring memories of the bargain—and the knowledge that we could relieve them of their precious superpowers any time we chose—would keep them in line when the moment came."

"So why kill Brain Stem?" Nancy demands. "Why now?"

"We always had the technology to mindwipe them," Moretti answers, "but his psychic abilities made the process much simpler. However, the little bastard had . . . *ambitions.* So we kept erasing his memories and rebriefing him whenever we had need of his talents. Eventually the repeated wipes took a toll on his mind, and he became useless to us. But he kept using those damn powers to dig for his lost memories. Finally we had to activate one of our more reliable agents to put him down for good."

Something about his story is bugging you. "He's lying. Why would he even tell us all this if it were true?"

"Because it's too late," Nancy says. "He knows he's already dead. I can see it in his eyes."

Supervillains often spill every detail of their nefarious plots to heroes they have in their clutches, but you're pretty sure the habit comes from an unconscious desire to fail, or just garden-variety stupidity. If Moretti truly has accomplished everything he's claiming, he can't possibly suffer from either of those. Is he stalling for time? Nancy, so close to answers she's been seeking for decades, insists on continuing the interrogation.

▶ *If you trust her judgment and hear Moretti out,* **turn to page 157.**

▶ *If you think you're only playing into his hands and walk away,* **turn to page 242.**

Really? You've come all this way, uncovered the alien plot, witnessed Nancy North's untimely death, built a spaceship out of a supersonic jet, and when finally called upon to do something truly heroic, you opt instead to save your own skin? Seriously, we were so sure you'd make the other call we almost didn't bother to put a choice in there.

And don't give us that "I was just checking this page to see what would happen" business either—you were checking the cowardly route to *see if you could get away with it*. Guess what? You can't. The mothership survives and throws a wave of 6,000 Cosmic Guardians at you, who disintegrate your jet on the spot. And don't try flipping back to the previous page and choosing the other path, either. You go right back and start over at the beginning.

You go back, and you think about what you've done.

THE END

Do they think you stole Jannsen's armor? "He totally gave it to me!" you shout through your loudspeaker. Then it occurs to you that they probably don't even speak English. But your armor can translate! You tell it to explain what happened to the rest of the Guard.

You swell upward and you support, it says. You can't actually determine if it's speaking to the other Guardians or to you. *Is assimilated this persona this duration completely, function immediately of verb the internal duration.*

Translation: not your armor's strongest suit. The blasts keep coming. Your visual display crackles back to life, so you use the opportunity to start your descent—you're afraid their continued attacks will short out your suit completely, and if that happens, you'd rather not be 10,000 feet in the air. However, they appear to interpret your actions as a hostile maneuver. A Guardian charges you, smacking you with several tentacles, and you lose control, plunging toward solid ground. You're cooperating, dammit! If they would give you some instructions, you'd be happy to comply. You start yelling commands to your battlesuit. "Open up a communications channel or something so I can talk to them!"

You right yourself just before impact, but then another Guardian slams you into the earth—your suit absorbs much of the impact, but it still knocks the wind out of you. You hear a click, finally receiving a transmission from your attackers.

"DESTROY ALL HUMANS."

Oh. You have to admit that you didn't see that coming. Your visor shorts out again, so you don't see the final blows that pummel the life out of you, either.

The End

We're just going to tell you straight up: this will end badly. You hobble out to the street and catch a bus back to the bar where your car is still parked, and it's past noon before you even manage to get out of Cleveland. You keep tabs on the situation in D.C. via news radio, and it's getting worse: a second group of villains soon joins in on the fun, and when the Justice Squadron finally does show up, instead of battling their foes, they jump right in on the monumental demolition.

Similar reports start coming in from all over the globe— heroes and villains joined together, destroying landmarks and national monuments, apparently just for kicks. The governments of the world send in their various armies, but they're ill-prepared to deal with the combined might of the planet's superpowered beings. As for you, it's a good seven-hour trip to the capital, and you haven't even reached Maryland when you see a putrid-looking brown smoke roll in over the hills.

Ew—you roll up your windows, but it gets in through the vents. And this isn't just your run-of-the-mill southern Pennsylvania smog. It's poison gas, and it's everywhere. You're dead in minutes.

Poison gas? That just isn't sporting.

THE END

Given the choice, you'd prefer to save the planet with as little murdering as possible. Octavia starts linking your mind with the approaching Guardians. Wait for it . . . wait for it . . .

Brain blast! You transmit the reprogramming protocol to the entirety of the Cosmic Guard and, suddenly confronted with the unfiltered anguish of their long-suffering hosts, they all shut down at once. But the psychic backlash of all that pain and suffering is too much for your system to handle. You black out along with the others.

When you eventually awaken, it's to the sound of Octavia's gentle sobbing in your head. You can't be sure how long you've been out, but you gaze down to the planet beneath you and instantly know that something's wrong. The blue and white swirls you admired on your first trip to space yesterday are now tinted with a deep, sickly brown.

They did it. They totally destroyed the world.

All around you, your fellow Guardians float listlessly. Their mechanical halves are focused almost entirely on comforting and tranquilizing their newly-empowered organic halves. After a lifetime of following directives, the host minds are eager for someone to tell them what to do—overall, they're a mess, but the common threads are pain, rage, and an overpowering desire for revenge on whatever power is responsible for their seemingly endless suffering.

You have a pretty good idea how to give it to them.

At this point, your own grief and anger is at least equal to that of your fellow Guardians, and when you start transmitting orders to them, they follow you without hesitation. You discover that two major alien settlements have been established

(continue to the next page)

around the huge terraforming stations erected at the Earth's North and South Poles. These are scientists and technicians, beginning the task of awakening the mothership's passengers for colonization after their perfect coup. Your Guardian army falls upon them like the hammer of god. They started the job of destroying every living thing on the planet, but within minutes, you finish it.

Wait, Octavia thinks after the last bits of alien encampment have been reduced to rubble. *Someone's still out there. I can sense it.* She directs you to New York City—or New Jersey, technically —and a secret base beneath Liberty Island. There you discover an unexpected pair: the Human Torpedo and a very old, very sick woman who you think might be Magnifica. They're both long-retired heroes and members of Octavia's old team, the Liberty Patrol.

After an emergency decontamination process, you let Octavia out of the backpack pod, and the Torpedo fills you in on the past day's events. "The air turned poison first, and people just dropped dead. There was no saving them. I can hold my breath for a long time, but most people . . ." He trails off. "Maggie wouldn't give up. She kept going back out to look for survivors, but never found any. They're all dead, Octavia."

"Not all of them," she says, her eyes closed. "There are scattered groups, all over the globe. An underground bunker in Japan. A bio-dome research project in deepest Canada. The alien attackers are gone. If we all work together, we can find a way to rebuild here."

Octavia can still read your thoughts, though. "Don't even consider it," she says. "The planet has never needed its protector

(continue to the next page)

more than it does now."

Your mind, however, is made up. "There's a backup battle-suit under the Pacific Ocean. I'll make sure it's programmed right, and then you can stick anyone in there—you'll have your Cosmic Guardian."

The Torpedo nods. "So that's what that place is—I was just there last night." His eyes light up with what's certainly the first glimmer of hope he's felt today. "In fact, if he's still safe down there, I know just the hero for the job."

Your concerns lie elsewhere. After a few days' preparation, you gather your raving, bloodthirsty troops and head for the stars. The enemy is still out there, spreading like a plague throughout the galaxy. You jump to light speed, your armor's intelligence taking the reins as your biological mind slips into suspended animation.

You plan to make them suffer.

THE END

The needs of the many, apparently, don't outweigh the needs of you. You sprint for the pod that brought you here, waiting just long enough for Ox to join you before hitting the big red button to launch the craft. Which is actually fairly magnanimous, when you think about it, considering you're already risking literally billions of lives in an effort to save your own hide. You rocket from the launch bay, and moments later the mothership jumps to light speed, back from whence it came.

As your craft travels toward Earth, you can't shake the sinking feeling in the pit of your stomach. Things might turn out fine, right? Once you get back, you'll marshal all of the planet's resources and fight off the alien invasion properly. Heroes and villains, united against a common enemy! The combined military might of every nation! Random alcoholics in crop dusters! There's still hope. How quickly could the Cosmic Guardians possibly get that enormous starship back on course?

Turns out: pretty quickly. About six minutes into your trip, the pod is rocked by explosions as the alien mothership overtakes it, sending you and your companion to your immediate, excruciatingly painful doom.

All of humanity soon follows.

THE END

Magnifica doesn't need much encouraging—you've barely said two words to her when she takes off like a rocket to hunt down and destroy the satellite. A second blast never comes, so from what you can gather she's successful. However, she doesn't come back. Is she off battling Cosmic Guardians alone? Rounding up the heroes of yesteryear for a dramatic final stand? You didn't actually get the chance to tell her about the alien plot, so for all you know she retreated to a secluded mountaintop somewhere to mourn. Clearly she and Nancy were close.

That leaves you in a bit of a tough spot. Are there ways to stop the invasion without the aid of an Orbital Death Laser or the world's mightiest hero? Sure, but at this stage they pretty much require all the resources of the Nightwatchman. If you so much as power up your wrist computer, the Guardians will pinpoint your location immediately and hit you with enough plasma bolts to kill you ten times before you hit the floor.

So you're relegated to making phone calls, warning friends and various public officials of the impending invasion. This results in quite a bit of panic (either about the fate of the world or your personal well-being, depending on each recipient's assessment of your sanity), but very little action.

When the poison gas starts rolling in late in the afternoon, you know that it was all for naught.

The End

It's a two-hour drive to Connecticut, and during that time things go from bad to worse. Cities across the planet are in supervillain chaos, and then the heroes show up, but only join in the destruction. Governments are marshaling their military forces, but you find precious little news about the blackouts. You worry that whatever's causing them is spreading so quickly that by the time it overtakes a region, there's no one left to file a report.

The hospital staff is glued to the cable news channel and seems quite flustered by the day's events, so the charge nurse doesn't give you any trouble. "He's the same as he always is," she says as she shows you to Tachyon's room. You've left your Nightwatchman gear in the car, of course. "He still wakes up for a couple of minutes every few months, disoriented. Asks what day is it, what year is it. The weird thing is, his vital signs never change, even when he seems lucid." She shrugs. "Oh, and occasionally he'll ask how the Canucks are doing, but I don't actually know what that means."

He looks impossibly old and frail. You remember seeing photos taken when he was active in the '60s and '70s, and he wasn't a particularly young man even then. As soon as the nurse leaves the room, however, his eyes pop open.

"I thought she'd never leave."

Tachyon! You can't believe your good fortune. Could it actually be possible to change the past?

"Aliens are attacking," you say. How can you explain this quickly? "I think they're poisoning the planet—you have to go back in time and stop them!"

"So today is the day," he says slowly. "I've spent a lifetime

(continue to the next page)

gathering information, and finally it has come to pass."

"You knew? Why didn't you do anything?"

"There's still time. There's always time. What do we know about the aliens' plan?"

You think for a moment. "We know that they've been here for years. That they're responsible for the current crop of heroes and villains."

"Not just the current ones," Tachyon says. "Poor Dogstar. They had already destroyed his homeworld, so he came here to warn us of the alien probe that might one day come, heralding our doom. He was too late. The probe was a testing unit, sent to determine how Earth's biology would react to their mutagens. Maggie and Charles and the rest of us—we were the result of those tests. By the time Dogstar arrived, that probe was already making the return trip to report its findings."

"So first they turn us into superheroes, and then forty years later they come back and poison us all? That doesn't make any sense."

"The first trip was just for reconnaissance. After that, they sent the Cosmic Guardian. Or the Guardian armor, rather—it bonded with the human Sten Jannsen and set up research facilities to gather data the aliens would need to terraform our planet. As we speak, they're transforming it into an ecosystem that can support them—the destruction of all pre-existing life is simply a side effect."

"But why keep manufacturing superheroes?" The pieces still don't quite seem to fit. "What's the point of creating the Justice Squadron and all the rest?"

"I was never sure of that myself. But I think now we have

(continue to the next page)

our answer." He gestures to the television news blaring from down the hall. "Look what's happening out there. The terraforming has already begun, yet all of the planet's defenses are being marshaled against a mishmash of spandex-clad fools trying to destroy the Eiffel Tower and the Lincoln Memorial."

You cringe. All the years you've idolized these people—this was their purpose all along? To run interference for alien Armageddon? "Okay," you say. "What do we do now?"

Tachyon's voice lowers. "I can travel through time, but only to give warning. I can't affect anything directly, and I'm not the one who makes this decision. That's something I learned long ago. I have to admit, I always thought it would be Nancy with me at the end of all things. But here I am, and here you are." He pauses, looking deeply into your eyes.

"So tell me, how do I save the world?"

Gulp. What should you say? To go all the way back to the 1960s and stop the alien probe before any of this begins? How much history would change as a result? You'd be living in a world without superheroes, for starters. What else? Would your father still wind up meeting your mother? Is that even *important* in the grand scheme of things? Maybe you should keep it simple, and tell him to warn you personally, far enough back that you can still make a difference.

▶ If you tell Tachyon to undo the planet's history for the past 40 years, turn to **page 34.**

▶ If you tell him that with enough warning you can save the world yourself, **turn to page 309.**

You've never had an intimate relationship that lasted more than five months—permanently merging your consciousness with an alien intelligence isn't something you're entering into lightly, to say the least. Besides, the Cosmic Guardian was one of the Earth's greatest heroes. With all his power at your disposal, you should be able to handle a few measly supervillains, right?

Well, not so much. You rush to D.C. and find yourself facing Doctor Diabolus, the Turtle, and Lightning Queen. Diabolus doesn't represent much of a problem—he can control weak-minded people with his thoughts, but your mind is at least medium-strong, so he's mostly harmless to you. And the Turtle is really just a poor man's version of the Ox—only dumber, weaker, and incredibly slow-moving, as his name would imply.

Lightning Queen, however, is another story. In fact, of all the Earth's villains, only Übermind and Lightning Queen ever gave your predecessor much trouble, and she was by far the more dangerous of the two. If you had access to all the records stored in your armor's memory, you'd know that. Just saying.

She immediately hits you with a bolt of electricity, and your armor seizes up. Her next two strikes finish you off completely. In fact, the mysterious puppetmasters behind the attack on D.C. are so impressed with her performance that later in the day they give her a Cosmic Guardian battlesuit of her very own. Hers doesn't have the same qualms about things like mental health or basic human decency, though.

They're very happy together.

The End

"Take my hand," Lightning Queen says. "Without the glove, sweetheart—I need to complete the circuit." You peel back the goo from your forearm, and the moment you place your hand in hers she calls a bolt of lightning out of the clear night sky that completely envelops both of you.

The pain is excruciating. When you can bear to wrench open your eyes, you find yourself in what appears to be an empty prison yard. The first thing you realize is that you're no longer covered in your protective shell. Was it left behind in New York? You attempt to summon more goo from your pores, but your whole body is crackling with electricity and it's impossible to concentrate.

"*¿Dónde está el Verminator?*" Lightning Queen screeches. You're beginning to understand why she acts so erratically—traveling by lightning bolt messes you *up* inside. Moments later a pair of swarthy guards—clearly putting their own best interests ahead of their internee's—drag a short, middle-aged man out into the yard.

Lightning Queen grabs him by the throat, and the guards flee. "You're the one who sent those space robots after me!"

Wow. This woman is bonkers. That's not at all what you were implying when you mentioned him earlier, but you're currently defenseless and not about to raise the issue. Verminator shudders, terrified. "What? I don't know any space robots, I swear!"

"Your meteor buddies! Tell me about the meteor!"

"What meteor?" A little mouse pops out of his shirt pocket, then scurries back in.

"You little bastard, your rodent friends can't help you now!

(continue to the next page)

The meteor that gave you superpowers!"

Verminator starts bawling. "I made it all up! I don't know how I got my powers. I just woke up hung over in an alley one day and I could talk to vermin. There was never any meteor!"

"You lied to me!"

"Not to you, specifically—I don't know, I just thought it sounded cool."

Lightning Queen screams like a banshee, and another bolt of electricity explodes from the heavens. At first you hope she's just teleported Verminator elsewhere, but the charred remains in her grasp tell you otherwise. She turns to you, her eyes glowing white-hot.

"You! I suppose *you* lied about the meteor, too!"

You desperately try to call up your goo, but it's useless. "No! I really did get my powers from a meteor!"

"That's even worse!"

What? "How is that worse?"

"I don't know, but it's the same!"

She's not making any sense, but you're learning that it's impossible to argue with a crazy person. Or pointless, at any rate. The next bolt has your name on it.

THE END

You have a distraction to create, and you figure this is as good a place to start as any. "Cut the crap, Moretti," you say. "I know who you really are."

His brow furrows. "Really? And what gave me away—was it my recent cover story in *Forbes* magazine? That whole black helicopter ruse was a simple test to find out what kind of moron we had to work with."

"Uh, the kind that's about to kick your ass," you say.

With a soft ding, the elevator behind Moretti opens and something in Guardian armor emerges, shaped like a human being but a good three feet taller than you and at least twice as wide. It opens its visor to reveal the now-familiar mug of the Ox. Oh, crap. This is the same villain who beat you to a pulp *without* the benefit of cosmic battle armor. And now he looks all veiny and jittery, as if his experience bonding with the armor hasn't been anywhere near as pleasant as yours was.

Well, you might as well put on a good show. "I'm not afraid of you," you lie. "I've learned a few tricks since last we met."

"Yeah, me, too," the Ox says with a cackle, firing a heavy disk from his chest plate that clamps onto your armor, connecting the two of you with a thick metal cable and sending an electric shock all through your body. "They showed me the training video."

Apparently, one of the helpful tips in that video was how to short out your opponent's armor, force open his or her helmet, and crush the enclosed head like a ripe tomato. If they graded for effort, the Ox would get an 'A' for execution.

THE END

If there's one thing you'd like to avoid, it's having your brain eaten by the half-living remains of a canine-mechanical hybrid. That much you're sure of. Also, the fact that the Cosmic Guardian was not what he seemed. You need some time to fit the pieces of this puzzle together, so you leave the apartment the way you came in and find a nearby coffee shop where you can sit and work things through.

Sadly, time to think isn't something you actually have. While you consider this new information, the space dog is alerting the Cosmic Guard of a breach in security. It takes them less than half an hour to find you, and before you even have a chance to finish your bagel, the entire café is obliterated by the force of several hundred Guardians firing upon you at once from high orbit.

At least you don't suffer.

THE END

You loom as large as you can in the shadows and whisper a single word:

"*Run.*"

That's all the encouragement he needs. Rockjockey turns tail and breaks into a sprint, bits of rubble dislodging from his body as he goes. Man, you could get used to this striking fear into the hearts of villains business. You duck into a corner and shut down your equipment. You're not sure who sent you that message, but if it was the Nightwatchman, and giant, rock-encrusted supervillains are that terrified of him, you definitely want to stay on his good side.

The computer screen goes blank, and your gloves and boots decompress, losing their custom fit. Somehow even your cloak feels heavier and more awkward, and the infrared in your goggles switches off, leaving you in darkness. Well, that sucks.

"Psst! Over here!" As your eyes adjust, you see a dark figure peeking around a corner down the alley, waving its arms at you. After a moment's consideration, you decide to follow it. Worst case scenario, you can always turn your costume back on and kick its ass, right? The mysterious stranger leads you a few blocks to a parked car and gets in, opening the passenger door for you. You peek inside, and in the car's interior light recognize a very familiar face.

"*Nancy North?* What are *you* doing here?"

"Waiting on an old acquaintance," she says, looking you up and down. "Although I somehow suspect he isn't coming. Who are you and what the hell are you doing in that outfit?"

"Um, I'm the new Nightwatchman? Sort of?" It's Nancy North! You try to maintain your cool, but the truth is you're

(continue to the next page)

geeking out a little. "Hey, did you just send me a text message?"

You get in the car with her and explain the incident with Rockjockey. Nancy says she didn't send the message, but she does have a theory. "Nightwatchman upgraded all his equipment in the '90s, using technology he borrowed from the Cosmic Guardian. The invisibility, the telepathic control—it's all alien tech. So the Cosmic Guard might be able to track the suit. If it *was* the Nightwatchman who sent that message, he may have just saved your life."

"But the Cosmic Guardians are the good guys. Aren't they?"

"The one we had on Earth was, but nobody knows anything about the organization that sent him. And if they're dealing with Reginald Thorpe, all bets are off."

You compare notes with Nancy—she's perturbed to hear about the murder of Brain Stem, but says she's uncovered something even more troubling. "I've found evidence that Crexidyne is working on a massive orbiting weapon built into a communications satellite. For lack of a better term, it appears to be some kind of doomsday device." She pauses. "Say, how would you like to assist me with a little corporate espionage?"

You're not sure if you should break off your search for the real Nightwatchman—if he's communicating with you now, surely you're close. Your first lead seems to have come to a dead end, but perhaps the safehouse in Philadelphia will hold some answers. Then again, working with Nancy would be a dream come true—you may have grown up dreaming of superpowers, but she's pretty much your journalism idol.

▶ *If you join forces with Nancy,* **turn to page 296.**

▶ *If you turn down her offer and continue your search in the City of Brotherly Love,* **turn to page 184.**

Moretti put you in charge, and your first command decision is that you'd just as soon avoid another ass-beating. "We bring him in," you say.

"Fine, but open your helmet once we get close so I can get out. If I go ahead and get inside his brain, at least we'll have a plan B."

You swoop down next to the van, carefully matching its velocity. The station wagon in the lane beside it wisely slows down to give you room (the look on the driver's face is priceless), and you tap on the Ox's passenger side window and wave. He does a double-take, then cocks his head for a moment, apparently considering his next move. Eventually he pulls the van over to to the highway's shoulder.

"Really?" the Ox says, getting out of the van and slamming the door behind him. "I do you the favor of not quite punching you to death, and this is how you repay me?"

"I'm not here to fight!" you say. You open and close your visor just a smidge, and your partner shrinks down further and slips out. "I'm here because I need your help."

He cracks his knuckles. "Well, too bad for you I don't run a charity for superheroes who suck at their job."

"Just hear me out!" Okay, time to turn on the charm. "The truth is, I'm new to all this. You were my first fight, and you know what? Being a hero sucks. I'd rather do what you do."

"So go rob a bank. I ain't stoppin' ya."

"Maybe you're not. But after I got the suit, some guy showed up in a black helicopter and started giving me orders."

The Ox nods. "Big mountain base out in the middle of nowhere? Yeah, I hate those guys."

(continue to the next page)

"Well, they have something in there that can shut my armor down by remote control if I don't do what they tell me to," you lie. "So I'm asking you to help me break in and bust up the place."

"Yeah? And what's in it for me?"

That's a good question. You're thinking on your feet, here. "Revenge?" you try. "Wanton destruction? All the miscellaneous, fancy, high-tech equipment you can carry?"

He taps his chin with his finger a few times, then points at you, smiling. "I like the way you think. Okay, I'm in. But if you double-cross me, I'm gonna kick your ass again." Since that's your backup plan, anyway, you can hardly argue with his terms.

"Besides," he continues, "I was just going to some boring supervillain thing tonight anyway."

Wait a minute. "What supervillain thing?"

"Just this big dumb meeting. I can totally bail on it, though."

Moretti said there was a supervillain conspiracy brewing. If you can talk the Ox into taking you along, this could be your chance to find out more. Or is walking into a hive of scum and villainy just plain stupid? Maybe you should just bring him back to the base and let the professionals interrogate him.

▶ *If you stick to the plan and keep luring the Ox back to HQ,* **turn to page 83.**

▶ *If you switch gears and try to infiltrate the supervillain meeting instead,* **turn to page 260.**

Octavia pinpoints a small tenement building across town. Magnifica flies you over there—less rapidly this time, although somehow being carried with an arm around your chest and your legs dangling wildly is even less comfortable—and drops you through an open window on the third floor. You bang your knee on the carpet with a yelp as Octavia is dumped right on top of you. So much for the element of surprise.

"Who's there?" a voice calls out from the other room. "Are you from the veterinarian's office?"

A little old man pokes his head into the room. "Yes, Mr. Patel," Octavia says, probing his mind while she picks herself off the floor. "You called us . . . Wow, you've called us every day for the past six years. We're here to take a look at Barkley."

She shakes her head at you as the man dodders into the other room. Apparently Mr. Patel is not the criminal mastermind here. "Barkley hasn't been feeling well," he says. "I'm very worried."

The thing you find on a pet bed next to a heaping bowl of organic kibble is not a dog. Or at least, it hasn't been for a long time. It's the barely living shell of a German shepherd, grafted to some kind of pulsating mechanical mass. The circuitry patterns almost remind you of . . .

"Holy balls," Magnifica says. "Is that *Cosmo the Space Dog*?" Back in the '80s and '90s, the Cosmic Guardian traveled with a canine companion. This could very well be that dog, if its little cybernetic mask and harness had swollen over the decades like a giant robotic tumor.

"Look at the wall." Octavia gestures toward a row of photographs featuring Mr. Patel and his beloved pet in a variety of

(continue to the next page)

matching holiday outfits. They were clearly taken over a span of decades, as Patel ages quite distinctly. The dog, however, appears just as it is now in every frame. This is not a recent development.

"I always figured the Guardian took the pooch with him when he split in '96," Magnifica says.

"There's no dog left in there," Octavia says, half in a trance. "But something's keeping it in kind of a wretched half-alive state. Something with a rudimentary consciousness. I think it's the machine."

"Is it serious?" Mr. Patel asks anxiously.

"It's been sending messages to Thorpe for years," she continues. "Not with direct mind control, but much more subtly —through dreams, maybe? There's a record of the messages, but there are far too many to sift through. Thousands."

"Obviously, those dreams drove Thorpe mad," you say. "Are you getting anything on the supervillain attacks? Can you see a larger purpose?"

"Hold on—here come the psychic defenses." She pauses, and smiles. "Nicy try, buddy. Just a lot of hostage-taking and destruction of major landmarks. I can't see any rhyme or reason to . . . oh, no. No, no, *no*. It's the Cosmic Guard. An entire army of them. This has been planned since . . . oh, my God. All that supervillain stuff is just a decoy. They're colonizing."

Your stomach drops. "They're here already?"

"The ship should be in orbit by now, but they can't breathe our air. They're erecting these vast machines at the North and South poles . . . they're terraforming. They're going to mutate the entire planet into something that will support them. Everyone will be dead in days."

(continue to the next page)

"We have to move out," you say. "I'll call the Justice Squadron and the Phenomenal Three. That Canadian team, whatever they're called. We'll gather every hero on the planet . . . "

"Stop."

Magnifica stands in front of you, arms crossed. "Those people aren't heroes. I swear to you, they're as bad as the villains these days."

"But Maggie," Octavia says. "Magnifico and the rest of the Squadron . . ."

"That little pissant is not affiliated with me. I'm telling you, you can't trust any of them."

"We can't do this alone."

"We're not alone," she says, pulling something from a chain around her neck. You look closely and see that it's her old Liberty Patrol communicator ring. "We're getting the team back together."

Magnifica might be on top of her game, but you don't imagine Octavia would be much use in a non-psychic fight. Then you glance at Mr. Patel, still waiting patiently for a diagnosis. What are the chances that the rest of Maggie's contemporaries will be in any shape to stop an alien invasion? The fate of the planet is literally at stake, and there's no time to let hard feelings get in the way.

Then again, the Nightwatchman's notes said Magnifica was the only person in the world you could trust. Should you trust her judgment now?

▶ *If you send out a distress call to every superhero on the planet about the alien invasion,* **turn to page 113.**

▶ *If you decide to rely on the former members of the Liberty Patrol alone,* **turn to page 193.**

Lightning Queen is notoriously unstable and needs to be returned to the slammer pronto, or innocent people are going to get hurt. With your enhanced strength and agility—and the fact that you can make any part of your body as adhesive as you want it to be—scurrying up three stories to the rooftop is a snap. You start forming a ball of goo in your left hand, ready to hurl it at Lightning Queen—

And immediately get tackled by one of the Cosmic Guardians.

"Wait! I'm on your side!" You realize this can't be the same Guardian that you witnessed in Cleveland this morning (for starters, it has twelve arms). Despite your continued protests, it pins you down with two of its massive limbs and starts pummeling you with the other ten. Your coating absorbs most of the force from the blows, but soon a blast of energy hits you from behind. The other Guardian is firing on you!

"Dude, I'm trying to friggin' *help* you guys!" Purely as a defense mechanism, you start pumping slime onto your attacker, and apparently the goo functions as an extension of your senses, because you can feel it seeping into the cracks in the Guardian's armor. Something flashes, and suddenly you see yourself through your attacker's eyes. Whoa. Are you psychic now, too? That's kind of awesome.

You're shocked, though, by the state of the Guardian's mind. It's a terrifying glimpse into what seems like two distinct entities: a malevolent, calculating intellect barely in control of a separate psyche, utterly consumed with madness and rage. You're certain that they both intend to kill you. And afterwards, possibly tear the limbs off of your dead corpse and suck the

(continue to the next page)

marrow out of your bones.

Before they get the chance, a white-hot bolt of lightning comes out of nowhere, breaking your psionic connection and blasting you halfway across the rooftop. That's one more item to add to your list of supergoo properties: it's an excellent electrical insulator, which is the only reason you're alive right now. You see Lightning Queen standing over the hollowed-out, smoking remains of the twelve-armed Guardian's armor. Its partner takes one look at the carcass and flees, quickly disappearing into the night sky.

"Thanks for distracting them," Lightning Queen says. "Jesus, what are you supposed to be? The Purple People Eater?"

"No, I, uh . . ." Should you even be talking to this woman? The truth is, after the beating you've taken, you're in no condition to fight. And she may be crazy, but there's no way she could be half as insane as that thing that just tried to kill you. Still, Lightning Queen is famous for her volatile temper and sudden violent outbursts, so you'd better play this carefully. "I don't really have a name yet," you say. "I'm new."

"Are you, now?" She takes a few steps toward you, one eye twitching just a little. "Tell me everything you know about our attackers. Do they have anything to do with that stupid space dog?"

Space dog? That's new. "There's a space dog?"

"Yeah, I paid a visit to Übermind a while back, in some horrid little apartment in Queens. You know Übermind, right? Little guy, super egomaniacal? Anyway, he's retired now, and completely obsessed with caring for some vile animal." She kicks the dead Guardian's helmet, and you see that it still con-

(continue to the next page)

tains a chunk of charred meat. "The pooch was covered in alien circuitry that looked just like this junk."

The Cosmic Guardian did have a canine sidekick back in the '90s, but you're not sure what the dog could possibly have to do with this. He was also rumored to be a member of a larger interstellar police force. "I think this was the Cosmic Guard," you say. "I saw one of them stop a meteorite in Cleveland this morning."

The same meteor, in fact, that gave you your superpowers. Now you're intrigued. What was it the Ox had said about meteors and superpowers? "Hey, do you know a villain who calls himself Verminator?"

"Sure, he's been rotting in a Mexican jail for years. Why? You think he has something to do with this?" Lightning Queen grits her teeth. "Well, perhaps it's time to check in on our incarcerated friend." She lifts one arm above her head, and her entire body crackles with electricity. "Feel free to join me if you'd like."

Hmm. If Verminator received his powers the same way you did, he might be able to shed some light on whatever's going on. You're not sure traveling with Lightning Queen is a good idea, but—other than the dog thing, anyway—this is really your only lead.

▶ If you travel to Mexico with the notorious, clearly bloodthirsty supervillain, **turn to page 222.** What could go wrong?

▶ If trying to track down Cosmo the Space Dog sounds like a better plan, **turn to page 116.**

You'll never make much of a supervillain if you run at the first sign of trouble. Besides, from what you've heard, the Ox breaks out of jail all the time. It's something you can do together. A villain bonding experience.

Magnifico charges the Ox, and you leap onto the hero's back like a crazed lemur. "Seriously?" he says with a note of surprise in his voice. "You guys have sidekicks now?"

He throws you across the room and you hit the far wall hard. In fact, the impact is enough to completely shatter your right arm—much to your surprise, it explodes with pain and then dissolves into purple goop. Something's definitely wrong here, and not just with your biology. Magnifico is supposed to be one of the good guys, but he just tossed you aside with enough force to *kill* a normal human being.

(continue to the next page)

As the glop spreads across your body, though, forming a protective coating and quickly reconstituting your damaged arm, you realize that you're *not* a normal human being. You clearly have some kind of disgusting gunk powers.

And now you're pissed. You leap back into battle, but this time when your opponent punches you, his fist smacks against the gelatinous coating on your chest and sticks like glue. Trapped, he delivers a blow with his other hand to your face, hard enough to cleave your skull in two. Your head, though, just melts into purple goo and reforms on the spot. Magnifico's eyes widen. "What *are* you?" he says.

"*I'm your doom.*" You shove one hand into his face and force a river of goo out of the pores of your palm, directly into his mouth and nostrils. You can feel it filling up his respiratory system, and instinctively know that you have complete control over this substance—you can make it flow into every crevice of his body and harden into steel with a mere thought. Your opponent collapses to the floor, choking.

"Jesus," the Ox says from somewhere behind you. "You're gonna kill him."

And why not? He definitely tried to kill you, and probably will again if you let him walk away. Besides, this is what being a villain is truly about, isn't it? Or is it going too far? You've committed to the life of a miscreant. This is your chance to kick that up a few notches, all the way to STONE COLD KILLER.

▶ *If you straight-up murder the world's mightiest hero,* **turn to page 291.**

▶ *If you back off and let him live,* **turn to page 54.**

Dale's plan actually works shockingly well. You fire energy bolts from your gauntlets to keep the Cockroaches away, and soon there are stretchy, purple tentacles shooting out from your back, smacking individual clones upside the head to knock them unconscious. More importantly, Dale is able to interpret instructions from your battlesuit and shout them back to you. Fighting the Cockroach is a matter of knocking out (or just plain squishing—you remind yourself that only one of the copies actually needs to survive) each unit before it has a chance to replicate into more. At first it seems like an impossible task, but you and Dale work as a single, well-lubricated machine, and before long your foes are utterly vanquished. It looks as though several of them were trying to haul a confusing-looking super weapon from the ship's cabin, but you take them out long before they can activate it.

The commotion has attracted attention from local law enforcement, so you figure they can call in their supervillain cleanup crew and perform the (potentially actually legal) search for any contraband that might be stowed away. Besides, you'd still like to keep as far under the radar as possible, so you take to the sky as the sirens approach.

"That was friggin' AWESOME," Dale says. And it honestly was. "Time for drinks, now?"

"Time for drinks," you agree. You head back to Cleveland, and the next several hours are an increasingly blurry vortex of celebration and alcoholism. You can't remember how you got there, but sometime late the next morning you wake up facedown on Dale's couch with one arm wrapped around an insanely heavy blue suitcase that you slowly recall is a camouflaged alien

(continue to the next page)

battlesuit. Dale is sprawled out on the floor across the room, covered in purple gunk.

As you roll over, for the second time in 24 hours, you see the glowing yellow eyes and unmistakable black cowl of the Nightwatchman.

This time he's just a few feet away, and creeping you the hell out with his stare. After you recover from the initial shock, you realize that up close he looks considerably smaller than you expected. Also, he kind of has an amazing rack. He removes his mask, revealing a face that's surprisingly feminine and extremely familiar.

"Melah? What the . . . *what*?"

"I followed him yesterday after the bank robbery, and found his secret equipment stash," she says. "After that, we sort of teamed up."

"That's amazing!" you say. "I ran into—"

She cuts you off. "I know. We've been monitoring both of you. You're the new Cosmic Guardian and Dale's . . . whatever he is. There's no time to go over it all now," she says. "The world's about to end, and I need you to help us save it." She explains that she and the original Nightwatchman have unearthed a vast conspiracy involving most of the Earth's superhumans—villains and heroes both—as well as an entire army of Cosmic Guardians. The Guardians, though, aren't the galactic peacekeeping force you've always thought they were. They're the frontline of an alien invasion.

"They've set up some kind of giant atmospheric conversion tower at the South Pole," Melah says. "Nightwatchman and Magnifica have gone to take it down. The thing is, they may

(continue to the next page)

already be too late. You've got one of their battlesuits, though. They're getting ready to deploy a second tower, and we need you to get to the mothership and find a way to destroy it before that happens."

"I'll go with you," Dale says. He looks like hell, but has a determined look in his eyes.

"Can you breathe in outer space?" Melah asks.

"I could get a NASA space suit, and . . ."

"There's no time. It's all happening *right now.*" She puts a hand on your shoulder. "Go," she says. "You might be humanity's only hope."

Dale sighs. "If our fate rests on your shoulders, then I can't think of a better pair."

The thing is, you *can*. You feel as if your entire life has been leading up to this moment, and can't believe you're even considering the idea. But the truth is that you can barely understand what your space armor is even saying to you, while it seems to somehow share a special telepathic bond with Dale. If you've got only one chance, wouldn't it make more sense to give the suit to your friend?

Then again, it's *Dale*. His heart is definitely in the right place, but his judgment can be a little suspect. Regardless of how well he understands the suit, can you trust him not to screw up saving the world?

▶ *If you take on the alien invasion yourself,*
  turn to page 249.

▶ *If you lend the suit to Dale and send him on his way,*
  turn to page 196.

You decide to file away the blowing-yourself-up idea as a potential plan B. Fortunately, you're already on course for the hangar, and in moments you're nearly there. The terraforming structures appear truly massive up close, but what startles you more is that hundreds of Guardians witness your approach and immediately stop what they're doing.

Uh-oh. Your commandeered suit may have the same basic propulsion system as theirs, but the burned-out, half-dead husk doesn't offer much in the way of handling. They quickly surround you, and although their blue energy beams don't damage your new body at all, the force of their blasts does manage to push you off course. That won't do. You coil yourself up and spring from your busted-up shell toward one of the attacking Guardians, intent on upgrading your ride.

It dodges. These things are fast! Now you're hurtling alone in the emptiness of space with no means of propulsion whatsoever. Yeah, you didn't think that through. You try reconfiguring into different forms to slow yourself down, but it's *space*. There's no atmosphere to create drag. Satisfied, the Guardians leave you to your fate and get back to preparing for the invasion of your planet. And although you don't need to eat, drink, or breathe in this form, you still have consciousness, and after what might be hours or might be days of drifting, you eventually fall asleep.

That's when your body instinctively reverts to flesh and bone.

THE END

"Even if what this guy says is true," you say, "he's only telling us because he has something to gain by it. You can stay and listen to his blathering all you like. I want nothing to do with it."

You leave, and soon Nancy rushes to join you. "You're right," she says. "I let my obsession with Crexidyne color my judgment back there, and I just want to say thanks for calling me on it."

"Uh, sure," you say. "So what do we do now?"

"I tied him up—we'll leave him to stew while we verify a few details of his story." She pulls a cell phone out of her bag. "Meanwhile, I think it's time for me to call in a favor or two."

Before she can dial, some kind of gray, misty portal opens up in mid-air behind her and two figures emerge from of it. You immediately recognize them as Jekyll and Hyde, a pair of low-rent supervillain thugs—wild, feral-looking twins with jutting fangs and big, nasty claws. You're not sure how they settled on Robert Louis Stevenson's literary classic as a theme, but one of them wears a lab coat, while the other dresses in rags and plays up his animal attributes. They're both dumb as rocks.

Jekyll grabs Nancy by the throat. You've got to save her! But if you turn on your superhero gear, you might draw the attention of the Cosmic Guard. You can't possibly fight these two with your bare hands, though. Can you?

▶ *If you risk switching on your gear to deliver a Nightwatchman-style beating,* **turn to page 122.**

▶ *If you try to save Nancy without it,* **turn to page 200.**

Your decision might have panned out a little better if the Cosmic Guard *had* any concept of mercy. Or courts. The truth is, the idea that they're any kind of galactic police squad at all is based on a lot of vague assumptions made about your predecessor. And if nothing you've read so far has led you to assume otherwise, well, sorry. Honestly, this book is kind of a bastard that way.

As the biological creatures inside the suits scream out silently in the throes of madness and agony, the synthetic alien minds that slowly drove them to that state follow their primary orders, which amount to something along the lines of "Kill all humans."

They start with you.

THE END

Fortunately, Tinker has been accumulating secret files throughout his sporadic jobs for Crexidyne, and one of the bits of information he's obtained is the address of Reginald Thorpe's personal residence. That, and a little time spent on Google Earth, is all Suong needs to open up a misty portal from Tinker's workshop right into Thorpe's living room.

You hop through it and immediately find yourself surrounded by gold-plated security robots. The Ox is carrying Tinker's anti-Cosmic Guardian weapon over one shoulder and grabs the paddle in his oversized hand. "Okay, let's see what this baby can do."

"Wait!" Tinker yells. It's too late—Ox presses his paddle against one of the approaching droids, but it results in electrical sparks and thick, black smoke coming from the box on his shoulder rather than his intended victim. Tinker is horrified. "It transmits a specific pulse that causes Guardian armor to short-circuit itself. It doesn't work on any old robot that wanders by!"

"I guess we're gonna have to do this the old-fashioned way, then," Ox says, throwing the box hard enough to flatten his attacker against the room's back wall. Cockroch starts splitting into multiple clones, and between the two of them—and Suong dropping robots into portals that open up to god knows where—the room is soon empty save for your crew and various piles of gold-plated scrap iron.

A sustained search of the palatial manor turns up Thorpe in a top-floor suite. At least, you think it's Thorpe. He's ragged, bearded, and wild-eyed, and crusted with enough filth to make you suspect his face hasn't seen a washcloth since the Clinton administration. You try engaging him in conversation, but he

(continue to the next page)

leaps onto his bed, wraps himself in a filthy blanket, and starts repeating something incomprehensible to himself beneath his breath. "If this guy is still calling the shots over at Crexidyne," Tinker says, "their current stock price is severely overvalued."

Before you can consider your next move, the room's bay windows shatter and a fleet of Cosmic Guardians tackles you and your companions. Man, that big metal contraption the Ox ruined would *really* come in handy right now—you cover yourself in a gooey shell and start flinging gunk at your attackers, but there are too many of them. There seems to be a limitless supply of space marines, regardless of how many you incapacitate with goo.

Although that's actually a surprising amount. You take down six alien heroes by yourself before they overwhelm you and you're torn to tiny little pieces. And that's pretty good. So, you know. You should be proud of yourself.

THE END

Hell, it's not like *you* had any jet fighter experience before yesterday, right? Ocean Boy will be fine. He makes a frankly worrisome little groan as you transfer the controls to him, but then Chuck leaps out of the open hatch, and you follow. It's business time! Hmm—that can't be the best superhero battle cry you can come up with. Walloping time? You make a mental note to give it more thought at some point in the future when you're not actively plummeting.

The Human Torpedo flattens himself into the most aero-dynamic shape possible to pick up speed and aims straight for Lightning Queen—probably a good call, since her electrical powers and psychotic disposition make her the biggest threat. You press the button on your touchscreen that transforms your billowing cloak into a hang-gliding contraption and choose your own target: Doctor Diabolus. You glide down and plow into him from behind at full speed. It works like a charm—he provides a soft place for you to land, and the resulting blow results in just enough soft tissue damage and head trauma to put your opponent out like a light. That was awesome! As you stumble to your feet and try to untangle yourself from your cloak, however, you glance up at the sky.

The jet is falling like a ton of bricks directly above you, black smoke billowing from its fuselage. Whoops. In retrospect, perhaps you asked Ocean Boy to bite off a little more than he could chew? Either way, you're crushed and then incinerated by the exploding wreckage of your own plane.

Which is a fairly humiliating way for a superhero to go.

THE END

You're not a hundred percent sure what's going on here, but it looks to you like a squadron of space police against Earth's most boring villains, so at least you know which side you're on. It also looks like they don't actually need much help. They dispatch most of the riffraff with ease, and although the Ox appears to be giving them a good workout, after about a minute he just passes out and falls to the floor.

That would be Migraine, you realize, still camped out in his adrenal gland.

One of the other Guardians skitters up to you (it's shaped like an enormous insect) and puts a pincer on your shoulder. "Uh, hi," you say. Soon the slug-like one joins it, pressing some of it's own armored flesh into your backside. You look around and see the others gathering unconscious supervillains into burlap sacks.

"Moretti?" You say as several more Guardians surround you. "You want to tell these guys that I work for you? Like, hands off the government employee and all?"

He just looks at you and smiles.

Even before they begin tearing you from limb to limb, you realize you've made a huge mistake.

The End

They're okay, but not great.

▶ **Turn to page 30.**

It has to be you—it's not that you don't trust Dale. It's that you don't trust him with *the fate of the entire planet*. You suit up and blast off.

You break atmosphere and spot an unnatural light just over the Earth's horizon. As you approach it, a dozen oddly-shaped creatures in armor like yours come out to meet you. They fire blasts of energy and you fire back, but there are far too many. It's all you can do to maneuver around them and get a better look at their ship. The thing is the size of a small city, and from a bay door you spot a platoon of Guardians working like insects around a giant metal cylinder. That must be the tower!

One by one, the worker bees peel themselves off and rocket toward you. Sustained fire from the ones you've encountered already is taking its toll on your shielding—you can't possibly take much more of this. If you don't come up with something fast, it'll be too late.

What about a suicide run? If you fling yourself at it, could you generate an explosion big enough to blow the tower up?

The primary increase delivers also bituiui momentum, your armor insists.

"I don't know what that means!" You don't have time to figure it out, either—Guardians are quickly surrounding you. "Ramming speed!" you say. "Go!"

You smack into the vast piece of machinery like a bug against a windshield. The impact doesn't do any measurable damage to the equipment, but it does knock you unconscious and take your battlesuit temporarily offline.

Prying, armored appendages and the harsh ravages of space do the rest.

THE END

You rocket through the ocean depths with your companions, half-blind from two-century-old rum, to avenge every baby seal who's ever met its end at the stubby little teeth of the dastardly orca.

This can't end well.

Oh, the actual whale fighting is a piece of cake. Ocean Boy, in particular, is nothing short of magnificent. They used to say that in his own element his strength and speed were a match for Magnifica herself, and from what you witness, you believe it. You, however, don't fare quite as well. The rapid acceleration and the excitement of a pitched battle prove too much for your poor stomach, and you suddenly find yourself violently ill. There's no genteel way to put this: before long the inside of your helmet starts to fill up with booze puke.

Your battlesuit normally has contingencies to deal with such issues, but, alas, Sten Janssen was a bit of a teetotaller and this is its first experience with binge drinking. It's actually fairly drunk itself just from being psychically connected to you, and is terribly confused. So your suit's artificial intelligence completely fails to keep you from choking to death on your own vomit somewhere deep beneath the Pacific Ocean.

It's no way for a hero to go.

THE END

You're not sure if a harder or more gelatinous shell will offer more protection from the fall, but suddenly you find yourself trying to engineer one of those middle school science project egg drops on the fly.

It's not your best work.

You create a soft shell, surrounded by a harder shell, surrounded by a medium-density shell, but before you've completed the third layer, the whole kit and caboodle hits solid ground with you inside. The thing is, normally your new body could easily withstand the impact by collapsing into purple goop and reforming itself. Except right now you're pretty freaked out by that idea, and your subconscious is actively directing your physiology not to do that.

So instead it collapses mostly to the standard kind of red goop, smashing up against the inside of your haphazardly-constructed cocoon and partially mixing with its soft inner layer. It would create quite the puzzle for some poor crime scene investigator-type if anyone ever happened to stumble upon your dead body.

But no one ever does.

THE END

Whatever Nancy has in mind is probably better than wandering around aimlessly, which is more or less what you've been doing up until now. "Okay," you say. "What's the plan?"

"If Crexidyne really is working with the Cosmic Guard, there will be records of it," she says. "I have passwords that should get us into their computer system. But we'll need to get in the building, and down into the secure sub-basement levels."

"With two-ton space armor, I'm not sure stealth is really my strong point."

Nancy smiles. "That's why you're going to be the diversion," she says. "Guardian, meet Nightwatch."

A dark figure pops out from the hallway, nearly giving you a heart attack in the process. Seriously, how many people are hiding in your apartment right now? As the shock wears off, you recognize the same black cowl and glowing eyes that you saw in the alley behind the bank this morning. "She's Nightwatchman's protégé," Nancy continues, "and we've been pooling our resources. Your job is breaking—she'll take care of the entering."

It makes sense that Nightwatchman would be training a replacement, you think—he's been active since the early '70s, which would mean he's pushing 60 at the very least. You stick out one hand and introduce yourself, but she just stares at you silently. It's a bit disconcerting. Also, it dawns on you that your visor is still open, making you the worst secret-identity-keeper ever.

Also, as far as Nancy's plan goes, aimless wandering is starting to sound a little better. "That's it?" you ask. "I walk into Reginald Thorpe's base of operations and start punching things?"

(continue to the next page)

"That's stage one," Nancy says. "Once we find out what their angle is, your mission will be to join the Guardians' ranks and disrupt them from the inside. That will require additional preparations, however—for now, this is strictly recon. And Nightwatch—if you find any evidence of the Guard's involvement at all, get out. That's an order."

Nancy's concern for your partner is touching, but you notice that she doesn't seem to have any similar concerns for *your* well-being. Decoy duty sounds pretty dangerous to you, and even if you succeed, what do you have to look forward to? A rematch with the alien creeps who tried to kill you earlier? Well, technically, it's not too late to back out and track down that telepath (honestly, page 24 is just sitting there waiting for you—knock yourself out), but otherwise it's time to put up or shut up. You wanted to be a hero. This is your chance.

"You know what? *I love this plan.* Which way to Crexidyne?"

Crexidyne central command is in New York City, and you offer to carry your new partner there, but she has her own transportation. She punches something into a little keypad on the back of her wrist and slides out the back door, firing a grappling hook and ascending effortlessly to the sleek black aircraft that's now hovering above your apartment complex. You follow her flight path to the city and prepare for stage one: finding out if the Cosmic Guard is in league with Earth's greatest supervillain, Reginald Thorpe.

As Nightwatch lands her jet in a secret underground hangar not far from Crexidyne, a message spits out on your visor's display. FIVE MINUTES, it reads. COVER ME.

For your part, you figured you'd just walk into the building's

(continue to the next page)

lobby and start busting up the joint. With any luck, Crexidyne corporate security will be more of the high-school-dropouts-with-stun-guns sort than the high-tech-robot-suit variety, and you can make a big ruckus without putting yourself in too much actual danger until Nightwatch sends you the all-clear. You walk in the front door and find that the building's lobby is surprisingly quiet. A lone security guard glances up from his magazine, looks at you, and shrugs. "Rooftop," he says, gesturing toward the elevators with his thumb.

Hmm—that seemed awfully casual. How many people in cosmic battle armor walk through those doors on an average weekday? It's time to start the diversion—should you continue with your plan and just go crazy on the spot? Or take the elevator up to the building's roof and see what there is to destroy up there?

▶ *If you stick to the plan,* **turn to page 288.**

▶ *One distraction is as good as another, right? If you take your senseless violence act to the rooftop,* **turn to page 38.**

"So what next?" Tinker asks. "I've got some ideas on how to get the poison gas out of this thing and replace it with oxygen. You want me to get started?"

"All in good time," you say. "First, get yourself down to the atmospheric conversion machines. I want you to study them, and be prepared to deploy by the time we reach Earth."

He pauses. "Um . . . why?"

You give him your steeliest glare. "So we can use the threat of planetary destruction to force the governments of the world to surrender. What did you *think* we were doing here?"

"Boss," the Ox says, "from what I know, the governments of the world aren't real surrendery. You think we really got the muscle to put up a fight if they call your bluff?"

Vicious as they are, your supervillain attack squad has dwindled to less than ten recruits. The Ox, however, is missing the point. You're not some posturing buffoon with delusions of grandeur and a self-sabotage complex. If you issue an ultimatum, world leaders can either accept your terms or they can be destroyed. "Look into my eyes," you say. "Do I look like I'm bluffing?"

The Ox meets your gaze, then exchanges glances with Tinker, Suong, Cockroach, Verminator, and the others. "No," he says with a sigh. "Sorry about this."

He reaches out and crushes the helmet of your suit with one hand. You gasp and thick, brown alien air fills your lungs —the stuff immediately goes to work on your innards, killing you within seconds.

"We're bad guys," the Ox says as your insides boil. "We're not friggin' *insane*."

THE END

You delve deeper. In fact, you descend as far as you can. The visions stored here are very different from what you've seen so far, not the product of a single observer, but ancestral memories of an alien world.

It started millennia ago, on a planet not unlike Earth. This was the Fatherworld. The inhabitants weren't humanoid in shape, but in spirit they could have been our cousins, full of hope and ambition, capable of incredible kindness and terrible destruction. They fought wars, made peace, and lived their lives, filling their planet to the very brim. Then they set their sights elsewhere. They developed the technology to terraform a second planet in their solar system, slowly transforming the barren world into a new paradise. This was the Motherworld.

The work took generations, and the Motherworld colony grew and grew. However, their hybrid mechanical/biological technology was unstable, and the carefully crafted ecosystem began to mutate beyond their control. The atmosphere turned to poison. The entire project was deemed a failure, and rather than risk contaminating their own planet, the Fatherworld leaders cut off all contact, leaving the entire colonist society to die.

Desperate, the colonists turned their technology inward. If they couldn't mutate the planet to suit their biology, they would mutate themselves to match the planet. They became twisted, misshapen mockeries of their former species, but they survived, and even prospered. Still, the Motherworld was slowly degenerating into the barren rock it had previously been. So, a century later, the colonists unleashed their fury on the Fatherworld that had long since forgotten them, launching a global attack and terraforming their ancestral home to fit their new needs, killing

(continue to the next page)

off the existing population in the process.

From there, they turned to the stars. After all, how could they trust that the Fatherworld wouldn't betray them and turn to poison as well? They sent probes to other solar systems, looking for living worlds to reshape in their own image. When they found one, they carefully studied the native biology over a period of decades until they had the information they needed. Then they struck quickly, ushering in complete destruction within days, and grafting a handful of natives to mechanical battlesuits to act as shock troops for the next invasion.

Now they've come to Earth.

You're wrenched away from the vision by a flash of pain. The alien intelligence has found you! It attacks, trying to overwhelm your intellect with its own. You don't even know how to begin to defend yourself.

▶ *If you flee, hoping to break the psychic connection before it can devour your mind,* **turn to page 284.**

▶ *If you fight, hoping to defeat Cosmo the Space Dog in psychic combat and uncover secrets that will save the world from the alien menace,* **turn to page 183.**

The ego is always a good place to start. "You're probably right," you say. "I can't risk putting a woman of your advanced years in harm's way. I'll find some younger superpowered heroes to help me."

"Reverse psychology? What are you, 12?" She pulls something from her robe pocket and tosses it at you. "You know what that is?"

It's a dirty little black rock. Is it the secret space element that robs her of her powers or something? Fortunately, your glove computer is already at work: 76% carbon, according to the readout. Oh. "It's coal," you say, trying to sound like you figured that out on your own.

She takes the lump from you and squeezes it for a moment, opening her fist to reveal an enormous, perfect diamond. Holy *crap*. "I could give a rat's ass what you think of me," she says. "Now leave me alone."

You're geeking out over the coal-into-diamond trick. "I'll make you a deal. Help me do this one thing and I won't tell the world about your secret hiding place. If you think *I'm* a pain in the ass, try dealing with autograph seekers and paparazzi."

"You little turd!" Her metal walker shakes, then starts to crumple in her wrinkled fists. "Fine. Where's Thorpe holed up? We'll go beat his ass until he confesses to the psychic twerp's murder or whatever." You were actually thinking you'd visit the crime scene and look for clues or something along those lines, but her plan is good, too.

▶ *If you decide to play to Magnifica's strengths and go with immediate violence,* **turn to page 50.**

▶ *If you insist on digging up some more information first,* **turn to page 164.**

Considering how your first attempt to battle the Ox turned out, backup does hold a certain appeal. The helicopter touches down on a giant elevator platform tucked away in a secluded mountain range, which descends to reveal an immense subterranean complex. It's everything you've ever imagined a top-secret government installation to be. Moretti hops out as soon as the platform stops moving.

"Guardian, meet Migraine, one of our most trusted agents." The man in front of you is either well into his sixties or has lived a *very* hard life, and is wearing a uniform that looks more like something you'd see on a COBRA operative than a federal employee. It only serves to emphasize his spindly legs, bulging waistline, and crooked posture.

"Another space freak?" he says, looking at your outstretched hand like it's been soaking in smallpox. Nice manners on this guy. "Well, whatever. Just do like I tell you, and we should both get out of this mission alive."

Moretti waves him off. "Actually, I'm putting Guardian in charge."

"You're *what*?" That was Migraine talking, but he echoes your thoughts precisely.

Moretti gives you a reassuring look. "If you think you're up to it, that is." Meanwhile, your new partner looks like he's trying to shoot tiny knives at you from his eyes.

▶ *Screw that guy! If you accept command of the mission,* **turn to page 78.**

▶ *If you defer to your partner's greater experience (considering your own resumé spans less than an hour and includes considerable time spent passed out and covered in dirt clods),* **turn to page 186.**

"Actually, a supervillain meeting sounds *super* fun," you say.

"Then you've never been to one."

"No, seriously! It would be a really good opportunity for me to network. We can do the meeting, grab some beers, and then plan our attack. What do you say?"

He shrugs, opening the sliding door on the side of the van. "Hop in," he says. The meeting is in New York, still several hours away, so you spend the time getting to know your new partner in crime. Despite yourself, you actually kind of like him.

"You know, if you're going to be a bad guy, Cosmic Guardian won't cut it," he says. "You need something scarier. Like, how about Cosmic *Tornado*?' Ooh, or *Galactivator*. Plus, you gotta do something about that armor, like put some spikes on it or something."

At the Ox's urging, you experiment with your battlesuit. It's shown the ability to shift and reconfigure on its own, and you discover that with focus you can will the exoskeleton into any number of different shapes like a Transformer. It's actually pretty fun.

The meeting is being held in the basement of a community center. You're not sure what you were expecting—a lair?—but it's fairly underwhelming. As you shuffle in, villains seem to be taking turns complaining about their particular nemeses. You wonder when the actual meeting will start, but after about 20 minutes it dawns on you that this *is* the meeting.

Then all hell breaks loose.

Agent Moretti bursts in the door, followed by at least a dozen armored figures. With a shock, you realize that they're

(continue to the next page)

all in battlesuits similar to yours, but in various shapes and sizes (one even looks like a giant slug). Is this the Cosmic Guard? Nothing Moretti told you led you to believe that there were other Guardians currently on Earth.

Something inside your head is telling you to run, and you realize that it's the Guardian armor. Maybe all the time spent bonding over armor spikes is making a difference, but instead of the badly translated audio messages you heard earlier today, it's as if the suit is trying to communicate via *emotion*. And with every fiber of its soul, it's screaming at you to *get the hell out of there*.

Moretti spots you. "There you are!" he says. "Quick, help us take these targets down!" You're getting conflicting orders. So who do you trust? Your government employer, or your apparently self-aware alien battlesuit?

▶ *If you trust Moretti and help round up the villains,* **turn to page 247.**

▶ *If you trust the suit and hightail it,* **turn to page 90.**

Something tells you that the Ox is the key to whatever is going on here. Octavia says she once had a therapy session with him and thinks she can track his psychic signature by returning to the scene of yesterday's bank robbery.

"Jesus," Magnifica says. "You're taking villains for patients now, too?"

"He was a mixed-up kid, Maggie. If they'd ever been treated with compassion, they might not have become villains."

"Oh yeah, and good job with all that. Pillar of the goddamn community *that* one turned out to be."

Magnifica grabs both of you for a gut-wrenching trip to Cleveland, where the Ox's psychic scent leads you to a cheap motel and then into Pennsylvania down a stretch of I-80, where you find an empty, overturned van on the side of the highway. From here, the trail leads northeast toward the Catskills. "Wait," Octavia says, her hands on her temples. "I think I've got him. So much anger and rage! Something else is controlling his mind, you guys. Something . . . cold."

She gasps. "Brace yourselves! He's coming!"

You dive out of the way just in time to avoid a dark shape that rockets to the ground, impacting with a boom and making a crater much like the one you witnessed yesterday, only smaller. As you stumble to your feet and dust yourself off, you're treated to another familiar sight: something crawls out of the hole that looks like the Cosmic Guardian.

Only *bigger*.

You realize that this hulking, armored figure is the Ox. Has he somehow become Earth's new Guardian? If so, the Earth is in trouble. Magnifica clenches her fists and takes a step toward

(continue to the next page)

him as he throws back his head in a furious wail. "Wait!" Octavia says. "His mind is a mess—he's not himself. I think the battlesuit is controlling him. Don't fight! We need to calm him down so I can get a better look inside there."

Magnifica scoffs. "Tell me you're joking. Are you suggesting we *hug this out*?"

▶ *If you follow Octavia's path of nonviolence and try to subdue the Ox,* **turn to page 39.**

▶ *If you agree with Magnifica that violence is clearly the solution,* **turn to page 182.**

You send one of your new lackeys (who has pterodactyl wings and apparently x-ray vision?) on a scouting mission to Crexidyne's headquarters in Manhattan, and she quickly returns with a report: the action is on the skyscraper's roof, where hundreds of Guardians are busy with some sort of massive construction project.

Guardians? You know how to deal with those. Suong opens a portal to the rooftop and you send the Ox through it with the armor-busting box. The rest of your horde charges in behind him, and soon you're witnessing a replay of the earlier altercation on a much larger scale: rampaging supervillains and helpless aliens of considerable variety being systematically eviscerated. It's a good thing you're a hardcore, badass criminal overlord now, because the level of blood and gore involved is straight-up *nuts*. What the aliens are building turns out to be a launch pad for big, silver capsules that look like spacecraft. Tinker inspects one, and reports that they have detailed memos taped to their consoles with piloting instructions.

"Hey, boss!" Verminator yells from across the roof. It's nice that they're calling you boss already. "I think I can communicate with this one."

He's found a Guardian shaped like a giant praying mantis, helpless and twitching but still in one piece. "I don't know if it's because it isn't proper vermin and I've got a bad connection or what, but its brain is a big, crazy mess." He pauses, squinting. "There's something else there, too. Something mechanical. A separate intellect for the battlesuit, maybe?"

His eyes widen. "I don't think these guys are taking orders from Crexidyne, boss—the invasion plan is coming from the

(continue to the next page)

Cosmic Guard. And unless there's some kind of quaint alien mistranslation for 'Kill all humans,' it's already started."

The night sky is illuminated by a sudden flash of light, and you look up to see a stray Guardian hurtling from the clouds on a collision course with Tinker's weapon. It crashes into the big metal box and explodes, sending fragments scattering in every direction. Tinker is mortified, and says it'll take two days, at a bare minimum, to construct a replacement from scratch.

"I think we've got bigger problems," Verminator says, still mind-melding. "The mothership is on its way. Unless my alien bug-translating skills are way off, it'll be here by morning."

"So we stomp 'em before they get here," the Ox says, gesturing toward a space pod. "Tink says he can fly these things. What are we waitin' for?"

You're supposed to be the villain here—is it really falling to you to save the world from an alien invasion? This *sucks*. You're pretty sure you fall under the category of 'all humans,' though, and the so-called heroes—Magnifico, at the very least—seem to have sided with the invaders. But should you go charging off into deep space to battle these things on their turf? It might be better to make your stand on-planet, since considerations like oxygen and gravity seem like sound tactical advantages.

▶ *If you commandeer a space capsule and take the fight to the alien invaders,* **turn to page 132.**

▶ *If you hold your ground and let them come to you,* **turn to page 93.**

Reginald Thorpe isn't even here, and you're guessing you won't get anything out of this Moretti guy. You tell Magnifica to back off. She sneers, drops him, and picks you up in his stead, leaping out the window and flying a few blocks down the street, where she deposits you on an empty rooftop.

"What the hell?" she asks while you catch your breath. "I thought we were gonna go bust heads real quick and be back for bridge."

"It looked like a dead end to me," you say, straightening your cloak. "And I figured there was no reason to fight the Justice Squadron if we didn't have to."

"You don't understand," she says. "If he does have those little bastards on a leash, they're coming for us right now, no matter what we do."

You scan the horizon and discover that she's right: Megawatt, Gravity Bomb, and Skyhawk from the Squadron are flying toward you, fast. And they're joined by a half-dozen other non-team-affiliated heroes as well. You recognize Luminati, as well as Doppelganger and Salamander (the latter pair quit the Phenomenal Five a few years back, ruining their alliteration).

"Get the hell out of here," Magnifica says. "Now."

"What? Surely this is a misunderstanding. We can just explain that—"

"Do your little invisibile thing and run!" she says. "I'll hold them off!"

▶ If you follow Magnifica's command and split,
   turn to page 304.

▶ If you stay, hoping to defuse the situation or at least help her fight the heroes off, **turn to page 190.**

Your ship breaks atmosphere and the pressure eases up. Ox starts pacing back and forth in the cramped cabin. "You and me, dude. Ox and Globulon. Kickin' ass!" See, that's just how these things start. You've got to nip this in the bud before "Globulon" sticks.

There's no way of knowing how fast you're traveling in the windowless ship. You putter around the craft and find a stash of space suits and what might be a set of weird alien tools. After less than half an hour, a clang of metal on metal rocks the cabin and machinery begins to whir. It sounds like you've arrived. The hatch, though, remains shut. You feel a rush of wind, and notice brown gas filtering through vents in the walls.

They're pumping the atmosphere out of the ship.

There's no time to get into a space suit, so you grab a helmet and oxygen tank and pop them on your head and back, sealing them to your body with supergoo. "I can hold my breath," Ox insists as you prepare a helmet for him, but you graft it to him, anyway—who knows how long you'll be up here? Once the chamber has been filled with sickly-looking smoke, the hatch jerks open and you can make out 20 or 30 bloated, splotchy figures in a hangar bay. They're not in battle suits. Your friend tenses up, ready to charge.

▶ *They haven't attacked you yet. If you attempt to communicate with them before resorting to violence,* **turn to page 173.**

▶ *Um, they just tried to poison you with brown gas. Plus, the fate of the entire planet is probably at stake! If you utilize the element of surprise and strike,* **turn to page 29.**

Magnifico charges, but Maggie holds up one hand, catching his fist and stopping the enormous man dead in his tracks. Wow. You had no idea she still had it in her. She launches into the air, slamming them both into the office's vaulted ceiling.

Has Magnifico gone mad? Your files include several complicated scenarios for dealing with a Magnifico-related catastrophe (one of which involves luring him to the Arizona-Nevada border so you can use the electricity generated by the Hoover Dam to knock him unconscious), but nothing about what might set him over the edge. He said he was taking orders. From whom?

You notice Moretti's tablet computer resting on the desk, lightly sprinkled with its owner's remains. Magnifico seemed awfully eager to get the Crexidyne executive out of the picture. You pick up the tablet and wirelessly jack into it. Fortunately, your equipment includes some really phenomenal password-breaking software, and the screen crackles to life. Meanwhile, Maggie has her own investigative methods. She now has her much larger rival pinned to the floor and is straddling his chest, literally beating him senseless. *Damn*, girl.

"So, you're a murderer now?" She doesn't pause to give him a chance to respond. "Who are you working for? Damn it, you wear that uniform, you use your goddamn powers to *protect* people, do you hear me?"

She finally lets up, and Magnifico speaks, coughing up a little blood with the effort. "They *gave* me my powers. They gave *all of us* our powers, and they can take them away with the flick of a switch."

A cursory search through Moretti's most heavily encrypted

(continue to the next page)

files seems to back him up. There are entries tracking literally hundreds of superhumans. Magnifico's own file has years of what appears to be basic surveillance, followed by something called "full memory reestablishment" just a week ago.

Before you can learn more, a blast of red heat knocks the tablet out of your hand. "I'd rather die than go back to that life!" Magnifico brings his wrist near his face, and you realize he's speaking into a Justice Squadron communicator. "Send reinforcements! Dammit, send everyone!"

Maggie pummels him a bit more until he falls silent. You check on the computer, but find that it's been melted to slag. There goes your information gold mine. Glancing out the window, you see a swarm of flying figures approaching on the horizon. You'd just as soon be elsewhere when they arrive.

However, you notice a tablet docking station on Moretti's desk and realize that the melted files were surely backed up. Your first instinct is to grab the computer and run, but there is no computer. The dock is connected to a port on a desktop monitor, which is connected to some funky looking jacks underneath the desk. This terminal must be attached to the larger Crexidyne network.

"Let 'em come," Magnifica says.

▶ *If you have Magnifica hold off the flying monkeys while you gather more intel,* **turn to page 65.**

▶ *If you'd rather get out while the getting's good,* **turn to page 204.**

You decide to ally yourself with the terrifying space creature. "Nightwatchman! Surrender to the combined might of the
Cosmic Guard and . . ." well, you still have no idea what you're
going to call yourself, so you just sort of trail off. He ignores you
and touches a panel on the back of his glove and his entire body
flickers and disappears. Whoa—if this guy's just some cosplayer,
he's put some serious money into his hobby. Nevertheless, it
turns out the Cosmic Guardian doesn't need much help from
you to apprehend him. It bathes the alley in a blue light that
neutralizes your quarry's cloaking technology. You see his
shimmering form hugging a brick wall across from you, trying
to remain as silent as possible.

Then the Guardian opens fire, incinerating him on the spot.

Holy *crapsicle*. Wherever this thing is from, they administer a harsh brand of justice there. It immediately turns its attention to you. Seemingly perturbed that its original target didn't
put up much of a fight, it snatches you off the ground with its
jellyfish tentacles and rips you into dozens of pieces, torching
each one individually.

You, my friend, clearly backed the wrong filly in this horse
race.

THE END

You make the connection. The first thing you sense is that the other Guardians are *not* like you. They're cold, mechanical intellects, grafted to kernels of utter, raving madness. And as you start to make sense of the wave of consciousness that washes over you, you quickly learn that the supervillain attacks—and there are more on the way, all over the globe—are a decoy to occupy the Earth's forces while the aliens put their real plan in motion. In order to inhabit Earth, they need to terraform it, a process that will kill everything currently alive on the planet within days.

You also immediately understand that you can pinpoint the location of each of the thousands of other Guardian units. Which means that, in return, they can pinpoint you.

You leap into the sky through the bedroom window, taking out a big chunk of Octavia's exterior wall in the process. Fifteen or twenty Guardians are approaching from the east, but you're ready for them, and adjust your energy field to absorb their blasts. You now understand that the Guardian armor is equipped with safeguards to defend against its own weaponry. The key to fighting these things will be coming up with avenues of attack they don't expect.

As the Guardians surround you, one suddenly drops out of the sky like a rock, and you hear Octavia's voice in your head. *I put the host to sleep, and the whole thing went down. Huge portions of their brains are dedicated to protecting the host.*

That gives you an idea. A gargantuan, slug-shaped Guardian swoops down, attempting to grapple. You know that if enough of them get a hold of you, they could pull your armor clean off. But instead of dodging, you let it grab you and form

(continue to the next page)

a mental connection. You know from your armor's past experiences just how powerful the host-protection protocol is. So your plan—it's really more of a harebrained scheme at this point, but you're flying by the seat of your pants here—is to couch a set of instructions within that protocol.

The host is at risk, you think, transmitting all of the data you compiled years ago while developing the unique graft method with Janssen. If you can convince this Guardian unit that the madness it has instilled in its occupant constitutes a mortal threat, it might accept the solution you're offering, which is to

(continue to the next page)

reconfigure its bond into an equal mind-partnership the same way you did.

It works! However, while you and your armor have a bond between two strong, independent minds, the other Guardian finds only a deep well of insanity in its host, with very little consciousness left. It freezes up and goes offline entirely.

Meanwhile, others are coming in for the kill. Armored hands, pincers, and tentacles lock onto you. *Octavia! Help!*

You feel her consciousness spread out, linking your mind in a web with the others. You send the rebonding directive in a blast, and the Guardians all disengage, falling from the sky as one and hitting the ground in a cacophony of thuds.

There's no time for celebration—the alien mothership is already in orbit. They'll already be preparing to launch their terraforming towers. You have to stop them!

Still inside your head, Octavia insists on coming with you. Into space? You recall an armor configuration that would allow you to carry a passenger in a giant pod like a backpack, but it isn't ideal for battle and would certainly slow you down. Besides, in the event of your—let's face it—incredibly likely failure and death, wouldn't it be better to leave her on Earth to gather the troops?

▶ *If you suspect you'll need all the help you can get and take Octavia along for the ride,* **turn to page 128.**

▶ *If you think it's more tactically sound to go alone,* **turn to page 180.**

What the hell, it's not *your* brain. You tell the Ox that shoving something called a mnemonic grub inside his head sounds like a swell idea. He cracks open the orb and sticks the wriggling worm in his ear. You expect the Squadron to jump you, but instead Moretti waves them back. The Ox falls to his knees, clasps his hands over his ears, and screams. His face contorts into a mask of pain.

It doesn't let up. After a few moments, he starts to slump. Whatever it's doing to him, you're worried that he may not survive it. Not knowing what else to do, you put your hand on your friend's head and send a tendril of gunk into his ear canal after the worm. You close your eyes and concentrate on the purple goo, trying to sense the path the grub made into his brain. It works—you manage to lasso the little bugger and yank it out of his head.

The Ox gasps and lets out a roar. "Moretti!" he shouts, veins bulging in his neck and forehead. "*You* did this to me!" He lunges just as a Cosmic Guardian leaps forward to intercept him, but he bats it aside with one hand, knocking it halfway down the street.

Gravity Bomb lifts a hand and you instantly fall to the pavement, immobile. The Ox is quite a bit stronger than you, though, and now he's truly pissed—he slows a little but doesn't stop moving. Coldfront hurls a volley of icicles at him, which only bounce right off his hide. The insectoid Guardian moves to intercept, only to get pummeled into the pavement by a two-handed blow.

The eyeball Guardian focuses on you, seemingly unaffected by the intensified gravity that's keeping you stuck to the asphalt,

(continue to the next page)

and wraps several of its tentacles around your midsection. Crap!
You've seen enough hentai to know where *this* is going. There's
not much you can do to defend yourself beneath the weight of
the gravity field, but you manage to send a few thin strings of
goo creeping across your attacker's armor. You pray that you can
find a vulnerability somewhere and force enough gunk into the
suit to mess it up on the inside.

As the goo seeps in, you hear something like a voice inside
your head. You were able to feel the stuff moving through the
Ox's brain and Magnifico's circulatory system—now it seems
to be opening some kind of communication channel with the
alien's mind. Except what you're getting isn't exactly speech,
and you wouldn't exactly call it a mind. It's like a series of psychic impressions coming from two distinct sources—the cool,
mechanical intelligence of the Guardian armor, and some kind
of insane, animal rage coming from what can only be the alien
eyeball monster. It's difficult to comprehend, but you get flashes
of something about global conquest. Or worldwide extinction?
Something to that effect.

Meanwhile, the Ox has the big bug pinned down and is
furiously raining blows upon it. Its armor has already shattered
to pieces, and its soft interior is steadily being mashed into
pulp. The Ox turns to face your attacker, and the thing's giant
eyeball does what through its battlesuit appears to be an exaggerated double-take. Both its mechanical and insane biological
thoughts converge into something approximating "uh-oh," and
it pulls away from your gooey tendrils and flees.

You feel gravity returning to normal, and look up to see the
rest of the Justice Squadron beating a hasty retreat. The helicop-

(continue to the next page)

ter pilot has already taken flight—the only person unaccounted for is Moretti. That's when you spot his tablet computer on the ground a few yards from the fracas and two telltale legs sticking out from under the busted-up Bug Guardian like the Wicked Witch of the East.

Ouch. That can't be a pleasant way to go.

The Ox's eyes are still wild with rage, and it seems that whatever memories he recovered from the worm have brought little comfort. "I remember a dark room," he says. "I dunno, it's all in bits and pieces. Moretti was there, and that Brain Stem guy from the Squadron. There were all these experiments . . ."

He shudders. "A lotta pain. I think they made me promise something? Like, I gave up something important?" His eyes narrow and he cracks his knuckles loudly. "Whatever. I'm gonna go kick some more ass until somebody tells me what the hell they did to me."

The urge toward global domination that you sensed in the Eyeball Guardian has definitely piqued your curiosity. But even though the pair of you managed to defeat Magnifico and the Bug Guardian, you're pretty sure you'd get clobbered if the Squadron pools its resources. Revenge sounds like a losing proposition. You suspect you'll both be better off if you can persuade the Ox to look for answers through self-reflection rather than storming off on some kind of suicidal rampage.

Then again, you're pretty much a supervillain now. Who are you trying to kid? People like you *live* for suicidal rampages.

▶ If you're on board with vengeance, **turn to page 136.**

▶ If you try to sell the Ox on inner peace instead, **turn to page 75.**

Screw this noise. You focus all of the suit's power into your rocket thrusters and blast off. The Ox manages to hold on for about 200 vertical feet and then falls to the earth, taking a big chunk of your suit with him. It's a chunk that was in some way responsible for flight stability, too, judging by the way you go careening off on a random trajectory and crash into a hillside about a mile from the freeway.

Ouch. You're not certain if your body is more busted up than your cosmic space armor, but you're pretty sure you'll need to be airlifted out of here, since the suit is no longer responding to any mental commands. But Moretti's crew is monitoring you, right? Surely they'll send someone along. As you lay motionless for 20 or 30 minutes, though, you start to have your doubts. They don't think you abandoned your mission, do they? I mean, technically you did, but it was a matter of life and death!

Then you see a strange orange glow in the sky directly above you. At first you think it's a rescue vehicle, but it's just a little pinpoint of light that's quickly becoming brighter and more intense. You might be getting paranoid, but now you start to wonder if Migraine was implanting one of those targeting beacons on you while he was riding inside your helmet. Before you have a chance to even panic properly, the light becomes an enormous orange beam and you're instantly burned to a crisp.

Let this be a lesson about trusting any organization that utilizes orbital death lasers. They implanted that beacon while you were still in the helicopter.

THE END

If Magnifica is going to force you to pick between them, you'll take geriatric muscle over ethically-questionable brains. The decision has two significant consequences: first, it makes Tinker cry (he tries to suck it up and exit the hangar with all the dignity he can muster, but it's not a pretty sight).

Second, when Conrad finishes making modifications to the jet, the results are less than breathtaking. "You're sure this thing will hold up?" you ask.

"Absolutely not," he replies. "But if it manages to break atmosphere we should be fine. And Maggie will rescue us if we just plain fall out of the sky before that point—right, Maggie?"

Magnifica just grunts. "Come on, you pansies. We've got a planet to save."

Conrad, it turns out, is able to pilot the craft using only the power of his mind, and he's as brave as they come. His grasp of aerospace engineering, however, is really only that of an enthusiastic amateur. The modified jet starts shaking violently as it gains altitude.

And then it explodes.

THE END

Nightwatchman's jet may be 1,300 miles away, but you still have access to another of his assets: absolutely staggering wealth. You find his credit card number on file, and quickly pay the obscene sum of money required to charter a Learjet from New York City to Broward County, departing immediately.

You switch planes at the rest home and head due north. By now, though, the situation has worsened. Huge chunks of the world's communications grid have gone offline, and when you reach the vicinity of northern Canada, you find out why. The sky around you turns a putrid brown, and the very landscape below is shifting. Snowy expanses are torn asunder while patches of greenery wither and die, only to be replaced by something creeping and mold-like. You realize that the alien's aren't just invading. They're *terraforming*.

That's why Crexidyne commanded its superpowered forces to attack various population centers of the world—to divert attention from all of this. And when a fleet of Cosmic Guardians flanks your jet, you know that you're too late to stop it. Their alien technology apparently trumps yours, because suddenly you lose control of the craft, spiraling to your doom.

The rest of the planet will be joining you shortly.

The End

MATT YOUNGMARK

You tell Dale you'll call him later—if you're really going to keep everything on the downlow, you'll need to find some genuine privacy. So you blast off into the stratosphere, flying halfway around the globe in about ten minutes to the general region where you imagine Nepal to be. If you can find peace and quiet anywhere, you figure it'll be Mount freaking Everest.

The suit keeps you at a toasty 78 degrees even at this altitude, so you begin teaching yourself to control it, slowly learning to communicate with the artificial intelligence through a kind of telepathic link. Other than a quick jaunt back to Cleveland to raid your apartment for snacks, you get lost in your project and spend the next 18 hours bonding with the suit. By the next morning (or morning Cleveland time, anyway), you've made some real progress, and even have your laptop's copy of Windows XP running in your visor's display under a subroutine. A popup keeps reminding you that it's an unregistered version that will expire in 30 days, but at least you've got internet.

And the internet has some news. A group of supervillains is making a full-scale attack on Washington, D.C.! It couldn't come at a worse time—you're on the verge of a real breakthrough in your studies. Plus, you're totally keeping it secret here. The east coast is lousy with superheroes—can't the Justice Squadron or the Phenomenal Three take care of this?

> ▶ *That's no way for a hero to think! If you storm off to join the battle,* **turn to page 188.**

> ▶ *If you stay put for now and let someone else handle the attack,* **turn to page 127.**

Is it the bravest thing you've ever done, or just the stupidest? It's both.

You step forward and wrap your arms around the Ox's hulking, armored form in the most loving embrace you can muster. He returns the gesture by squeezing you so tightly that your spine crumples, your organs liquefy, and the marrow damned near goes squirting out of your bones.

Octavia may be compassionate to a fault, but among her strengths is a willingness to take responsibility for her own shortcomings. She admits to Magnifica that in retrospect attempting to hug a supervillain mid-rampage was a spectacularly awful idea.

THE END

You've already limited yourself to the world's most decrepit heroes, so the last thing you want to do is split your meager forces. You head for the North Pole—Magnifica, the Human Torpedo, and Princess Pixie under their own power, and the rest of you following behind in the jet. Torpedo apparently makes a detour to pick up his old sidekick, because by the time you catch up to the others at your destination, Ocean Boy has joined the team as well.

The battle is epic. You find the tip of what must be an enormous alien tower poking out from beneath the polar ice sheet, and Tina the Tank leaps out to pound the thing with her bare fists. You open fire on the swarming fleet of Cosmic Guardians —aliens of all shapes and sizes in armored battlesuits—while your teammates wage war beneath the ocean's surface. Ocean Boy proves to be particularly majestic, breaking through the ice and hurtling through the air after the occasional foe who attempts to escape his underwater fury. If he's this badass above the water's surface, you can't even imagine what he's like underneath it.

You reduce the terraforming tower to rubble with your all-out attack. It's not a particularly speedy process, however, and therein lies the problem—by the time you've emerged victorious, the Cosmic Guard has sent reinforcements from their southern encampment. And they bring along a weird, glowing orb that robs your teammates of their superpowers, shutting down your telepathic link to the Nightwatchman's jet as well.

You're not sure how the others fare, but you crash into a glacier and explode.

THE END

You pull the trigger. It takes about six seconds for the satellite weapon to receive your signal, lock on to its new target, and fire.

"Crap in a hat," the Ox mutters, then drops Moretti and smashes through the wall behind him, vacating the premises just as a ten-foot-diameter column of orange light tears through the ceiling. It momentarily blinds you and utterly disintegrates everything it touches, right down to the building's foundation. Needless to say, that includes Agent Moretti.

"Noooooooooooooooooooooooooo!" You fall to your knees and cry out to the heavens (or, technically, to a non-collapsed segment of the room's fluorescent lighting). You just killed your boss, and somehow didn't even manage to take out the rampaging supervillain with him.

As your eyesight returns, you see a dozen large shapes descending slowly through the newly-blasted hole in the roof. They're encased in armor that looks just like your own, only in a variety of freaky alien forms. Oh, no. You've caused the death of an innocent being—surely that's against whatever code of conduct you theoretically signed off on when you took this job. Has the Cosmic Guard come to discipline you? To make you turn in your badge and gun?

▶ If you humbly throw yourself upon the mercy of cosmic space court (assuming that's what this is), **turn to page 243.**

▶ If you run like hell, **turn to page 202.**

The alien entity comes at you with full force, but you quickly withdraw your slime away from the machine, breaking the psychic connection. It has no power over you here. Well, almost no power. Suddenly an odd thought pops into your head.

MAN, ALL THIS ALIEN INVASION STUFF IS SUPER-DEPRESSING. YOU SHOULD TOTALLY JUST TAKE YOUR OWN LIFE RIGHT NOW.

Wow. You have to at least give Cosmo points for trying. If the Cosmic Guardians are used as shock troops, you think, the invasion may have already begun. Is that why they attacked Lightning Queen? To take out the competition?

Speaking of which, the charred Guardian battlesuit from last night is probably still on the roof of the liquor store where you left it. From what you gathered, it didn't possess anywhere near the brainpower of the space dog—if its mechanical memory is intact, it should be easy to dig through it and pull out any useful information.

You use your elastic arm to slingshot yourself back across town, since traveling this way is faster than dealing with city traffic. It's a bit disturbing when you think too much about it— you can make your limb as solid or gelatinous as you want with just a thought. Clearly there is no musculature or bone structure in there. And yet the hand on the end of it still functions normally. You wonder about the rest of your body. Can you turn your other arm to slime as well? What about your internal organs? Could you function with goo lungs? A goo brain?

Well, you'll have time to experiment later, assuming the world doesn't end. You reach the rooftop and find the Guardian armor undisturbed (also, still filled with cooked flesh). You

(continue to the next page)

cover the scorched helmet in purple tendrils, establishing a link to the artificial intelligence inside. Without its host body, it's not in good shape. *Tell me about the invasion plan*, you think.

HE OR YOU THE DESTRUCTION WHICH IS ETERNAL UNDERGOES FROM THE BOAT OF THE MOTHER WHO IS TO METHOD.

Well, that's just gibberish. This isn't getting you anywhere. BOAT OF THE MOTHER ARE FOUNDATION PROCESS. BEFORE GOING ROUND A STANDSTILL, POLICY DOES NOT HAZARD.

Wait, boat of the mother? Does it mean "mothership?" *Tell me more about the boat of the mother*, you insist.

Suddenly, various pieces of Guardian armor jerk to life, assembling themselves through some unseen force into a rough sphere, and launching straight into the clear blue sky. You, of course, are still attached. Before you have time to react, you're rocketing through the air and already starting to break atmosphere, seconds away from blacking out. You were wondering what would happen if you tried transforming your entire body into the purple slime? Now would be the time to find out.

▶ *If you will yourself into goo, internal organs and all,* **turn to page 197.**

▶ *Wait! You NEED your internal organs. If you disengage from the battlesuit and try forming a goo cocoon to protect yourself from the inevitable impact waiting below,* **turn to page 251.**

"It has to be Tina," you say. "She's willing to give everything to save us all—I'm sure that's more than enough humanity for the job."

Octavia briefs Tina on the task at hand while she and Conrad attach the alien technology to her back. "It's all about willpower," she says. "Once you get to the tower, press up against it and use the strength of your will to overpower the alien intelligence. It's like smashing, but with your brain!"

"Tank strongest brain there is!" Tina says, blasting off in her newly-upgraded chair. She's famous for being an unstoppable force of destruction—surely, if anyone can get past the tower's guardians, it's her. Now the fate of the planet is riding on the willpower of a woman who . . . hmm. Who apparently couldn't manage to cut out sweets despite the advanced stages of diabetes, you realize. You're starting to have second thoughts about your decision.

The Cosmic Guard attacks her in force, obscuring your view of the proceedings. Octavia sprints toward the action, trying to get close enough to attack them with a mind blast, and Conrad heads back toward the jet, hoping to build something from the wreckage. For lack of a better plan, you just stand there and watch the action.

It's over in minutes. You can't know if Tina made it to the tower and failed in her task or if they stopped her from ever reaching it, but soon all the Guardians are flying toward you and your companions.

They take their time finishing you off.

THE END

As soon as you think it, your armor splits open in front and you fall from its embrace onto the cold, tiled floor. You're overcome with a sudden loneliness. It's not just the suit itself that feels missing—it's as if it took a little part of your consciousness with it. Technically, that's just the telepathic link that you were beginning to establish, but it leaves a small hole in your psyche nonetheless.

"So what now?" you ask. You know full well that Moretti holds all the cards—he can still kill your associates if he chooses (not to mention you), but what else could you have done? "Reginald Thorpe's little flunky gets to play superhero dress-up?"

"Seriously?" he says. "Have you *seen* what happens to the sorry sons of bitches they stick in those things? No, thanks. I'll leave that particular honor to some other flunky." Several engineers in lab coats enter the room and start loading the battlesuit onto a kind of high-tech forklift.

"I do want to thank you for being so accommodating, though," Moretti says. He pulls a small-caliber handgun from his jacket pocket and fires it, point blank, right into your forehead.

"I'll be sure to make a note of it in my report."

THE END

Okay, here goes. It's ruckus time.

Before you have the chance to start, though, you see someone hustling toward you, waving his arms frantically. It's Moretti. "Thank God it's you," he says. "We have a critical situation!"

Is he still pretending to be a government agent? "Yeah, I know," you say. "And you're here because . . . ?"

"Because I'm deep under cover," he whispers. "I've been worming my way into Thorpe's organization for years. Listen, I know you want to remain a free agent, but I really need your help."

Does Moretti think you're dumb enough to buy that? You're supposed to be covering for Nightwatch's espionage mission—you should probably tell him the jig is up and get on with it. Then again, maybe if you play along you can find out what he's up to. Plus, who are we to say how dumb you are? It's *technically* possible that he really is a government mole. What better place for a secret agent than at the very top of Reginald Thorpe's corporate ladder?

▶ *If you tell Moretti you're on to him and commence with the ruckus,* **turn to page 224.**

▶ *If you go along with his ruse to see where it leads,* **turn to page 198.**

"Fire!"

Everything goes orange again, but this time the flash is followed by an explosive force that rocks your craft, toppling it end over end. *There's* the concussive blast you were looking for.

The temperature in your cockpit drops suddenly. "I think it's a hairline crack," Tinker says. "We're losing pressure. Fast."

"It was a pleasure working with you both," Conrad says.

You try to respond, but the air is already too thin to speak. It's only a few more moments before you black out.

* * * * *

When you regain consciousness, Magnifica is standing above you. "You know how hard it is to stay mad at you," she asks, "when you go off like that and save the whole goddamn world by yourselves?"

You're lying on a dirty blanket in Nancy's hangar, back on Earth. "We did save the world, didn't we?" Tinker muses. "That doesn't sound like the sort of thing I'd do at all."

"Get used to it," Conrad says. He already has the jet torn apart and is reconfiguring it into something that looks like a Japanese battle mech. "We're going to need some new recruits if we're getting the old team back together."

"We still have a buttload of evil heroes and supervillains to deal with," Magnifica agrees. "And Christ knows how may Cosmic Guardians." She turns to you. "We're definitely going to need the Nightwatchman on our side."

"I can't even turn the suit on without alerting the whole alien army," you say.

The old bird looks at you and smiles. "Bring 'em on."

THE END

What good will it do to charge off into battle half-cocked? If you're going to fight supervillains, you at least intend to make sure you're cocked all the way. The answers you need right now lay within. You turn off your suit's internet connection (in fact, you consider dumping the Windows install entirely, but decide that you may want to squeeze in a few relaxing games of Bejeweled later), and focus on *you*.

And anyway, it's been quite a while since you've slept. After a few more hours of AI-bonding meditation, you find yourself drifting off. In this state, it's hard to determine where your dreams end and your armor's begin—as you slumber, you have visions of some vile alien race with plans to completely transform the Earth's ecosystem and atmosphere, killing every living thing on it in the process.

The thing is, the plot in this book moves pretty fast, whether you choose to participate in it or not. And while you've been puttering around on a mountaintop, a lot of the stuff you're dreaming about is actually happening. Your battle armor may know to switch to its internal oxygen supply when blasting off into deep space, but unless it has reason to believe otherwise, it assumes the air on Earth is safe for you to breathe. By early evening, the toxic alien gas reaches the top of Mount Everest, seeping through your suit's filters and turning your entire body to brown sludge while you sleep.

You die alone.

THE END

You've spent your entire life studying superheroes, but have actually given surprisingly little thought to the villains. You're pretty sure you know why they always fail to take over the world despite repeated efforts, though: it's because they're stupid. Or at least egomaniacal to the point of stupidity—every time they have the hero in their clutches they stand there gloating, or worse, going over their plans in fine detail instead of simply pulling the trigger. If you're going to be a villain, you decide you're damn well going to be a smart one.

You solidify the molten sludge inside Magnifico and pull with all your might, dragging his internal organs out through his face in a spectacular, bloody mess. They say that death is never final when it comes to superheroes, but there's no way anyone is getting reincarnated from *that*.

"Holy crap," the Ox mutters.

The weirdest part about all of it? It felt *good*. You've turned a corner now, and there's no going back. You're going to be the baddest-ass supervillain the world has ever seen. The question is, how to go about it? You've already taken out one costumed buffoon, and you can definitely see yourself doing more of that. Perhaps a superhero murder spree is in order? Or are you more the type to consolidate power, build an organization, and rule over the underworld as the kingpin of villainy? They may be a superstitious, cowardly lot, but Magnifico's head on a stick should buy some serious street cred in the bad-guy community.

▶ *If hero thrill-killing is for you,* **turn to page 162.**

▶ *If you prefer the idea of building a criminal empire,* **turn to page 96.**

You made the call to put Migraine in charge, and now you'll just have to put up with his crap. Maybe this is some kind of Mr. Miyagi thing, and by the time you're done washing, you'll be able to instinctively block karate kicks?

"So, does it matter if I wash them up and down, or side to side or anything?"

He's already gone. And it turns out some of the trucks are really filthy. Other than a short break around midnight when an intern brings you a sandwich and a can of orange soda, you spend the next ten hours scrubbing. By morning you're exhausted, and someone leads you to a cot where you immediately pass out right in your armor.

It's a pretty big day, but you're fast asleep so you miss it. Seriously, it starts out with coordinated global attacks by dozens of supervillains and ends with an honest-to-god alien invasion. And things might have turned out differently if you were on hand to change them, but you made your choice.

And your choice was washing cars. The air around you fills with thick, brown, poisonous smoke before you even get a chance to wake up.

THE END

Involving the Justice Squadron may be a crapshoot, but if it means getting complete sentences out of your battlesuit, it's worth the risk. You try to talk it into opening up a web browser on your viewscreen, but it either can't understand you or doesn't have internet in deep space. Sigh. After a short trip at light speed, you're back to Earth, trying to enter your apartment building as quietly as possible. Your desk chair creaks ominously under the armor's weight, but you pull up the Justice Squadron exposé you wrote in journalism school. You were fairly certain you'd narrowed Brain Stem's secret identity down to one of two people: either a Jamie Kramer or a Barney Llewelyn. Kramer turns up about a million hits on Google (although you're pretty sure he wasn't Miss Maryland 2003, at least) but Llewelyn only turns up—

Oh, no. A man named Barnaby Llewelyn was found murdered and stuffed into a refrigerator in upstate New York last Tuesday. That can't be a coincidence. Could the superhero traitor have done it? Or the government agents? *The Cosmic Guard?* You start to panic. *Do they know where you live?*

Get a hold of yourself. Nobody knows you're the Guardian. And even if they do, they won't find you here. You're a *freakin' superhero* now. So what would a superhero do? Check out the crime scene. You take a moment to slap together a sandwich, dig up an address, and get ready to head out. Then you pause for a moment, and decide to check your email. Fifty-seven comments forwarded from Facebook? Lord. Hit the "like" button on your cousin's wedding pic just once, and suddenly you're in the loop for every little—

"Cosmic Guardian. Long time no see."

(continue to the next page)

You almost choke on your sandwich. The woman standing in your apartment is Nancy North, a legendary TV journalist with ties to the superhero crowd going back to the 1970s, when she worked for the *Daily Globe* in New York. "Wha . . . ?" you stutter. You realize your visor is open, and she can see your face. "You're . . . How did you . . ."

"You're a new one," she says evenly. "Relax. I was covering the Ox's bank job and saw you fly toward this building. You left the door open." You're flabbergasted, and not just because you're almost certain that door was *locked*. Nancy North's illustrious career inspired you to write that superhero exposé in J-school to begin with. One night after a few drinks, you even mailed her a copy. Seeing her in your apartment right now is blowing your *mind*.

Nancy, on the other hand, seems less thrilled to meet you. "I hear you stopped a meteor in front of a bank, and then had your ass handed to you by the Ox twenty minutes later," she says. "Care to tell me what's going on?" You pause for a moment, then decide to come clean. If Nancy's been investigating this, she might have some useful information for you. And besides, you're not sure how well you'd hold up under her steely gaze— she's a famously tough interviewer. She made Schwarzenegger *cry*. You explain that the original Guardian didn't survive the meteor strike, that the suit was passed on to you, and that you've uncovered what you think is Brain Stem's murder.

"It all leads back to the Crexidyne corporation," she says. Crexidyne is an international megacorp run by Reginald Thorpe, a criminal mastermind who can count any number of superheroes among his arch nemeses. "I've been investigating

(continue to the next page)

a Crexidyne black ops division that snoops on various heroes and villains. Brain Stem and the Ox were both under their surveillance."

If Reginald Thorpe is involved, you may have stumbled onto something big. "Hey, do you know a man named Agent Moretti?" you ask. "Little guy, tablet computer, rides around in a black helicopter?"

"That's *Carlo* Moretti," Nancy says. "He's Thorpe's second-in-command. Jesus, do you not have the internet?"

"I was going to look him up, but I got attacked by space aliens." She gives you a blank look. "Maybe I should start over from the beginning."

You tell Nancy the whole story, from the bank robbery to your trip to the sun, and how you hoped Brain Stem could help you commune with your battle armor. "That's actually not a bad idea," she says. "There's still someone who might still help with that—she's a better telepath than Brain Stem ever was. But I'm worried that the Cosmic Guard might actually be working with Crexidyne—if that's the case, time is of the essence. How would you feel about infiltrating the Guard?"

"Infiltrating?" You swallow hard. "Last time I ran into them them, I barely survived it."

She smiles. "Yes, but this time you'll have a plan."

▶ *If you like the sound of infiltration,* **turn to page 252.**

▶ *If you think that decoding your battlesuit's gibberish should be top priority and contact Nancy's psychic friend,* **turn to page 24.**

Your search for Nightwatchman can wait. Nancy tells you that her first choice would be to send you into Crexidyne headquarters with your cloaking device activated to break into their computer network. If they're in league with the Cosmic Guard, though, she can't risk it. "You've stayed off their radar so far, but if they can detect the suit, you'd better not push your luck," she says.

Instead, she decides to have you kidnap Crexidyne's chief of operations, a man named Carlo Moretti, and bring him to her for interrogation. You could argue that the Nightwatchman would make a more intimidating inquisitor, but you've seen her conduct celebrity interviews—Nancy North could get a tearful confession out of a turnip. She gives you an address and tells you to meet her there with Moretti as early as possible tomorrow morning.

After collapsing for a few hours in a crappy motel, you find yourself at Crexidyne corporate headquarters just after dawn. The plan is simple: you're wearing your powered-down suit underneath a big overcoat, and as soon as you locate Moretti, you'll switch the power on, grab him, leap out a window, and use the suit's built-in hang glider to coast straight to Nancy's hideout before any Cosmic Guardians even know to look for you. It'll all be terribly exciting. Potentially deadly if anyone catches you in the act, but exciting nonetheless.

You're surprised to find a woman working so early at the reception desk on Moretti's floor. And according to her phone conversation, Moretti is in as well. "I'm sorry," she says to whoever is on the other line, "Mr. Moretti has a 7:30 meeting with Standards and Practices. He'll be unavailable until late this af-

(continue to the next page)

ternoon." Well, that's better than the the photocopy repairman ruse you had planned. You march in and introduce yourself as the new junior executive from Standards and Practices, whatever that is.

"Right," the receptionist says with an exaggerated wink. "Standards and Practices." She winks again, and giggles. "I can't believe we get to go on a real spaceship! Whoops." She makes a zippering-her-lips motion and winks awkwardly several more times. "Go right in! Mr. Moretti will see you right away!"

Okay, that was weird. You assume his office is the big one at the end of the hall, and find a thin, completely average-looking man in a tweed jacket poring over a tablet computer there.

He looks up at you. "My god, what the hell are *you* doing in here?"

Crap. "Um, Standards and Practices?"

"I can see you're wearing a big, stupid costume under your coat," he says, tapping at his screen and scrolling though a list he finds there. "Which one are you supposed to be? Are you with the D.C. contingent? Dammit, if you're with group A, you should be on site already."

This is it—you should switch on your equipment and grab him. His questions have caught you off guard, though. Clearly he thinks you're someone else. Perhaps you should play along for a while and find out where this goes.

▶ *If you jump him and put your original plan into action,* **turn to page 207.**

▶ *If you wait and pump him for information using guile and cleverness,* **turn to page 92.**

Magnifica refuses to accompany you, so you make your way toward D.C. alone. You research your opponents en route—the Turtle is strong but slow, so you don't think you'll have much trouble outmaneuvering him. Doctor Diabolus has control over the weak-minded, but you're pretty sure your brain will make the cut. The real threat is Lightning Queen, who has electrical powers and a notoriously volatile disposition. You'll need to use your suit's cloaking device to sneak up on her and take her out as quickly as possible.

By the time you reach the city, however, additional villains have joined their ranks. You didn't count on that, or on the fact that even though he can't mind-control you, Diabolus can sense your presence, cloaked or otherwise. He calls out your position when you've only just started sneaking, and before you know it you're dog-piled by half a dozen thugs in identical brown leather armor. They pin you down and start tearing away your gear—soon your cloaking device is ripped from your utility belt and you flicker into view.

"It's Nightwatchman!" all your attackers say in unison.

A howl echoes out over the city streets, and a figure in black rushes you. You recognize him as Axemaster, which is weird, because you thought he was in a maximum security prison, serving a number of consecutive life sentences after being brought to justice by . . .

Oh. Yeah, he's nursing a bit of a grudge, and has been meticulously planning his revenge on Nightwatchman for years. If anything, he's even angrier that he didn't get to execute the first six stages of his plan. He makes up for it though, by executing the final stage with extra enthusiasm.

THE END

You see Megawatt transform into blinding yellow light, and his space suit falls through his body to the floor. You're spared the obligatory evil laugh, since you can no longer hear him through the helmet's audio system. "Ox!" you say. "I have an idea, but I need you to hold them off!"

Cosmic Guardians are still piling into the hangar as you speak. "Yeah, okay," Ox shoots back. "Hurry up, though. I usually pass out pretty quick once he starts with the brain torture thing."

You spot what looks like a computer access panel on the wall. A group of Guardians rushes to intercept you, so you form a thick bubble of goo around yourself and the console, willing it to harden. You put your palm up to the mechanism, and let the goo flow into it. *Is there anything in there? Computer?*

(continue to the next page)

Meanwhile, you can hear Ox's trash talk through your helmet's speaker as he singlehandedly takes on the horde. "That's right! You want some more of that? Aauuugh! Crap! He's inside my—eeeeeaaaaargh!"

You'd better hurry this up. *Computer! Respond!*

ACKNOWLEDGED. You're in! Your cosmic space goo must be working as a kind of psychic conductor. INSTRUCTIONS?

You're interrupted by more screaming. "He's in my head! I can hear him laughing while he friggin' zaps me—eeeeeeeaaaagh!" Your shell is keeping the Guardians at bay, but if Megawatt comes for you, it's all over. *Self-destruct!* you command.

SELF-DESTRUCT PROTOCOL NOT FOUND.

It was worth a shot. What else? Can you send the ship somewhere else? *Change destination!*

NEW TARGET INSTRUCTIONS?

Anywhere! *Jupiter!* you think.

TARGET UNKNOWN. COORDINATES?

You certainly don't know the coordinates of Jupiter off the top of your head. *The sun! The star at the center of the original target's orbit!*

TARGET UNKNOWN. COORDINATES?

This isn't working. Ox is just screaming now, without any of the intermittent banter. *List known coordinates!*

The computer spits out a string of numerals and letters, which mean nothing to you. *Set target to farthest known coordinate!*

TARGET RESET TO FATHERWORLD. TIME TO ARRIVAL: 65,000 YEARS AT LIGHT SPEED. JUMPING TO

(continue to the next page)

LIGHT SPEED IN TWO POINT FOUR MINUTES.

Light speed? *Can you travel any faster than that?*

NOTHING TRAVELS FASTER THAN LIGHT SPEED. JUMPING TO LIGHT SPEED IN TWO POINT THREE-TWO MINUTES.

You did it! You soften the top of your shell and poke out your head. The Guardians—several dozen of them now—have given up trying to get to you and are hovering in a wide arc around Ox and Megawatt. A scattering of armored body parts around Ox's feet make a pretty good case for giving him a wide berth. While you've been messing with the computer, his screams have ebbed to a soft, constant whimper.

"Ox, the ship's jumping to light speed! We have two minutes to get out of here!"

Your friend is on his knees, with Megawatt's noncorporeal hands phasing right into his head. "Heh," Ox chuckles softly. "You hear that, you bastard? You lost." He stumbles to his feet. You're not sure he understands that you really don't have time for the whole bloody-but-unbowed schtick. Megawatt holds his ground, shifting his hands to keep them in Ox's brain.

"Nnnng. That hurts, all right." He takes a step forward, his body overlapping Megawatt's torso slightly. "Owwwwww. Yeah, you told me already. Made out of pure energy. You know what I'm made out of?" He takes another step, and Megawatt disappears entirely into Ox's hulking frame.

"*Pure kicking your ass.*" Ox lets out a bellow that threatens to short out the speaker in your helmet. Megawatt's form goes hurling out of his, reverting to flesh and bone before it hits the wall on the far side of the hangar. Unconscious, he takes a

(continue to the next page)

breath of alien air and immediately begins to swell up and turn a splotchy white. That brown gas is some toxic stuff, you think.

Which reminds you. "Ox, we have to get out of here. The ship is leaving!"

He gasps, gesturing timidly at the Cosmic Guardians. "Won't they just reprogram it to come right back?" You didn't think of that. If this ship truly has the power to destroy your entire world, you can't risk leaving your enemies alone on it. But you could stay on board to clean up shop, and if light speed is a universal constant, any Guardans left on Earth could never travel any faster than you to catch up. They couldn't even call ahead, because if nothing travels faster than light, you'd arrive before the communication did. By the same token, though, you could never risk turning the ship around, or even slowing it down, because they could be right on your tail. It's a one-way, 65,000-year trip.

▶ *You know what comes with great power? Yup. If you sacrifice yourself and stay on board to ensure the Earth's survival,* **turn to page 140.**

▶ *What? You can't leave the Earth behind! Think of the sandwiches! If you flee while you still can and hope for the best,* **turn to page 216.**

Dale has always been a bit too touchy-feely for your taste. But now you're fighting dozens of Savage Cockroaches, and certainly you'll need at least a pair of heroes to pull it off.

It's rough going—Dale separates and you immediately lose him in the fracas. Cockroaches dogpile you, and for every one you blast with a bolt of blue energy, three more are doubling themselves into six right behind. You see a handful approach you dragging a big metal box with what looks like an emergency-room heart paddle attached to it. The whole scene is pretty unsettling. And it gets even more so when they start to talk.

"When I heard Cosmic Guardians were rounding us up, I paid a visit to my old buddy, Tinker," the clones say. They don't talk particularly loudly, but they all say it in unison (except for the two whose faces you're currently smashing together). It's creepy as hell. "He designed this for Übermind back in the '90s. Let's see if it still works!"

Cosmic Guardians are rounding who up? Also, what Cosmic Guardians? Before you can try your hand at banter, a Cockroach presses the paddle against your helmet and a massive electrical surge pulses through your body. You fall to the deck, your armor refusing to respond to your commands.

Übermind was the original Guardian's arch nemesis, you recall, and was always concocting devious plans to destroy him. He might have done it, too, if Guardian didn't have the entire Justice Squadron watching his back.

All you have, alas, is Commander Goo.

THE END

If Magnifica says you're in trouble, you believe her. You switch on your cloaking device and your body shimmers, turning invisible—fortunately, you had some time to study before bed last night. You also know that your cloak transforms into a really spiffy hang glider, so you spread your wings and jump from the rooftop's edge, gliding effortlessly down to the city streets. The invisibility tech burns through battery power like crazy, so you find an empty alleyway and switch it off. What now? You check your wristscreen and are surprised to find a short message on the display.

SHUT DOWN YOUR SYSTEMS.

What? Could that be Magnifica sending you a text? Crap —maybe the real Nightwatchman has found you! For all you know, though, Thorpe's goons have tapped into your network. You're not about to fall for that. Are you?

Before you have the chance to make the call, a huge figure descends into the alley in front of you. It's the Cosmic Guardian! At least, you think it is—he's enormous, at least twice the size of the hero you saw stop that meteor in Cleveland. And even more startling, you feel your boots and gauntlets decompress, expanding to their original size and losing the custom fit they'd formed around your extremities yesterday. You check your wristscreen and find it blank. It appears that your systems have made the decision to shut down without you.

The Guardian armor features any number of advanced weapons—shoulder missiles, energy blasts, high-powered plasma bolts. Your opponent doesn't bother to use any of them. Instead, he reaches out with one hand and crushes your skull like a grape.

THE END

"Thorpe's not going anywhere," you say. "Let's go see if the citizens of Washington need our help."

Magnifica flies you and Octavia to the city and deposits you on a rooftop to get a better look. "What the hell are they doing?" she asks.

You're not sure. It doesn't look like they're stealing anything, or really even trying to hurt people. "They're just kind of wrecking stuff," you say. "Octavia, can you get a read on what they're thinking?"

"It's like they're at work," she says. "As if someone hired them to destroy some national monuments today."

As you watch, several members of the Justice Squadron arrive on the scene. Instead of trying to stop the carnage, however, they start helping the villains destroy the Lincoln Memorial. That's troubling.

You check for media reports on your gauntlet computer, and find that heroes and villains are teaming up all around the globe—Paris, Tokyo, Mumbai, and Mexico City are suffering similar fates. Even legendary foes La Legión de la Matanza and Los Vengedores Robotico have joined forces for mutual destruction. You don't know what to make of it.

You've got a more immediate problem, though. The collected group of superhumans in the streets below has been alerted to your presence, and it goes on the attack. Magnifica charges them, but this means there's no one on hand to defend you or Octavia against the fleet Cosmic Guardians who immediately begin hurling plasma bolts at you from above.

It looks like you've managed to piss *somebody* off.

THE END

With every single speck of life on the planet at stake, you can't afford to take any chances. And even if there's an innocent victim deep inside each of those enemy soldiers, an end to their long suffering can only be a blessing.

Even the ship's less-complex artificial intelligence has a biological component to it, just like your armor—that's what allows Octavia to link with its mind. They must not have telepathy on the alien homeworld, you think, because this seems way too easy. You tell the ship to skip the usual countdowns and warnings, and set two courses for opposite ends of the galaxy. The onboard computer is very excited about this prospect— it gets to take two trips! Making the decision to sacrifice the Guardians was tough, but if anything, you almost feel worse about the ship.

You configure your armor for the jump to lightspeed—and not a moment too soon, because the Cosmic Guard has arrived in force. At the last possible moment, you make your own jump. In a flash, everything goes white.

How long do you need to travel to avoid the blast? It's light speed—any length of time should be more than enough. You put on the brakes and get your bearings. From this distance, the Earth is just a faint blue dot among a sea of stars. *Did it work?* Still curled up in her pod, you sense that Octavia is holding her breath. There's only one way to find out, so you warp back to Earth.

At the coordinates where you left the alien ship, there's just . . . nothing. You try opening a channel with the Guard, and get no response whatsoever. Octavia scans for brain activity, and gets the same result. Were they vaporized in the explosion?

(continue to the next page)

A spectral analysis of the area confirms it: microscopic debris, and plenty of it.

You did it! You totally saved the world.

Next stop: Washington, D.C. Mopping up a group of bargain-basement villains may be anticlimactic after stopping an alien invasion, but the work needs to be done. Once there, you discover that the Justice Squadron has beat you to it— Magnifico, Megawatt, and Skyhawk are already on the scene. Hold on a second. They seem to be helping the villains trash the place.

Is the whole damn Squadron in on this? Do they not know that their alien overlords have already been atomized? You drop Octavia off on the sidewalk and reconfigure your armor for full battle readiness.

This is going to be fun.

THE END

There must be another way! "I won't do it," you say, putting the trigger away.

The Ox stares at you, then throws Agent Moretti across the room and turns, bursting through the wall behind him. He manages to destroy three additional walls on his way out of the complex, and there are a number of injuries caused by collapsing masonry and bullets ricocheting off his impenetrable hide, but no fatalities. All in all, it's not much of a rampage.

Moretti peels himself off the floor. He doesn't look pleased. "Come with me," he says. "There's something I want to show you."

You follow him into the power-dampening chamber. It's strangely empty except for a table upon which you see a small glass ball. "The truth is, our power-dampening technology won't even work on the Ox," he says. "This entire mission was simply a test to see how you'd perform in the field."

Suddenly something clamps onto your back and electricity surges through your armor. You lose control and fall to the floor in a heap. "A test which you failed," Moretti adds.

You're starting to wonder if he works for the United States government at all. You realize that he's definitely better at luring people into that room than you are, though. Then his goons storm in and start trying to crack open your shell with steel crowbars and diamond-tipped drills.

They're not particularly careful, and you don't survive the experience.

THE END

Tachyon smiles, and closes his eyes. He doesn't open them again.

Is that it? Is he off altering the past, or just back in his coma? You step into the hallway and find the hospital staff still glued to their news broadcasts. As you watch them, your vision starts to fade. Slowly, everything turns white. You don't know much about the space-time continuum, but you're guessing this is what happens when the timestream unravels.

It's all up to you now. Even with advance notice, is there anything you can do to save the world?

▶ *To find out,* **turn to page 1.**

ALSO AVAILABLE FROM
CHOOSEOMATIC BOOKS:

You're a stuffed bunny and it's the end of the world.

Between you and safety are forty or fifty zombies gorging themselves on the flesh of the living. If you disguise yourself as one of them and try to sneak past the feeding frenzy, turn to page 183. If you grab a tire iron, flip out and get medieval on their undead asses, turn to page 11.

In **Zombocalypse Now** you'll be confronted with undead hordes, internet dating, improper police procedure, and the very real danger that you'll lose your grip on reality and wind up stark raving mad.

With 112 possible endings (at least 7 in which you don't die) the zombie apocalypse has never been this much fun.

For news, author commentary, and a
secret map to the really good endings, go to

chooseomatic.com

ACKNOWLEDGEMENTS

It may be officially dedicated to a pair of my childhood idols, but this book is double-secret-extra dedicated to Dawn Marie (and not just for naming Professor Medium Maximus, the Gentleman Mentalist). Also, it was made readable through the efforts of my crack editorial team (in reverse alphabetical order this time, to Krystal's undoubted dismay), Neal Starkman, Melodie Ladner and Krystal Abbott. You went above and beyond to read this on an insanely abbreviated schedule, and I'm deeply indebted to each of you.

I'd also like to give a shout-out to all the coffee houses in Seattle's Ballard neighborhood where I sat nursing a mocha and working on this book (in particular, Blue Dog Kitchen and Grumpy D's). And to Debi at the gliffy.com support desk, who was incredibly patient with me when I somehow managed to replace my graph for the entire Nightwatchman arc with a copy of Cosmic Guardian. Also, of course, thanks to Ryan North for the initial spark of inspiration. I don't know if it's possible to build an entire career out of a single Dinosaur Comic, but I'm damn well going to try.

ABOUT THE AUTHOR

Matt Youngmark has written *Zombocalypse Now* and *Thrusts of Justice*, and is currently hard at work on Chooseomatic number three, *Time Travel Dinosaur*. He lives in Seattle.

CPSIA information can be obtained at www.ICGtesting.com
Printed in the USA
BVOW041749170612

292822BV00001B/13/P